Playing the GAME

KAREN FRANCES

Alistair
Hope you enjoy
the game
love Karen
x

Playing the Game

ISBN 978-0-9934154-6-3
Published by: Clydeside Publishing

Cover Design by
Kari March, Kari March Designs

Photographer
Max Ellis

Model
Chris Spearman

Editing by
Karen Sanders

Interior Design and Formatting by
Christine Borgford, Type A Formatting

Dedication

Maxine and Suzie.

This one is for both of you. I wasn't sure anyone would love Fletcher as much as me, but I know you do. You've both been here for me, encouraged me throughout writing this story. Thank you, not only for #fallingforfletch, but your friendship.

Acknowledgements

THIS PART DOESN'T GET ANY easier, and with this book, *Playing the Game,* there are so many people to thank, because truthfully, I would never have got to the end of this without them.

This book has been challenging to write. My characters, Fletcher and Jess, were very demanding and at times draining. For me as an author, this was a highly emotional storyline to write, given the subjects discussed. Yes, there were a lot of tears shed and a lot of time walking away from my computer until I felt ready to write again.

Firstly, my wonderful husband Paul. You let me live my dreams, even when it may seem they are breaking me in two. And with this story, there were plenty of tears. I'm lucky and blessed to have you in my life. Thank you for putting up with me and tagging along on this journey with me. There's no-one else I would have beside me.

Thank you to my amazing kids. Not only do you drive me insane, especially my older boys, but you all make me so proud of you, each and every single day. Life is never boring.

To my family and friends—you have all done so much for me throughout my journey, and yet you may not even know it. Thank you for being there; for looking after the girls when I've needed some extra peace and quiet. For also helping out with promotions and telling anyone who would listen to you about my books.

Cheryl, Fiona, Maxine, and Suzie, thank you for reading my very first draft of *Playing the Game.* Your love for Fletch encouraged me to go on and make this story better, which I hope I've achieved. I appreciate all each of you do for me more than words can say.

Krissy, what can I say? You are an amazing friend, and thank you for, yet again, agreeing to read over and offer constructive criticism.

Karen, it has been an absolute pleasure to work with you on this project. E 'stato un viaggio interessante. Sorry, I couldn't resist. Thank you.

Laura, thank you for doing a final read through for me, especially at short notice.

LP, what can I say about you, lady, that hasn't been said before? Not a lot. I'm so glad we've finally met. I have to say you are professional in all that you do. And I'm sorry that it was so cold and smelly out and about in Dublin. Thank you for just being you and for your friendship.

Max, it was an absolute pleasure working with you. Your sense of humour had me laughing on more than one occasion during the photoshoot, as you know. Thank you for everything, because without you, I wouldn't have the shots I wanted.

Chris, I don't have enough words for you. From our very first conversation, about you looking better in the football strip than of the picture of a certain footballer you sent me, I'd like to say we hit it off, and for me, you have become a friend. For the photoshoot, you went higher than my expectations and I hope you love the covers to *Playing the Game* and *Playing to Win* as much as I do. So from the bottom of my heart, thank you for being *my* Fletcher.

Kari, you went above and beyond with the cover for this book. Especially when I had no idea what I wanted. And now I'm excited to share the cover for *Playing to Win*, as well. Thank you, and I look forward to working with you again on my next project.

Christine, you do what you do best, and that is make my books perfect on the inside. Thank you, again for another project complete.

To the ladies in my readers group, I love you all. You make me smile on a daily basis. Thank you for believing in all that I do.

Lou, thank you for being you. After our almost daily conversations, I'm so glad we finally met, and now I can look forward to the next time we see each other.

To every blogger around the world, thanks doesn't seem enough for all you do. You work your socks off doing promotions for us authors. Each of you have a very special place within the community.

I've made some amazing friends within the book community, there are far too many to mention, but you all know who you are. Thank you.

Thank you to my wonderful readers. I hope you all enjoy Fletcher and Jess' journey.

Contents

Prologue

Fletcher

PEOPLE CAN OFTEN GIVE YOU recollections of days and times that stand out. A significant moment in time. Like where they were and what they were doing when J.F.K was assassinated on the 22nd of November, 1963. Or on the 8th of December, 1980, when John Lennon was shot dead in New York City. I can understand people remembering these incidents; they're written into our history books.

Me? I can tell you when, where, and what I was doing when I realised my life was fucked up. And when I say fucked up, I mean with a capital F. Some things will be forever burned in the deepest part of your memory. It will stay with you for life. At times it will haunt you.

Tonight, the Hilton hotel in Manchester, and I'm just about to slide between the legs of yet another blonde fucking bimbo.

She's unbuttoning my jeans and her hand slides beneath my boxers. My eyes rake over her body beneath me, and it's not a bad body. It's actually pretty hot, but she's not what I want. My eyes roam the room as she purrs in my ear like a fucking pussycat. One of the lads has a young girl bent over the table, there's someone else on the floor, and the noises coming from the bedroom . . . well, it leaves nothing to the imagination.

I'm getting too old for all this bullshit. Situations like this are what get me into bother, and do I really need the hassle that comes with this?

I grab her hand and remove it from my boxers. She looks at me and pouts. Those sad eyes are doing nothing for me. Fastening my jeans, I turn my back to her and walk out of the room, not saying a word to anyone.

As I stand in the elevator, I look at my phone. Four a.m. It's too early to make the call, so I send a text instead: *I want a transfer. I don't care where I go but I can't stay here. And the sooner the better.*

It's about time I grew up.

The boss will get this; he will understand. I might be a good footballer, but even he must be getting sick of the shit that comes with me. I'm probably doing us all a favour.

I need to sort my shit out.

Chapter ONE

Fletcher

FUCK. FROM THE HIGH OF last night's international game to this. I'm not sure my head can take everything that has been thrown my way this last week. I'm not usually an emotional man, but I'm not afraid to admit I'm struggling.

Sitting here, I stare at the front door, wondering if I should get out of the car. Everything looks exactly as I remember it. I remember my granddad painting that door the same shade of green it is now. I remember running past him and getting paint all over my white t-shirt. Gran and Granddad laughed about it, but not my mum. She lost her temper and gave me a good hiding. I must've only been about six at the time. That hiding she gave me was the first of many. It was my gran who consoled me that day, her soothing voice telling me repeatedly everything would be okay.

My life has never been okay since that day.

I thought my gran had died when I was in my teens. Well, that's what SHE told me anytime I asked about her. So, it feels strange being back here, sitting in my car in front of her house. But this time she's gone, and I won't get a chance to say everything I wanted to tell her. No second chances to put right everything that went so horribly wrong for us all. All I want to do is have one last conversation with her, tell her how much I loved her, and that I never forgot about her, even though SHE, my mum, saw fit to keep me away from her.

I'm not sure why I chose to believe what my mum told me about my gran. I should've questioned it when I got older, because the older I got, the more I realised everything that came out of her mouth was a pack of lies. When she took off away from here, away from my home, I'm surprised she took me with her given the small fact that she never cared for me, let alone loved me.

No, my mother was a selfish bitch who only ever cared about herself. It's no wonder that's how I've been the last few years, and it's only in the past few months I've realised just how much like my mother I've become.

It's time for changes in my life. The woman who gave birth to me was nothing but a bully. She resented everything about having me, and she told me on numerous occasions that she should have got rid of me when she had the chance.

Talk about giving a kid a complex.

My gran was a lovely, sweet lady; always put others first, even my mum, when all she did was cause her pain and sorrow. I loved my gran. She always said I was the apple of her eye. In her opinion, way back then I could do no wrong. God knows what she would make of my life the last few years. I cringe at the thought of being a disappointment to her. I'm sure if Gran knew half of what I've been up to, she would've given me a telling off along with a good old clip around the ear. She might have been a sweet lady, but by God, she had one mighty fiery temper; not that I was ever on the receiving end of it. She was old school; wasn't afraid to speak her mind.

Things in my life might have been different if I'd had my gran around all those years.

She was a beautiful woman. I can remember her features so clearly. She had the most amazing soft blue eyes that reminded me of the ocean. Sounds stupid, I know, because as a child, I had never seen the ocean. But I always pictured it when I looked into her eyes. I remember her long blonde hair, and she always wore it in a bun.

A lump forms in my throat and tears fill my eyes. What would the boys say if they saw me like this? 'The great Fletcher Adams, crying,' I'm sure a lot of them would say as they laughed at me. Yes, I'm sure this would make for a great conversation in the dressing room. But which dressing room? I have an important decision to make, one that could shape my future, and I'm not sure what to do. Do I stay on in England and see out my contract, or move on? The only offers on the table bring me back home to Scotland. Could I restart my life here in Glasgow? Would I be given the space to do that?

A fresh start is what I need to put recent events behind me. Would I be able to stay out of trouble for long enough? Or is it just going to follow me wherever I go?

I don't have the answers to any of these questions.

Today is going to be harder than I thought it would be. I hope I can do it. I've never had to take care of someone's belongings. When my mum died last year, I called the local charity shop and let them take everything they wanted. The rest of her belongings went to the recycling centre. I didn't want anything that belonged to her; not that she had much, and what she did have came from me.

I should get out of my car and go inside the house. There is nothing I can do sitting out here.

Leaving my car, I walk up the path toward the front door. I turn and look at my baby, my Porsche Panamera; it looks so out of place in this street. I'm sure Gran would have loved to go for a spin in my baby. She would've ensured I kept my speed down. I smile at the thought because I've lost count of the number of times my lawyer has gotten me off speeding charges. I know I should watch what I'm doing, but what's the point in having a flash car that can do those high speeds and not taking advantage of it? I love being on an open road and pushing it to its limits.

There's a lot of things in life I love pushing to limits.

Hearing a commotion, I turn to the house next door. There's a lady crying, rushing out of the door, throwing items in her handbag. A man dashes out behind her. The woman's whole body is shaking, and the man is trying to lock their door, but his fingers are fumbling with the key.

"Elaine, sweetheart," he calls after her. "You need to calm down. You won't be able to help in the state your in. Please . . ."

"I can't help it," she cries, standing by the car, waiting on him. "She doesn't deserve this. Why would he do this to our beautiful daughter? I still can't believe we're just hearing about this. She's been there all night on her own. No one to hold her hand and just be with her. She's been all alone."

The man reaches her and wraps her tightly in his arms, trying to console her. I don't think I've ever seen a woman so upset. He opens the car and helps her inside before walking around and getting in to the driver's side. I wonder what's going on with their daughter. With the woman's crying, it doesn't sound good.

Turning my attention away from the couple, I rummage in my pocket for the key the solicitor gave me earlier today to open the front door. I pause and turn back to the other car. I can see the man is having problems with it. I know I should just go inside and mind my own business, but I'm a sucker when it comes to hearing a woman cry. My mum always used that side of me to her advantage. When she wanted something, she turned on the water works.

I walk back down the path and around to the driver's side of the car, and knock on the window. "It sounds like a flat battery," I tell him when he opens the door. Now I can hear the woman's cries louder; she sounds in pain. "If you have jump leads, I can start it for you."

"Christ, no. They're in my daughter's car."

"For pity's sake, Jim!" she shouts through her tears. "We need to get to her. She needs us with her!"

"Elaine, calm down. It will be fine. We can get a taxi."

"Excuse me, sir. I can take you if you need to be somewhere urgently," I say without thinking.

"Fletcher, isn't it?" he asks, studying me.

"Jim, we don't have time for small talk," Elaine snaps.

"Yes, sir, it is. Now, where is it you need to go?"

"The hospital, son."

"Well, let's get you both there."

Why do I feel the need to help them? This is so out of character.

I walk around to Elaine's side and offer her my hand to help her out. She takes it and gives me a small smile.

"Thank you. You have no idea what this means to me," she says, wiping away her falling tears.

From looking at her, seeing her appreciation, my small act of kindness means the world to her. Women don't usually appreciate me unless there's money or sex involved, so this is a first for me.

"You're welcome."

"Do you know the roads, or do you need directions?" Jim asks when we're all in the car.

"No, good old sat-nav, but which hospital are we going to?"

"The new one, son."

That's good, because it should only take about twenty minutes to get there. Less if the traffic is quiet. I don't put the radio on because, under the circumstances, that would seem rude, especially when they're so concerned about their daughter. I hope it's not as serious as it seems.

"You know, Fletcher, your gran has followed your career over the years," Jim says, breaking the silence in the car now his wife has stopped crying.

"Did she? My mum told me years ago my gran was dead," I tell him. Why, I don't know, because he's a complete stranger to me. I smile and then frown thinking about Gran following my career, reading about my antics in the papers. My thoughts drift off; why did she never try to make contact? Was I that much of a disappointment to her? There's an ache in my chest as I think about her being ashamed of the man I've become. *Fuck*, I'm ashamed of myself.

"If it makes it any easier, she knows none of it was your fault. She always spoke fondly of you to us. She was very proud of you." I can see Elaine agreeing with him in my rear-view mirror. "Elaine isn't a football fan, but your gran, well, she would watch all your games on the TV. Over the last few months, I kept her company when they were on, and I loved seeing her reaction to you playing. She would burst with pride at the mention of your name. When she watched you playing for your country, she always had tears in her eyes."

My heart tightens and I feel sick at what he's telling me. But I do know she would have been proud of me for playing for my country; it's every young boy's dream, after all. It doesn't matter what goes on in my personal life, I always pull on my Scotland jersey with pride. There's no better feeling than playing for your country.

"How long have you known my gran?" I ask.

"We moved in about five years ago and we took to her straight away. In the last few years we've helped her out around the house, doing odd jobs, and getting her shopping."

"Thank you, both of you, for looking out for her." My gut churns at the thought my gran had no family around to look after her. If I'd known, I would have been here with her.

"If you need anything while you're here, please let us know."

"That's very kind, but I can only imagine you have enough

going on in your own life."

Elaine starts crying again.

"I'm sorry," I say. "I don't mean to upset or offend you."

Jim explains that their daughter, who is six months pregnant, has been found unconscious and badly beaten up in her home. The neighbours reported a disturbance last night to the police and they found her when they called at her house. According to the neighbours, they think it was her partner. I can hear the pain in his voice as he speaks.

Bloody scum. What kind of man attacks a pregnant woman?

There's nothing worse, in my opinion, than a man attacking a woman. I've done many stupid things over the last few years, some have been well documented, but I couldn't lift my hand to a woman. My heart goes out to the couple and their daughter. I hope and pray she's okay, but from what Jim is saying, it doesn't sound like it.

He changes the subject back to my career. "What are your plans now?" he asks.

I tell him I'm not sure yet but have options open to me here in Glasgow. He smiles. At a guess, Jim follows the goings-on of Scottish football and has probably heard the teams I've been linked with. Maybe I should watch what I'm saying; nothing has been decided yet. But I get the feeling Jim wouldn't repeat anything I tell him. Not sure why I feel like this, I just do. Maybe it's because he seems approachable, easy to talk to. He makes me feel at ease. Or it could simply be because I know he's helped my gran over the past few years.

We talk about last night's game. He says it was a thrilling high-speed game to watch from beginning to end. "And that goal, son. What a way to end the game. I've never seen anything like it."

It's not very often Scotland wins against other teams, but last night's friendly game against France was fantastic, with goals from both teams. I scored the opener, but never for one minute did I think I would score the winning goal. *What a night*.

The traffic is quiet, and we get to the hospital in under twenty minutes. I drop them off at the main entrance and give Jim my phone number, telling him to call me if he needs anything. They both thank me for what I've done for them. In all honesty, I've not done very much.

Now, it's time to go back to Gran's house and do what I came here to do, which is pack up her things and then try and sort my own life out once and for all. Or, do I say *fuck it* today, and deal with all this shit the only way I know how; get pissed, find a nice, although not too nice girl I can lose myself in for a few hours and forget about my fucked up life? Let's face it, you only live once, and I've still got plenty of time to grow up.

Or maybe I'll be like Peter Pan, the boy who never grew up.

Chapter TWO

Jessica

"CAN YOU PLEASE STOP FUSSING?" I ask calmly, although I'm silently counting one-to-ten under my breath as my mum tries to help me stand up. But she doesn't stop fussing. She hasn't listened to anything I've said to her this last week. I don't know how much more of this I can cope with. It's only going to get worse when I leave the hospital and go home with her. At least here she's had to go home at night, and I've gotten a bit of peace and quiet. My mum means well, but this is too much, even for me.

"Oh, for FUCK'S sake! Leave it!"

Her expression changes; her soft features sadden at my words. Shit! Now I've only gone and upset her.

"There's no need for you to be cursing. I know you've been through a lot, but there's no need to take it out on me." She turns her head away from me, not wanting me to see the hurt in her eyes.

"Sorry," I say weakly. None of this situation is my mum's fault; I shouldn't take it out on her. But I can't seem to help it. What's the saying? 'You hurt the ones you love the most.' In my case, it's certainly true. When I've not been sitting, staring blankly into space, ignoring everyone, I've been damn right rude. Under any other circumstances even I would have to admit to being a right bitch.

"Sweetheart, it's fine. I just want to help you." She takes my arm, and I let her this time. There's not a single part of my body that's not sore. My eyes drift downward, and they fill with tears when I forget and look for the bump that's no longer there. And here was me hoping I was all cried out. I didn't think I had any tears left.

"Oh, my beautiful baby girl." Mum takes me in her arms as my tears fall. "Ssh, ssh. Everything's going to be okay. Cry all you like."

What can I say to that? Everything is not okay. Not in my mind. So much has changed in the last week.

Only a week ago, I had so much to look forward to; a job I love, a man I thought I loved, a beautiful home, and a baby on the way. Now? Now . . . I've lost so much. It's all gone; my happiness, my hopes, my dreams, and my home. Gone . . .

If I could go back in time, I wouldn't have worked so late, then maybe I would still be carrying my baby and life would be as it was. But it's not, and I'm not sure it will ever be the same again.

We stand huddled together, both of us crying, until the room door opens. I lift my head and see my dad standing there looking at us. I offer him a weak smile. He frowns in return.

"Come on, you two. It's time to go." He grabs my belongings. "Jessica, let's get you home."

Home. I don't have a home anymore. Well, not one I want to go back to. I know my parents mean well, and going to stay with them for a few days will help because I'm not ready to step foot inside my house. Although, I know I need to sort out my house at some point in the next few days. Because it is *my* house. The mortgage is in my name only and there's no way HE is getting to stay there rent free. But I don't think I'll ever be able to stay there again. I shiver at the thought.

My house was the first thing I bought when business took off. Some people buy flash cars, fancy jewellery. Me? I wanted a nice home that would one day become my family home. I fell in love with it the moment I saw it; it was perfect and in a great area for local schools. I bought it before Scott and I got together, and when things became serious between us, it made sense for him to move in with me. He stayed in a flat in the city centre, and all in all it was nice enough, just not somewhere I saw myself staying. My house was perfect.

But not now. No. I can't live there again after what's happened. Too many memories; it would be too painful.

I'm going to sell it. That's what I'll do. When I see Lee, I'll tell her to start the ball rolling.

Lee is my best friend and has been for thirteen years, since we were twelve-years old. I love her; she's the sister I never had. She's been here in the hospital with me every night as soon as she's finished work, even though she's had extra work to do with me being stuck in here. She's much more than just my best friend; we're also business partners. We run a very exclusive estate agency in Glasgow. Our clientele includes some of the country's rich and famous. I love my job and I love working with Lee. Sometimes we can go the whole week without actually seeing each other in the office because we're both so busy.

My steps are slow as I walk. Mum has her arm linked with mine and is walking at the pace I've set. I didn't expect to feel as bad as I do leaving here. I thank the nurses as we pass their station. They've all been great with me. I know our NHS sometimes gets a bad name, but I really can't fault the staff that have cared for me.

As we get closer to the exit, I can see a taxi waiting. Dad opens the door for me to get inside. Where is his car? I don't ask the question, because in all fairness, I don't actually care.

As I sit in the back of this taxi, I feel myself shutting

everything out. My parents are talking beside me, but I couldn't tell you what they're saying. I no longer care about anything or anyone. It wasn't just my baby that died last week. When the doctors removed my baby, they took a piece of my heart along with it. A part of me is missing, and I don't know what to do. I feel so broken. So empty. I'm struggling to see how my life can move forward.

I'm not sure my life is worth living anymore.

I'm powerless.

I have no control over anything that happens. No control over my feelings.

The therapist that spoke to me at the hospital wants to see me again. He says how I'm feeling is understandable considering what I've been through. But how would he know? I can guarantee he's never experienced pain or suffering, not to this extent, anyway. How would he know what it feels like to wake up in the hospital and have the news broken to you that the baby you've been carrying for the last six months is gone? That I'll never see my baby celebrating birthdays or getting married. That I won't have chance to love my baby as much as I do right now.

When the consultant broke the news, my hands instantly flew to my stomach. I screamed and screamed when I realised he was telling me the truth. The nurse that was in the room held on to me, comforting me until my parents arrived.

It was the same caring nurse who brought my tiny baby boy to me. He was wrapped in a beautiful handmade white shawl. I'll never forget how he looked. So tiny and perfect. I sat holding him, just staring at him. The whole time I had him in my arms, I never cried, not once. He just looked like a sleeping baby. I kept expecting him to wake up. But he never did.

The nurse encouraged me to name him. She said it might help me deal with my grief in the long term. I know her heart was in the right place, but how can I move on from this loss? I can't imagine moving on with my life after this.

I called him James, after the most important man in my life; my dad. The only man a girl can truly depend on.

The hospital priest came to see me and we talked about what I would like to do. Yesterday, in the hospital chapel, we had a very short service for the baby I've lost. My parents stayed by my side the whole time, and we all shed more than a tear. There is a remembrance garden within the hospital grounds where I can go anytime. One of the nurses took me earlier today. I wanted to go and say a final goodbye.

So far, everyone has told me each day will get better. But I can't see how when I've lost so much. I keep asking myself what I've done so wrong to deserve what's happened to me. Am I such a bad person? I don't think I am. Had I done something to provoke Scott? I've tried to think about the answer to that, but I don't think I did.

Yes, we had been arguing a fair bit, but not once did I think things would come to this. I put our arguments down to the fact that he was concerned about all the hours I was working. God, how wrong was I?

My phone buzzes and I look to see a text from Lee: *Have you left hospital yet?*

Me: Yes. Going to mum and dad's x

Lee: Do you want me to come over after work?

Me: No. I'm just going to try and sleep. I will speak to you tomorrow x

Lee: Ok. I love you xx

Me: Me too x

I will see her tomorrow. For the rest of today and tonight, I just want to be left on my own with my thoughts, however dark they may be.

I know Lee and I have things to discuss about work. We have a meeting with a developer who wants us to market his new development of apartments down by the River Clyde. I know I should spend some time working on our proposal for them, but I'm going to leave that to Lee. The initial ground-work for the deal is already done. I finished it only last week, and I'm certain we have the deal in the bag, but truthfully, I couldn't care less right now. I'm not interested in work.

We both fell in love with the apartments when we saw them a few weeks ago. Lee said she wants to buy one for herself. At the time I said it was unsuitable for me because of the baby. Now, though, that could be an option. The apartments . . . what can I say about them? We were only in the penthouse, but oh my God, the views from there are amazing. I don't think I've ever seen that far along the river before. Now that I think about it, I've never really appreciated the beauty that's sitting on my own doorstep.

The taxi stops and I look at my surroundings. I'm outside my parents' house. God, we've not stayed under the same roof for the last six years. I expect my mum is going to continue to fuss over me. It should be fine, though. I'm going to stay out of the way, lock myself in my room away from everyone, from the world, because I don't know when or if I will be strong enough to face the world again.

Dad comes around and opens my door for me. I might be lost at the moment but I can still see the sadness in his eyes as he helps me out of the taxi. If my head was in the right place, I'm sure I would be telling him not to feel sorry for me. But I can't.

"Come on. Let's get you inside. Mum has made up the back bedroom for you. It's quieter at the back of the house."

"Thanks, Dad." He gives me a cuddle and that makes me want to cry again. Dad isn't the most overly affectionate person.

He's never been one to show his affection, especially in public.

Mum comes around and takes hold of my arm to help keep me steady. I'm not sure I have the energy to stay standing on my own.

"One step at a time, Jessica," she says in a soft voice, trying to coax me into moving. My feet seem rooted to the spot. Dad had moved away to collect my belongings from the taxi, but is back by my side, asking what's wrong.

I can't look at either of them. Run . . . That's what I would do if my legs could take me. I hear the taxi drive away; the driver must think I'm a complete weirdo.

"Sweetheart, please. We need to get you inside." My mum's voice is pleading with me but I still can't look at her. "Jim . . ."

My tears fall and I'm helpless to stop them. My head is in a spin. I feel so dizzy and tired. I need to sit down before I fall down. My legs are weak. My body is shaky. I grip my dad's arm tighter as my body moves forward. I close my eyes, wanting the darkness to take away my pain.

"Jim!" Mum's voice cries over everything else. "Do something!"

There's lots of noise, and I can't make out who's saying what. My eyes flutter open and look at my mum; she's crying as she holds me in her arms.

"Mrs Taylor, let me," a deep male voice says calmly. I'm suddenly in someone's arms, being carried through the air. My eyes close; I don't want to see pity on this strange man's face. I can hear my dad trying to calm my mum down.

"I can't bear to see her like this, in so much pain," she sobs.

"Ssh. Let's get inside and try and get her settled. I think we should give her the sleeping tablets the doctor prescribed. They might help her."

This is all my fault; I hate myself for causing them more pain. They shouldn't have to worry about me or look after me.

I'm meant to be big enough to take care of myself.

There's a slight wind blowing on my face; it's refreshing as I'm carried toward the house. I know I'm inside when I can no longer feel it.

This stranger who has me in his arms carries me effortlessly. I hear my mum fussing as I'm laid down on the bed. I turn my back to all of them and curl up into a ball, hugging my legs.

The weight of the bed shifts, and I don't have to turn around to know my mum is lying next to me.

"I should go back next door and leave you all alone," the deep voice says.

"No, you don't have to. Come on through to the kitchen and we can talk," my dad says to the stranger. "Elaine will be fine with her for a while. You would be doing me a great favour if you want to talk to me about your situation. It would give me a distraction."

The room door closes, and the only noise that can be heard is both my sobbing and my mum's.

My mum is crying for me, and I'm crying for everything I've lost; all my hopes and dreams that have been ripped away from me in the cruellest of ways.

Chapter THREE

Fletcher

"FOR FUCK'S SAKE, WHAT IS wrong with you tonight? No, change that. What's been up with you the last few days?" Logan asks as we enter the club. He's dragged me out tonight, telling me I'm turning into an old man. His exact words were, 'boring as fuck,' so I thought I'd show him. But in all fairness, I really don't want to be here. I'm just not in the mood to be out drinking until I'm rat-arsed and can't stand on my own two feet.

There has to be more to my life than this. This is what I was hoping to leave behind in Manchester.

"Nothing's fucking up with me. I'm trying to keep my head down and stay out of trouble."

"As I said earlier, 'boring'. Come on, lighten up. Let's get pissed and leave with a couple of hot girls."

We walk toward the bar where there are a few guys I recognise. I really wanted a night away from anything football related, but as I look around the club, I realise that's not going to happen. Every second guy I look at is a player or an agent. Then I look closer. The women in here all look like they're up for anything. The sort you have a whole load of fun with, but fuck waking up to them in the morning. All that make-up smudged over their faces. Everything about them screams 'fake'.

"Well, looky who is finally showing his face. Fuck, we all

thought maybe you'd decided to be celibate and become a priest," Jackson says as he slaps me across the back. "You never came out to celebrate with us after the Scotland game. It's good to see you. I hope you're closer to making a decision on your future. We could use you up here, and let's face it, you must be getting sick of the same slappers you hook up with down south."

"Good to see you, and let's just say there are a few issues I need to sort out before any announcements can be made."

"What will it be, boys?" the bartender asks.

"Beer for me," I reply. Obviously, Logan has other ideas as he orders shots for all the boys at the bar. And here I thought we were just having a few drinks. I should've known better.

The first round of shots gets knocked back quickly, and I feel the alcohol spread through my veins. A feeling I've missed. Granted, I was out last week, but I avoided all the popular hang-outs; I wasn't ready to see the boys. I had one thing and only one thing on my mind that night—getting laid, and I did. The bonus was, she had no idea who I am.

"So, are you going to share what's up?" Logan asks, not letting up. I wish I'd just come out at the start of the week, or even after the game, then he wouldn't be constantly asking. But I don't have an answer for him. Well, not one I'm telling him, anyway.

"There's nothing wrong," I tell him.

"You might fool everyone else, but not me. Is it some chick hassling you?"

I laugh.

"Hey, don't knock it. Some of us would love to have your problems with the chicks."

If I thought Logan would give me a sensible answer, I would tell him what was wrong.

I've thought about a girl all week long; couldn't get her out of my mind. I was concerned about her. I spent a lot of time talking to her dad this last week and her story saddened me.

But after seeing her today and carrying her into the house . . . Christ, I can't explain it to myself, so what chance have I got of Logan understanding? None, and he would only take the piss out of me for it.

I had to help when I saw them getting out of the taxi, and when her body fell to the ground, my heart stopped beating. I did the only thing I could to help and picked her up. Jesus, her battered and bruised body looked so tiny and fragile in my arms. Not once did her eyes open the whole time I held her protectively.

Fuck. I didn't want to let her go.

"No, just dealing with my gran's stuff. It's got to me," I tell him.

"You know you can talk to me anytime."

"I know. Thanks." Just not about Jessica. Not at the moment.

"Now we've got that out of the way, let's get pissed," Logan says loudly, and the rest of the boys cheer. Why do I have a feeling this could get messy? The boys are up for a good time and no one has training in the morning, so maybe I should try to relax with them. It might help take my mind off Jessica. Although why she's in my thoughts, I have no idea, but I'll say this for her, even with all the bruises she's covered in, she's fucking gorgeous.

You know that saying, marry, snog, avoid? Well, she's the type you would marry, because snogging would never be enough. But she might just be the type I should avoid, because a guy like me would never be good enough for someone like her.

I still can't get my head around what her boyfriend did to her. He must be a right bastard to hurt someone he's meant to love. Jim never thought for one minute that he was capable of doing what he did. From what Jim has said about him, he liked him before, but obviously not now. Now he wants to fucking kill him for what he's done to his daughter, and after seeing her today, I wouldn't blame him.

Fuck, I've read about situations of domestic abuse, but this . . . this seems so much worse. Yes, she's battered and bruised, but she looks as though she's given up. Given up on life. I hope I'm fucking wrong.

Drinks are coming thick and fast, and all the boys seem to be having fun, laughing and joking. It's not long before we draw attention to ourselves. Attention of the female kind, as a group of girls approach us.

Alcohol flowing through my veins, music pumping, and girls, lots of girls, is not a good combination. This is why I've been keeping a low profile since I arrived in Glasgow. Girls are good for one night, but it's a risk. They might want more than the one night of sex and don't take rejection well, which has led to problems for me in the past. Women selling their stories of our nights together to the papers. Seriously, who wants to read that shit? Everyone, it seems.

"You're Fletcher, aren't you?" a tall blonde with legs that go on for miles asks, resting her hand on my shoulder. Logan smiles with a look that says *you've pulled tonight*. She is pretty tidy looking, but has overdone it in the make-up department. I rake my eyes in appreciation over her body. Curves in all the right places, and those tits, bloody hell . . . I could have a lot of fun with those as I slide between them, but of course, they're probably fake.

"Yeah," I say, even though I shouldn't, but I'm sure the rest of the guys are loving the female attention they're getting. "Drinks all around," I call out.

The bartender smiles as he looks at our company. Even he has an idea of how tonight will end.

The blonde tells me her name, but I don't take any notice. I don't want to remember her name in the morning, or whenever I creep out of her bed. Makes it easier that way. As the alcohol flows freely, the blonde keeps trying to persuade me to get on the dance floor with her. She seems the type that wouldn't mind putting on one hell of a floor show. I might be on the drunk side now, but I'm still cautious. I've definitely learned my lesson over the years; you just never know who is lurking around, ready to get pictures. She can do what she wants for me in private later on, though.

Our party has doubled in size and noise. The volume has been getting louder since the girls joined us. I'm sure if it wasn't for the amount of money we're spending behind the bar, we would be asked to leave. Some of the girls' high-pitched screams are fucking irritating.

She leans in closer and whispers in my ear. "I think it's about time you and I leave the party and have a party for two. Or if you would prefer, I can bring someone else along."

Fuck! Has she really just offered me a threesome? Yes, and I can't hide the smile on my face. "Well, handsome, I take that as a yes?"

She walks away to one of the other girls, wiggling her hot as fuck arse at me. Maybe I should just take her on her own, but if a girl is going to offer a threesome, am I really going to turn her down?

Fuck no.

I'm a warm-blooded man, of course I'm more than willing to accept what is offered to me on a plate.

The line I'm walking tonight is tight, but in my present state, I'm not thinking straight. Blondie walks back to me, arm-in-arm with a stunning brunette.

"You lucky bastard." Logan grunts in my ear. "How the fuck do you do it? No, don't tell me. Go on. Run along. Don't keep the ladies waiting, and I use the term 'ladies' loosely because for what they have in mind tonight, they're certainly not ladies."

They hook their arms with mine and we walk away to more than a few wolf whistles and shouts. Yes, the boys are going to have a field day with this. Outside, I flag down a taxi, and the blonde tells the driver our destination. Thank fuck for that, because if she hadn't, it would've been a hotel. I might be a lot of things, but I can't disrespect my gran's memory by having them at her house.

I'm not that much of an arsehole.

I climb out of the bed and look around. Where the fuck are my clothes? They must be here somewhere, but all I see is the skimpy outfits the girls were wearing.

"Fletch, that was amazing. Stay," the blonde says, with the brunette nodding in agreement. I flash them a smile and they both swoon. A man would never tire of seeing that look on a woman's face. It would be easy to slide back into bed between them, but I'm starting to sober up. At the time, this seemed like a fucking brilliant idea, but now . . . ? Christ, what was I thinking? So much for staying out of trouble and keeping a low profile.

"Can't, sweetheart. I have a busy schedule in the morning," I lie easily. She doesn't know I don't have training.

Blondie climbs out of the bed, and my eyes travel the length of her body as she moves toward me. Her skin is flawless, and those tits jiggle only a little as she moves. I'm enjoying the way her body sways as she walks toward me. My head says, 'get out of here before you end up in trouble,' but there's a part of me that wants more of what she's offering.

"Can't I tempt you?" she asks breathlessly, standing in front of me, gloriously naked. She is making it hard for a man to restrain himself. She runs her fingers along my jawline and leans in. Fucking hell, this girl can kiss. My dick stands to attention. She breaks away and looks down. "See? I can tempt you."

She takes my hands and leads me back to the bed. I sit down. Her friend kneels down on the floor in front of me, licking her lips. Blondie joins me on the bed and starts kissing me again. I moan in her mouth as her friend's mouth starts work on my dick.

I think I've died and gone to fucking heaven. Women are my weakness. And I'm sure there's no man on the planet who would turn down my current situation.

Well, there might be one, but I'm not him.

Chapter FOUR

Jessica

I CLOSE THE DOOR BEHIND me and sag against it, kicking off my shoes. My feet feel as though they're on fire. I knew I should've taken sensible shoes with me to work, especially considering I've been showing clients around houses today then doing a presentation tonight. We're trying to impress a new contractor; I think it went well but I'll have to wait and see what they thought about our company. This is an amazing opportunity for our business.

What a day and night it's been. Lee and I are going to have to advertise for another agent because she won't be able to cope with this workload on her own in a few months' time when I go on maternity leave.

There's music coming from the living room, which means Scott's home; he's meant to be working nightshift this week. Why is he home? Did he have the night off and I've forgotten about it? Walking into the living room, something seems off. He's sitting slumped in the chair, with a beer can in his hand. Bloody hell, this isn't good.

Why tonight?

He looks pissed. He's not had a drink in over a year and has decided tonight is a good time to start again. Oh, God, no. I really should've left him last year when his drinking spiralled out of control after he lost his job. It was awful seeing the confident man I love turn into this drunken weakling who didn't care about anything or anyone. I helped him to help himself. He finally sought out help and turned his life back around.

I turn away from him and hope I can slip away un-noticed and go for a bath in peace to soak away all my aches and pains. It's late, and right now I just need to unwind after an eventful and tiring day.

"Where the fuck do you think you're going?" His voice is slurred as he shouts at me.

I turn around slowly to face him. He pulls himself from the chair and staggers, with the beer can still in his hand.

"I'm just going for a bath. My body is sore and my feet ache. Why aren't you at work tonight?"

"Because, Jessica, they let me go. Told me I'm bloody useless."

"And you thought, 'I'll just sit here and get drunk', whilst I'm out working."

As I look at him, all I can see is a drunk man who wants to waste his life. He is nothing like the bank manager I first met. This is not the man I fell in love with. If I'm honest with myself, that man is long gone.

"No, I thought I would sit here, have a few drinks, and watch the Scotland game on TV."

Scott has always been a good-looking man. He's a few years older than me, but when he lost his job, he started to change. He went from always taking pride in his appearance to not giving a shit. Now he only bothers when I moan if we're going out together, and that's not often anymore.

"It's late. Where have you been?" he shouts as he moves toward me.

"I told you this morning, I had a presentation to do tonight with Lee."

"And you expect me to believe that? Are you sure you had work to do? You say you're working, but I don't think you are. I think you're seeing someone else."

I laugh at him. That is fucking ludicrous. I don't have the time or inclination to be seeing someone else.

"Scott, can we not do this now? I'm too bloody tired to have another argument with you. I've been out the door since before eight this morning, my back is killing me, and as for our baby, it seems quite happy to do somersaults all day and night." I rub my swollen belly.

"Our baby? I don't believe this is our baby. You spend far too much time away from me for this to be my baby."

"If this is what you think, why are you still here?" I shout at him. I know I shouldn't be shouting considering how late it is, but he's trying to push me into an argument.

I turn my back on him and walk down the hall. I can hear him shouting after me, but I don't hear the words, just the damn racket he makes moving around the living room. The sound of something smashing startles me. I don't even want to know what it is.

"Don't you fucking walk away from me! Do you hear me?"

I turn my head slightly to see him stagger into the hallway toward me. I shake my head in sheer disgust then carry on walking. This idiot is the father of my child. God help us both.

If I just ignore him tonight, he might fall into bed and straight to sleep. When he's sleeping, I can go and sleep in the spare room. There is no way I'm waking up to him in the morning. All he'll want is one thing, and he sure as hell isn't getting it from me.

"I was fucking talking to you." He grabs my shoulder. I stop and turn to him in time to see his hand coming up fast and making contact with the side of my face.

"You bastard!" I shout as I slap him back. "Get out! This is my house. I don't want you here. So, go on, leave! Now. I will pack up your things tomorrow."

"Sweetheart, you really shouldn't have done that." He grabs my hair and drags me to the bedroom. I struggle against his hold the whole time, but my body is exhausted. "Jessica, why are you struggling?"

"Because I'm not letting you hurt me. You can't hurt me."

He stops in the middle of our bedroom and pulls me to my feet. I slap him hard across the face, leaving the palm of my hand stinging.

"You fucking bitch." He kicks me, swiping my feet from under me. I fall to the floor in a heap. Turning away from him to protect my baby, I wrap my arms around me and pray this will be over quickly.

No!

I cry out in panic, opening my eyes, taking in my surroundings. Fear grips me. A dream . . . It was just a dream. My body shivers and my breathing is laboured. I lift my hands and rub them against my face; beads of sweat are dripping down my forehead. I scour the room, looking for him, because I'm certain I heard his voice; it was so clear. My body relaxes into the bed when I see the room is empty.

Bile churns in my stomach as I remember every last detail of my nightmare. Everything felt so real; it felt as though I was going through it all again. The conversation, the beating . . . then blank . . .

The bedroom door flies open as my mum rushes in. Straight away, she's beside me on the bed, with her arms around me. Dad rushes into the room moments later to witness me falling apart again. It can't be natural to be crying all the time. The slightest thing can set me off when I'm awake, but it's my dreams that cause the most damage.

Everything that took place that night is still so clear in my mind.

"What time is it?" I ask.

"Two-thirty in the afternoon," Dad says. "Are you hungry?"

I shake my head.

"Jessica, you need to try and eat something now." My mum's voice is soft yet firm as she speaks. "Please . . ."

"I could try," I say, knowing it will please her. "I think I should get up and at least go for a shower."

"Can you manage on your own or do you need me to help?"

"I'm sure I'll manage."

"Okay, in that case I'll go and make you something. Is there anything in particular you want?"

"No, Mum. A sandwich is fine."

Dad kisses her as she leaves the bedroom with a smile on her face.

"Jessica . . ." His doleful eyes look down on me, and his voice is taut. He sits on the bottom of the bed and takes my hand. "The police were here this morning to see you."

"Why?" My heart rate quickens and panic sets in.

"Because they want to speak to you about what happened last week, and for you to press charges. They called at the hospital but we didn't think it was the appropriate time. If it makes it any easier, the officer is a lovely lady."

"It doesn't make a difference. I don't want to talk to them."

Dad looks taken aback with my declaration. I take a deep breath, filling my lungs with some much needed air as I try to compose myself.

"You have to. He can't be allowed to get away with what he's done to you."

"Dad, I don't expect you or Mum to understand. It's bad enough that I have to re-live it every time I close my eyes. There's no way I can go through the process of a court case and having to tell everyone what he did to me." My composure is gone as I fight back the sobs building inside me. "Please, Dad. Please don't make me."

I stare at him and can see he's battling with my request. He moves to sit beside me and holds me close. "Okay, okay. But this is breaking my heart. I feel so helpless. I don't know how to help you through this. The police are coming back to speak to you, but it will be up to you what you decide to do about HIM."

"Dad, I'll get through this because of you, Mum, and Lee. I need to figure out for myself how to move on because at the moment, there is no light at the end of the tunnel for me. Only darkness."

"Oh, baby. I want you to know that I'm here for you, no matter what."

"I know that, but I don't want you and Mum putting your life on hold."

"Jessica, you're our daughter, our only child, and we will do whatever it takes to help and support you through this."

"Thank you." I kiss his forehead. "I'm going to go for a shower then I'll join you for lunch."

He smiles, moving from the bed.

The shower was just what I needed. I should've gone for a shower yesterday when I got here, but I was mentally exhausted. Now, though, I realise I've spent nearly twenty-four hours in my bed. I stand in front of the full-length mirror in the bedroom with a towel wrapped around me. The bruising is still visible on my face, arms, and legs, but I know I need to look at the rest of my body.

Dropping the towel, I gasp. My body shakes uncontrollably at the vision in the mirror. I hardly recognise myself.

There is bruising everywhere; all over my tummy, along with several deep cuts. My eyes travel downward to the scar that is now on my bikini line. My constant reminder of the attack that took away my son's life. They had to do a C-section because of my condition when I arrived in hospital; I was unconscious. All this was explained to me, but this is the first time I've been able to look at my reflection. I asked the nurse to cover up the mirrors in the bathroom of my hospital room. I wasn't ready to see myself then.

No wonder my dad wants me to press charges. If this was Lee standing before me looking this bad, I would be urging her to press charges. But as I said to my dad, I can't relive it. I'm not strong enough to face him. And if I press charges, I would have to come face to face with a man I once loved. A man who, in one night, destroyed my world.

I'm not going to cry. I'm not going to cry. It's taking every ounce of energy I have not to cry as I look over Scott's handy work. I feel dizzy and sick, but I try not to dwell on those feelings.

Turning away from the mirror, I see a pair of my shorts and a t-shirt laid out on the bed, along with some underwear. How did they get here? They were in a drawer in my own bedroom. Someone has been to my house. Dressing quickly, I brush the knots out of my long, light brown hair, and pull it back into a bobble. I've only towel dried my hair; I can't be bothered with the hairdryer. Even the thought of holding the hairdryer makes me feel sore.

I'd like to say I look normal when I leave the room, but how can someone with so many bruises look normal?

Normal; what's that again? Looking at the bruises, I'm not sure when they will ever go away. It's been a week and they still look so raw and fresh.

No. Nothing about my life is ever going to be normal again. I'm a broken shell of my former self, and nothing can repair the damage that's been done.

Making my way toward the kitchen, I hear voices, and there's one that stands out. I recognise the thick Glasgow accent from yesterday, but I have no idea who it belongs to.

Do I want to see who is in the kitchen with my parents?

Yes, of course I do. I'm more than a little curious.

I feel a tad self-conscious about my appearance. Then I think of how I looked to him, whoever he is, when he picked me up in his arms yesterday, carried me into the house, and laid me on the bed. I don't suppose I look any worse.

Closing my eyes, I take a deep breath and count to ten before opening them and entering the kitchen.

Mum is busy washing dishes at the sink, and she turns, hearing my footsteps on the cold tiled floor. Dad and the stranger stop talking and turn toward me.

Panic takes me by surprise, grabbing me by my chest and squeezing tightly until I feel unable to breathe as he looks at me. His eyes don't leave my face.

My body sways and starts tumbling downward. He pushes out of the seat quickly and his strong arms catch me once again, stopping my fall. This already feels as though it's becoming a habit. A habit that needs to be broken.

"Here, let me help," he says in a husky voice that could turn any woman into a quivering wreck. Lee would fall in love just hearing his voice. He guides me to the table and I sit down. I can hear water running then Mum is beside me.

"Jessica, take a drink," Mum insists, handing me a glass of water. I can feel three sets of eyes on me as I take a large gulp of water.

"Sorry," Dad says. "I should introduce you. Jess, this is Fletcher Adams. Mrs Adams from next door . . . this is her grandson."

"Hi," I say, avoiding eye contact. "I'm sorry about yesterday, and I'm sorry to hear about your gran."

"Thanks, and don't apologise. I'm only glad I was here to help."

I lift my head and finally look at him.

He has the most mesmerising blue eyes I have ever seen, and they're studying me closely.

Chapter FIVE

Fletcher

MY EYES LOCK WITH HERS and I can't pull my gaze away. Holy fuck. She is fucking beautiful. Those gorgeous hazel eyes are holding me captive. Jessica moves her hand as though she's going to run her fingers through her hair, only to stop suddenly, realising it's all tied back. I smile.

Her breathing quickens as her eyes are upon me.

She doesn't look as frail as she did yesterday. Christ, I can't imagine how bad she looked last week. Her lips are luscious, and what I wouldn't do to hold her in my arms and press a soft kiss to her lips.

Fucking hell, Fletcher Adams. Pull your shit together. I can't be thinking about her like this. I shouldn't be thinking of kissing her; it's so fucking wrong.

She sits before me in an almost trance-like state, staring at me.

I can't believe I've been so affected by her. I've never been affected by any woman, not like this. Every single thing about her draws me in and I feel totally helpless.

God, under normal circumstances this girl would be mine. I want her, but I know I can't have her.

Chapter SIX

Jessica

"HOW ARE YOU FEELING, SWEETHEART?"

My mum's voice distracts me from looking at Fletcher, who I have to say, is very easy on the eyes. Lee would love a lot more than his voice.

"I'm a bit cold, to be honest. Do you have a jumper or something I could wear?" I'm suddenly aware that I'm sitting in front of a complete stranger with very few clothes on. He might be a handsome stranger, but I don't feel comfortable sitting here like this, especially with all my bruising on show. I wish I'd left my hair down. It would fall over my face and hide some of the marks on my neck.

I catch the slight smirk on Fletcher's face; he knows I'm uncomfortable in his presence.

Why is he here?

"Yes, sweetheart. I'll go and get something for you to put on," she says, leaving the kitchen. My dad and Fletcher return to talking. I'm lost in my thoughts. I shiver, my dream from earlier still playing heavily on my mind. Shit. Did Fletcher hear me crying out as I woke from my nightmare?

I try not to think about that as I attempt to pour a cup of tea from the teapot sitting in the middle of the table. My hand shakes, making the teapot lid rattle.

"Let me." Fletcher takes the teapot out my hands, and for the briefest of moments, his fingers touch my skin. A charge of electricity passes between us. I look at him and see sadness in his eyes. Turning away, I pull my hand quickly from his. I don't want or need to have some stranger feeling sorry for me. Pitying me.

He pours the tea into my cup and starts talking to my dad again.

"Here, you go," Mum says, handing me one of my own hooded jumpers. Taking it from her, I look at it and then at her. "What's wrong?"

"Who's been to the house? Did Lee get some of my things?"

"No," Dad tells me. "Fletcher took me the other day. I knew you would need clothes."

"B . . . but why? Why would you take someone I don't know into my house?" I shout at him. I'm not happy at the thought of this man being in my home, touching things that belong to me.

"Jessica, can you calm down, please?"

"Why should I?"

"Maybe I should go," Fletcher says, pushing his chair back and standing. He's tall. Very tall. My gaze travels up him until I reach his face, those dazzling eyes, but that's not what I see. His eyes have darkened and all I see is a hollowness as he watches me. As I look at him, I know he feels sorry for me, and my blood begins to boil. "I'm intruding on your grief."

He knows about what's happened to me. A complete stranger, and he knows all my business. He doesn't need to know this. Why would my parents talk to him about me? Why?

"Yes, I think you should."

"I'm sorry," Fletcher says as he turns and walks away.

"Jessica. You should apologise to him. There was no need for you to be so rude," my mum says, sliding a plate of sandwiches across the table to me.

I pause, stopping myself from speaking for a few minutes, giving myself time to calm down. "Maybe not." I sigh. "Why was he at my house?"

"Because, if I'm truthful with you, if Scott was there I knew I wouldn't be able to stop myself from wanting to kill him." Dad's words hit me hard. "It was Fletcher who brought your mum and me into hospital the day we were given the news about you. My car wouldn't start. Your mum was so upset and crying. He offered and we accepted because it meant we got to you quicker. Fletcher had a look at my car but it needed to go into the garage. When I spoke to him about going to your house, he offered again, and I didn't hesitate to accept. You needed some of your things here."

I didn't know about Dad's car. That's why we got a taxi home yesterday. "I guess."

"He's also a young man who could do with a friend at the moment. He's suffering too, yet still went out of his way to help us. There's a lot more to Fletcher Adams than what the press report."

I catch the scowl on my mum's face at his words. Why does that name seem oddly familiar to me? What am I missing?

"Sorry."

"Sweetheart, you have nothing to apologise to us for. We understand how hard this is for you, but maybe if you feel up to it, you should go and apologise to Fletcher later."

"We'll see."

I sit quietly at the table, drink my tea, and think about what's been said. Maybe I was a bit harsh and jumped the gun. I manage a few bites from one of the sandwiches. There's a brooding look in my mum's eyes when I push the plate away.

"Sorry, that's all I can manage."

"Jessica, if you don't start eating properly, you're going to end up sick."

"Elaine, that's more than she's eaten all week, so it's an improvement." Dad smiles at me. "Your phone has been going non-stop this morning." He grabs my phone that was sitting on the work surface and brings it over.

Six missed calls from Dale, the property developer, and a text:

Jess, been calling you all morning but Lee has just told me what's happened. I'm so sorry. If you need anything, I'm here. Lee has the contracts for you to sign, but don't worry about a thing. We can talk when you're ready.

I smile at his message. Dale is lovely, and I'm pleased he's given the contract to us. I'm certain we will have no problem selling the apartments. Dale's company isn't a national company with all their own in-house teams, that's why he needs us to do all his marketing and selling, but these apartments will sell themselves. I don't think we'll need to do much to get viewers through the doors.

There's a text from Lee:

Coming over soon to see you. We have something to celebrate.

Just as I'm about to type out a reply to her, my phone buzzes in my hand. I freeze, looking at the screen, and drop the phone on the table. Panic sets in. I can't speak to him.

Scott!

Dad grabs it and answers.

"What the hell do you want? . . . No, you can't see her . . . She doesn't want to see you . . . The baby? You have a fucking cheek to ask. You killed the baby . . . What did you think? Did you think everything would be okay when you beat my daughter up to within an inch of her life . . . Yes, the locks have been changed . . . Your things? I'll bag them and put them out with the rubbish . . . DO NOT try to contact Jess again . . ."

He ends the call and sighs heavily, taking my hand.

"When did you change the locks?" I ask.

"The other day when I went with Fletcher. The front door had been secured, so I had to get someone out to let us in. I've also arranged for someone to go in and clean it up. I didn't want you to go back and see the mess it was in. Scott has completely wrecked it; everything is smashed and there's glass everywhere. I just took what I thought you would need for a few days and then left. I'm more than happy to go back with you if you need anything."

"Thanks. I'm going to lie down. I'm feeling a bit sore."

"Can I get you anything?" Mum asks.

"No, but if I fall asleep, can you wake me when Lee gets here? We have something to discuss about our new contract."

"This sounds exciting. How about I make a nice dinner for the four of us?" She half smiles at me, and I suddenly realise I miss seeing her smile. Mum has looked sad and broken the last week as she spent many hours with me at the hospital. She has such a beautiful smile when she does have something to smile about.

"Yes, Mum. I'm sure Lee would love some of your cooking."

Lee said recently that she missed my mum's cooking. When we were growing up, Lee would make sure she was at our house at least once a week for dinner. Her excuse was that she hated her mum's cooking. And it has to be said, her mum isn't a very good cook.

I go back into the bedroom and lie down on the bed with my dad's end of the conversation with Scott playing on my mind.

I wonder if he even remembers what happened at the house. Because he was so drunk, he might not remember. If that's the case, he needs to seek help before he does it again to someone else, because it won't be me. I can never forgive him for what he's taken from me. Never.

He's taken the most important thing he could from me. Our baby would have wanted for nothing, especially love.

I had my reservations when I found out I was pregnant. I was worried about being a good mum and running the business, especially given how hard Lee and I have worked to build up our reputation. I would have hated to let Lee down or leave her struggling to run the business. I might have the majority share; a sixty-forty split, but we both work damn hard.

That brings me back to Scott. There are things that need to be sorted out between us; there's bills in both our names and a bank account that will need to be closed down. I'm glad he had nothing to do with my business. Lee and I did think about having him do some work with us, but it was me who decided against it.

I'm not looking forward to the day when we need to sit down like adults and discuss things, and I know I can't ask for my dad's help with that, given how he feels about him. Lee has also made it clear how she feels about him. I think she might kill him before Dad does. I'm not sure when I'll be ready to meet Scott face-to-face. I know it has to be done soon, but I will need someone with me because I don't want to be alone with him.

I lie and stare at the ceiling, and try to block out my feelings, my emotions, but it's hard. The last week has been tough to get through, and I have no idea how I'm going to get through the weeks and months ahead. It's going to take a miracle to pull me back into the land of the living.

And right now, I don't believe in miracles.

My eyes roam the room and stop on the box of memories that one of the nurses made for me. It sits on the dresser by the window. I've not been able to look through it yet. I know I will open it one day, but everything seems so raw. Part of me is scared of letting go. Scared of how I'm going to feel as I look through it. She asked if I wanted a picture of James, and also of his handprints and footprints. I said yes. She said, when the time is right, I will take great comfort in looking at my memories.

Comfort. I don't think I will ever take comfort from a memory box. Having my baby in my arms would be a comfort. Tears I thought had all dried up start falling again, flowing like a river out of control down my face.

The only memories I have at the moment are of everything Scott has taken from me. All that would've been great in my life. All the joy that comes from bringing up a child. I won't be enjoying the feeling of becoming a mum now.

There's a knock on my room door before it opens.

"Sweetheart, the community midwife is here to cheek on you," my mum says, coming in with the midwife behind her. The midwife asks my mum to leave us alone for a few minutes. I catch the surprised expression on her face; I think she wants to stay and hear what the midwife has to say before she leaves. I'm glad she's left us, though. I have a lot of questions to ask about my body. All the changes are playing havoc with my emotions.

She is very thorough in her detail. I feel as though there is a piece of rope wrapped around my heart, with someone standing pulling the ends, squeezing the last ounce of life out me. To think that after everything I've already gone through, there is still more pain in store for me as my body adjusts to not being pregnant. She does tell me I should consider going on the pill, stating it might help with my hormones, not something I wanted to think about, yet. She cleans and checks my wound, putting on a fresh dressing, the dressing had fallen off whilst I was in the shower.

We talk about how I'm feeling. I guess this is just part of her job; she needs to discriminate between grief and depression. And as she speaks, I have no idea what she thinks of me. We talk briefly about my other injuries. She thinks I should see a big difference over the next few days in the bruising. I hope she's right because I hate looking in the mirror and seeing how badly marked I am.

She tells me, because of my operation, I'm not allowed to drive for a few weeks. That should be interesting when I decide to go back to work.

Work. I will need to go back, I'm just unsure when I'll be fit and emotionally okay. This is when it hits me; all the uncertainty in my life. In a life I had planned for.

When she finally leaves, my tears fall until my eyes close and darkness takes me away for a short time.

Chapter SEVEN

Fletcher

THIS HANGOVER IS BAD, BUT after hearing Jessica's screams, I can't sit here and feel sorry for myself. I swear her screams are going to fucking haunt my dreams. No one should have to relive what she's gone through. I don't think I'll forget the look of pain and fear on Elaine's face when we heard the first scream as we sat talking at their kitchen table.

Helpless . . . there was nothing I could do to help. When I heard her, I had an overwhelming urge to run to her, take her in my arms and hold her tight. But it's not my place, no matter how much I wanted to.

Jim has been great in listening to me for the past week, but I shouldn't have been there today. I know he and Elaine are being friendly to me because of Gran, but I've intruded on a private time, so I can understand Jessica's anger. Although, in my defence, I've been in the right place at the right time when it comes to her.

Yesterday, I watched from the window as she arrived home with her parents. She looked so tiny and frail, and when I saw her fall, I had to go and help. I ran from the house and picked her up from her mother's arms, leaving Jim to console his wife.

I carried her lifeless body inside the house. Looking at her, I had a lump in my throat. She looked in so much pain. Even with all her bruises and cuts, it's clear to me she is fucking beautiful. She's perfect.

This doesn't make any sense to me. I'm blaming the hangover from hell for all these wild thoughts.

As I sit on the floor, going through a box of pictures, my phone rings. "Logan, what's up?"

"Just calling to see how your night ended up?"

I bet he is.

"My night was interesting," I say, as memories come to me. Fuck, the sex was hot, but I don't want to think about it.

"What you doing now?"

"Going through another box of Gran's things."

"You fancy some company?"

"Yeah, why not?"

"Okay, be there soon."

One of the advantages to being back here in Glasgow is Logan. We first met about ten years ago when we both played for a youth football team down south. He's always been a cocky shit, but I suppose that's why we work as friends. I'm sure he wants to talk shop with me. He's desperate to know if I've made a decision on what team I'll be playing for in the new season. Which side of the old firm I'll be joining. I'm either going to be on his team or the opposition.

We've played together many times for the national team over the last few years. Logan has been capped twenty-five times, and I've been capped thirty-two, scoring twenty-one goals. My record is pretty impressive, even if I do say so myself. I was first called into the national squad at the age of sixteen, making me the youngest ever player to score in my very first game for my national team.

Logan is one of the best goalkeepers in the country, and that might just be helping make up my mind. Even I struggle to get the ball in the back of the net when he's standing between those posts.

It's strange looking through pictures. There are so many of my dad, and yes, I now know who I take after. Mum never had any pictures of him when we left Scotland. I'm certain she sat and burned them all one night. I get that she was angry with how he had been taken from her, from us, but I could never understand why she shut everyone out. My dad, John Adams, died a few weeks before I was born. He was in the wrong place at the wrong time when a fight broke out. All I know is he died after being stabbed several times. I suppose this one tragic accident is what shaped not just my mum's future, but mine and my grandparents'.

I used to wish my mum had left me with my gran. I know Gran loved me, and she would never have hurt me or lifted her hands to me.

To this day, every time Mum hit me, I have no idea what it was for. I wasn't that bad as a child, but that woman fucked up my life in more ways than one. I've realised these last few months that's just how she was. If my dad had been alive, I'm sure things would've been different. Maybe she wouldn't have been drunk all the time, feeling sorry for herself. She never really moved on with her life. There was never a someone special for her. And that part makes me sad.

I pick up a photo and smile as I see how happy my parents were. It has to be said, Mum was a good-looking girl when she was younger, but I don't remember her looking like this. She always seemed so sad, distant and angry, and always with me.

I glance around this room; it's going to take me longer than I originally thought to clear and sort through Gran's things. And I'm not sure what I should do with the house. Should I sell it? Or stay in it? I do feel a sense of belonging here. Something I've not had since I left Scotland as a boy. I never really settled anywhere else.

I'm still sitting on the floor when the front door opens.

"Fletcher," Jim calls out. "Sorry, son. I did try knocking."

"No, no. It's fine. Come in," I say, surprised to see him.

"I just want to apologise about earlier."

"Don't be stupid. I'm the one who should be sorry. How is she?"

"I don't know."

I tell him to take a seat. He looks tired; there are bags under his eyes that I haven't noticed before. It's no surprise that he's not sleeping. His concern for his daughter is clear. I sense he wants to talk. He's been there for me, so I can only return the favour.

"I don't think she'll ever get over this. The midwife has been in to see her this afternoon. I don't get it. A midwife comes out to check on a baby when a new mum comes home from hospital, but there's no baby to check on." He's holding it together, but only just. "I shouldn't be bothering you with my problems. You have enough going on. Have you made a decision yet?" he asks, changing the subject.

"You've been here to listen to me, so why can't I do the same for you? And no, but my friend, Logan, might sway my decision."

"As in Logan Walker, the goalkeeper?" His face lights up and I now know his team of choice. I nod. "Well, I'm sure you'll make the right decision. I only wanted to apologise for earlier. If you need me for anything, you know where I am." He leans over me and looks at the picture in my hands. "Your dad? You look a lot like him, and I know you've had it hard, son, but you need to try and move on. Your mum? A good-looking girl."

I smile as he leaves. He's right; she was beautiful back then. Maybe this is what I should focus on about her. I might not feel so bitter and angry then about the life we had.

I hear Logan's voice saying hi to Jim.

"Who was the man leaving?"

I look up to see him standing in the doorway with a box of beers in his arms.

"That's Jim from next door. I met him and his wife last week when their daughter . . ."

"A girl? Is this what's been wrong with you? Fuck, why didn't I put two and two together? I expect you to finally tell me what's going on, and I know it's more than your gran."

After putting the beers down, he goes in search of a bottle opener. He sits down opposite me and opens two bottles then hands me one.

"Well, I believe you have a story for me?"

I start at the beginning and tell him how I met the Taylors. He sits quietly but looks taken aback when I tell him about Jessica, and how her boyfriend beat her up so badly she lost her baby. I tell him about yesterday, and I'm not sure what I see on his face, but he looks at me funny. You would have to have a heart of stone for this not to affect you. He smiles when I tell him about carrying her in my arms.

"So, you feel sorry for this chick? God, I feel for her and I've not met her," he says.

"Yes, I suppose I do, but there's more to it than that. Even with every bruise on her, I can see how beautiful she is."

"Shit! Have you really just said that?" I close my eyes and shake my head. "I've sat here quietly and listened to you. You seem to have it bad for some chick you've met briefly for five minutes. This is why you've been blowing me off all week?"

"I know it sounds fucking crazy," I say, opening my eyes.

"Why didn't you say anything last night?"

"What, for you all to take the piss out of me? I don't think so. Look, I know how it sounds, and I had no idea how to explain it."

Logan takes a long drink from his beer and stares into space. "So last night, disappearing with the two dolly birds. What was that all about?"

"You know me, never one to look a gift horse in the mouth. No, seriously, I hoped they might take my mind off Jessica, but it didn't work. Yes, I enjoyed them at the time, but as soon as I left she was in my thoughts."

"Fletch, she comes with too much baggage. Surely you know that?"

"No, she doesn't. Not in my mind."

"You're heading for trouble. Even if you stood a chance with her, do you really think her dad is going to be happy about you spending time with his daughter after what she's been through? If I had a daughter, I wouldn't let you anywhere near her."

He makes a very good point. My reputation with the ladies is not good, and let's face it, it's been well documented over the last few years. I've well and truly fucked up before I've even got the chance to get to know her.

Story of my fucking life. A fuck up.

Chapter EIGHT

Jessica

"ARE YOU SURE YOU'RE UP to this today, Jessica? You don't have to go in. I'm sure Lee would understand." Mum watches me as I finish putting some light make-up on.

Oh, Mum. I don't have the heart to tell her Lee wouldn't understand. It's because of her I'm going through the motions of getting ready for work. She has been patient and understanding, but has given me the kick up the backside I need to get me out of the house. Lee said she can't sit back and watch me give up on life, so she demanded I return to work today, even if I don't want to. I love Lee dearly, but she can be a right bitch at times.

We had words only two nights ago, or rather Lee had words with me. At the end of it, we were both crying, and I agreed to come into work today. So here I am, four weeks after everything, and trying to put on a brave face, if only to keep everyone else happy.

Lee made me look at how I've been behaving, closing myself off from everyone, including my parents and her. But the thing with all three of them is, they would only allow me to sink so far before throwing me a life support to pull myself back into the land of the living, and that is what Lee did.

Since our conversation, I suppose I've done a lot of soul searching. Learned lots about myself; some things I would never have associated with me. Like becoming a victim. Letting Scott affect my life the way he has. Not venturing outside my parents' front door. Refusing at times to speak to my family and friends.

My grief for my son consumes me. And yes, I know everyone deals with grief differently, but I fear my feelings are way past the normal stages of grief. It took Lee to pull me back into the present from the darkness I was in. The darkness was comforting in a strange sort of way. It meant I didn't have to focus on anything. Not Scott, not work, and not my family and friends.

"No. I need to start doing things, and what better place to start than going to work? The longer I stay here feeling sorry for myself, the harder it's going to be." I try hard to force a smile. A smile my mum is almost certain to see through. I'm not even sure I believe the words I'm saying. Mum has always been able to see through me. She could always tell when I was lying to her when I was growing up. She has no idea how hard this is for me. To go through the motions and pretend I'm okay, forcing myself to get out of bed each day when all I want to do is fall asleep and never open my eyes again. All I want is darkness, because then I don't have to feel the way I do. Alone. I feel so very alone and scared, but most of all, I feel lost. I'm hoping that doing something normal helps me before I sink deeper than I already am. Anything has got to be better than staring at the four walls of this darkened room.

"I understand that, I really do, but I just feel as though you haven't given yourself enough time to deal with things. The bruising has only just faded from your face." She moves closer and reaches out to me. "Jessica, I'm worried about you. You've hardly moved from this room, and you've not spoken about what's happened. It's like you're in denial."

"Mum, please don't worry about me. I'm not in denial. I'm only too aware of what's happened these last few weeks, but I'm dealing with things in my own way. It may not be the right way, but at the moment, it's the only way I know. And as for not speaking about things, I have an appointment with the therapist later on in the week. He called and wants to see me, to see how I'm coping."

Mum raises her eyebrows as though she's surprised by my words but then smiles at me. His phone call came after the midwife had been out a few times, so I suppose I have her to thank.

"I'm glad, but just remember you don't have to go through this alone. We're here for you."

"Thanks, Mum."

I know she's trying to help, but I *am* going through this alone. No one else, just me. None of them will ever understand how empty I feel inside. It's strange because I've always thought of myself as strong and independent, but at the moment, all I feel is weak and helpless.

"Now, what about lunch? Do you think you'll have time to meet me today?"

"Sorry, not today. Maybe Wednesday. Lee and I are having a lunch meeting. She's out of the office this morning so she wants to meet and go over a few things for later in the week."

"That's fine. Now hurry up, and your dad will drop you off in town," she says before leaving the room. I should make the effort to go and collect my own car; I don't want to depend on my dad all the time.

Dad got his car back the other day. I'm sure Fletcher took him to the garage. I've heard his voice a few times in the house, but I haven't seen him. I know I should've apologised to him at the time. Now, though, I know it's too late. And anyway, if I'm truthful, I couldn't care less about him. I don't know him and I don't want to know him.

My parents were very fond of Mrs Adams. I only met her a handful of times, and she was a lovely old woman, so I can understand Dad spending some time with this Fletcher.

I glance in the mirror and I don't like what I see; even with my make-up on, I'm still chalk-white. My face is thin and gaunt, my eyes have dark circles underneath them from lack of sleep, and when my eyes slide down my body, I look fucking hellish. I've lost far too much weight. Looking at me now, you would never know I'd been pregnant.

With a sigh and a shake of my head, I leave the comfort of the room, not sure if I'm ready to take on the world, but today is already better than yesterday because today I'm prepared to at least try.

"You look lovely," Dad says with a smile full of warmth as I walk toward him.

"You don't have to lie. I look like shit."

"Jessica!" Mum scolds me.

"What? It's true."

"You are always beautiful in my eyes." Dad kisses my cheek. I smile, and for the first time in weeks, it's not forced. He really has no idea how saying such a small thing like I'm beautiful makes me feel. "Now, we should go before you're late for work. What would the boss say?" We both laugh at his awful sense of humour but it's worked. Not only has he made me smile, but laugh as well.

Maybe, just maybe, things aren't so bad after all.

Mum tries to give me a slice of toast as we leave; I tell her I'll get something on my way. She raises her eyebrows and shakes her head as if questioning my statement. I kiss her and walk outside to wait by the car. It looked as though she wanted a quick word with my dad. Me. That's what she wants to talk to him about. Why do I have the feeling they're going to be checking up on me all day? I'm certain Mum will leave the checking up to my dad, and he will agree to do it, just to keep the peace.

As I wait for them to finish their conversation on the front door step, my eyes drift to the car sitting in the driveway of Mrs

Adams' house. A Porsche. The man has expensive tastes. Red, though, is not a colour I would have thought for a man. Maybe it's not Fletcher's. It could belong to his girlfriend, or even his wife. I don't know him, so he might have a wife.

The front door opens and closes, and out comes a very attractive Fletcher, dressed in sports gear, with a bag in his hand. I take a moment to appreciate how he looks. Tiny hairs on the back of my neck stand to attention as he walks toward me. Those mesmerising sky-blue eyes hold me captive, and I'm unable to look away as he very slowly and deliberately drags them over my body. I feel the heat rise in my cheeks and goose bumps break out across my skin. A lazy smile plays on his lips as he watches me.

He's taller than me, but that's not hard with me only being five-foot-three. I feel small in his presence. His brown hair isn't too short, but sits perfectly; it's styled to perfection. I don't remember him having stubble along his jawline, but then I don't remember much about him other than those amazing blue eyes. I have to admit, he's hot. Bad boy hot. Probably sees himself as a bit of a player, and it's not hard to see why. I shouldn't be paying this much attention to him and how he looks.

"Nice to see you again, Jess." His voice is smooth and confident as he speaks—the kind of voice some girls could listen to all day and still want to hear more. "You look better." His smile shows off his dimples and his perfectly white teeth.

"Thanks. I wish I felt it. About the other week, I'm really sorry. I'm not usually so rude."

He frowns. "It's my fault. I was intruding on what should've been a private matter, so for that, I'm sorry. And for what it's worth, I was only too glad to be able to help your dad out. He's done so much in the past for my gran and I can never repay him for that. And as for going to your home, I'm glad you didn't have to see it. You had enough to deal with. So, are you going to work today?"

"Yeah, thought I should. Can't stay locked away forever, no matter how much I want to." I can hear the sadness in my own voice.

"You're too beautiful to be locked away," he says, his voice softer than it was only moments ago.

"Thank you for the compliment, I think, but I would have to disagree," I say quietly, embarrassed and surprised by his words.

Fletcher leans closer to me, resting his hand on the car behind me, his eyes sparkling. "Take the compliment. I don't give them easily."

His statement both surprises and pleases me. My breath hitches and I have to force myself to breathe.

"I should go. I have somewhere I need to be," he tells me. "But I'm glad to see you looking better than the last time I saw you, although, you need to eat. I'll see you soon, I hope."

He turns away and walks to his car, and I smile again. Twice in the one day. A new record. I watch as he throws his sports bag in the back seat and gets in his car. He flashes me a huge smile, pulls out of the driveway, and speeds away along the street.

My morning in the office goes by quickly. I've spent most of my time replying to emails and dealing with phone calls. It's kept me busy and kept my mind occupied, and for that, I'm grateful. It's twelve-fifteen when I leave the office and walk the short distance to the local bistro to meet Lee. It feels good to be out in the fresh air. Although, being in the city centre, it's highly polluted, but today it's not bothering me.

"There you are," Lee says, standing to greet me as I enter the bistro. "I was beginning to think I was being stood up." She gives me a hug and a kiss before pulling away and taking in my appearance. "You need to put on a few pounds."

"You're not the first person to say that today."

The usual waitress comes over and takes our order after telling me how sorry she is. This is what I had been dreading today; seeing that sympathetic look on people's faces when they speak to me. If people keep doing it, I'm never going to be able to move forward.

"So, how did you get on in the office this morning?" Lee asks, taking a drink.

"Good. I have a few meetings set up for later in the week with new clients. And Dale called about the opening at the apartments on Friday."

"Oh, crap. I knew I had something else to talk to you about. The designer, Matt, is in the penthouse this week, putting in the finishing touches. Dale wanted to know if we would both be there on Friday. What do you think? Are you feeling up to socialising?"

"Yes, I'll be fine for then." She eyes me sceptically. "What?"

"Just because you're back at work, doesn't mean I'll stop worrying about you." She frowns. "I know you're hurting, and it kills me seeing you in pain. Especially when I know there's nothing I can do to help you."

"Oh, honey!"

"Jess, please at least tell me things aren't as dark as they have been? Because, I'm not sure . . ."

I don't let her finish. I know what she means; she sat with me in her arms the night I told her I had nothing to live for. She stayed with me that night, afraid of what I would do on my own. I've not told my parents about that, and I'm sure Lee hasn't either. She made me promise if I ever felt that bad, I had to get in touch straight away. When I see the counsellor this week, I suppose I should tell him how bad things got. I'd never really given death much thought, and even when I tried to reassure Lee that wasn't what I meant by my words, I could already see the panic on her face.

"Lee, honestly, I'm past that place now. I'm trying hard to look forward. I'm not going to sit here and lie to you. It's hard, and there's not a day when James hasn't been in my thoughts."

"You promise me if you need to talk anytime, you'll talk to me."

"I promise." I smile.

"That's more like my best friend. It's been a long time since I've seen your smile."

"Would you be surprised if I told you that's not the first smile of the day?"

"What are you hiding?" Lee asks as the waitress brings over our lunch.

"Me? I'm not hiding anything," I tell her as I start eating. I can feel her eyes on me but I'm not about to tell her that Fletcher, a guy I hardly know, made me smile by paying me a compliment. Actually, I can't remember the last time a guy paid me a compliment.

We eat lunch and chat, just as we have done many times before. Lee doesn't treat me with kid gloves. She's not tip-toeing around me; she always tells me how she sees it but she has been my rock these last few weeks, the shoulder I've needed to lean on, and the comfort her arms have provided when words have failed.

"What do you have planned for this afternoon?" Lee asks as we finish eating.

"Just a few things in the office, why?"

"Could you be at the penthouse for two-thirty? We have our first viewing," she says with excitement.

"Of course I can. Do we know anything about the clients?"

"A footballer. That's all I've got. I have a meeting on the other side of the city with Mr and Mrs Richardson." She sounds disheartened, as though something about the Richardson's is bothering her; probably something she hasn't shared with me.

"What's wrong?" I ask, not liking the way she said their name.

"Mrs Richardson doesn't want to drop the asking price. Now, you and I both know the price she wants is unrealistic. She's never going to have someone put an offer in at the current price. But she wants me to put in more work trying to market it."

"Let me know how the meeting goes with them and we can discuss what we should do. I don't want to spend more time on this when the clients are reluctant to help. She was told that at the current price it wouldn't sell, but she wasn't happy with my valuation. I'm starting to wish they had taken their business elsewhere."

"I'll call you tonight and we can discuss it." Lee pauses and takes a drink before taking a deep breath. "What about Scott? Is he still sending messages and calling?"

"Yes. I've not replied to any of them, but it's starting to get to me. I'm going to need to change my number. Dad has also had the house number changed, so remind me to give you it. When I wouldn't answer my mobile, Scott started calling the house non-stop."

Scott's messages all say much the same; that he's really sorry and there are things we need to talk about. But in my opinion, there's nothing left to say between us. My ties with him are well and truly broken after that night in my home.

"What are you going to do about him?" she asks. "I know what I want to do."

"I don't know yet." The police called back around, but I was adamant I wasn't going to press charges. But if he keeps hassling me, I will be left with no choice.

"We could go out after work tomorrow and sort out a new phone, if you want?"

"Okay."

Lee pays our bill, saying it's her treat today and I can pay for lunch later in the week. We hug before going our separate ways. I need to go back to the office and collect a few things before going to the apartments, and she has to go across town.

Chapter NINE

Fletcher

MY PACE QUICKENS AS I try to push my thoughts about Jess to the back of my mind. Thoughts I shouldn't have. It's been a long time since I've pushed myself this hard during a training session. I only jumped on the treadmill to warm up and I'm still running flat out nearly thirty minutes later.

"What the fuck are you doing this morning? You said you wanted to work out. If you wanted to run a fucking marathon, that's what the streets are for, not this poor treadmill that will probably need a service by the time you've finished with it," Logan says loudly. I turn toward him. He's on the treadmill next to me, puffing and panting.

He's right, of course. My mind has been on other things since we started our workout.

I've not been able to concentrate on anything since I saw Jessica earlier. I didn't expect to see her as soon as I walked outside the door, but there she was, standing by her dad's car, looking mighty fine. She watched me intently as I walked toward her. The flush on her cheeks, the goose bumps on her skin. Yeah, I noticed it all.

I'm certain I embarrassed her with my compliment. I meant every word of it; she *is* too beautiful to be locked away. And the strange thing is, she doesn't know it. She looks completely different now her face is bruise free. I knew underneath all the marks her ex inflicted on her there was beauty, I just hadn't realised how perfect she was. Her beautiful light brown hair was shining in the early morning sunshine; she had obviously spent some time on it. And her deep hazel eyes; today is the first time I've seen life in them. Granted, I've only seen her a couple of times, but each time all I saw was sadness and pain.

I can't get Jessica Taylor out of my mind today no matter how much I try.

"One word. Jess?" he asks, even though he knows the answer. "Fuck! Do something about this because if you're like this when we start training with the team, it will be a long time before you get a game."

I know he's trying to help, and I need to pull myself together, especially since tomorrow it will all become official. I will be playing the next four seasons here in Scotland, with, in my opinion, the biggest team in the country. And the bonus is that I get to play alongside one of my closest friends, and I don't have to try and score into him.

"What the hell can I do about it?" I shout, causing a few people in the gym to turn and stare at us.

"No use shouting at me," he says as I finally stop on the treadmill. "I'm not the enemy here. Speak to her, ask her out on a date, anything. But, you, my friend, need to get your head on the game because you will only get one chance here. You fuck up, and your career will be over, no matter what your name is."

Yes, I've made mistakes, and I know the next one could cost me my career, but for me, being here in Scotland is all about new starts. I should have thought about that when I left the club with the blonde and the brunette. That was a mistake, no matter how much I enjoyed it at the time.

"I can't. It would be insensitive after what she's been through."

"Well, in that case, can I suggest you go out tonight, pick up some random girl, fuck her all night long and forget about Jess?"

"Don't you think I've tried that the last few weeks? I've even kept my distance from her, but seeing her this morning . . . She's perfection."

"You never said you saw her."

"She was leaving at the same time as me," I tell him before taking a long drink of water.

"Where was she going? And I think it's about time I meet this girl you can't get off your mind."

"Work, and how the hell am I going to introduce you to her?"

"As I said, a date."

"There is no way I'm asking her on a date. What part did you not get when I told you she lost a baby only four weeks ago? Even I know you don't move on from that sort of thing overnight. It's going to take time. Jim, her dad, is really worried about her."

"So, you're still on talking terms with her old man?" I nod. "Well, that's something. Look, I don't know what to say. I've never been that hung up on a girl who comes with baggage."

I understand what he's saying, and yes, I have to move on and stop thinking about her because I know she's never going to be interested in someone like me, given my reputation. She definitely doesn't need someone like me in her life.

Jessica Taylor is far too good for me, but maybe that's part of the attraction. Or maybe it's the circumstances I've met her under. Yes, I'm appalled at what she's gone through at her ex's hands, but I don't think it's just the fact that I feel sorry for her. Of course, I do feel sorry, I would have to be a heartless bastard not to, but there's something else. Something drawing me to her. Pulling me in.

"Right, lover boy. Time to get that head of yours out of the clouds. We still have more to do."

"Yeah, yeah. I hear you." He has no idea how much more we have to do.

We continue to move around the gym doing exercise after exercise. Poor Logan. He's red-faced and can barely breathe. I don't think he's worked this hard in weeks, maybe even months. He'd better start getting used to it, because my head might be on a beautiful girl next door, but I will always push myself hard when it comes to training. And from the look of it, Logan is going to struggle to keep up with the pace.

"Bloody hell, Fletch. Seriously, I can't do that every morning. You're going to have to find a new training buddy."

I laugh at him as he exits the showers with a towel around his waist. He stops and stares at me. "What?" I ask.

"I thought we were going for lunch? You look as though you're going on a date."

"We're still going for lunch, but I have an appointment this afternoon to view an apartment." I made this appointment a few days ago after speaking with Jim, and I was sure it would be Jessica's business partner I would be seeing today. But after seeing her this morning, I'm hoping it's her I'll be meeting at the apartments.

"You never mentioned you were house-hunting. I have a few things on this afternoon or I would've come with you. I presume it's the new apartments down by the Clyde?"

"Yeah."

"They do look amazing. Have you decided to sell your gran's place, then?"

"I don't know what to do with it. Part of me wants to renovate it and stay there, but another part of me says I should move on. It's a great house. It could be a great home for a family."

"So, the great Fletcher Adams doesn't plan on settling down, then?"

"Fuck, no. That shit's not for me. Why settle for just one

woman when there are so many to choose from?"

He laughs and returns to getting dressed, and again, my thoughts go to Jessica. Now she might be the one woman that might, just might, make me re-think my last statement.

Fuck! Maybe I should cancel this afternoon's appointment because I'm not sure I should be around her. She has me thinking crazy thoughts, and my thoughts are crazy enough without adding her into the mix.

We leave the gym, and there's a restaurant just around the corner where we head for lunch. I look at my watch. I have plenty of time before my appointment. We're passing a newsagent when the headline of a national paper grabs me. 'Has Fletcher made a decision yet?' Really, there's no way this should be front page news.

I take a copy inside the shop to pay for it. I want to know what crap they're writing about me. As I hand my money over, the guy does a double take. "Well, have you made a decision yet?" he asks.

"All in good time," I say with a smile.

"Let's hope you pick the right team to play for," he shouts as I turn and walk away.

And here was me thinking maybe I would have a quiet life here in Glasgow. Glasgow is a city of two halves when it comes to football—the great divide. I know I've made the right decision, but will the fans agree?

The news article is actually pretty accurate for a change. It mentions the offers that have been made to me by both clubs and gives arguments for and against each. Little do they know, my decision is already made and an announcement will be made tomorrow. At the end of the day, it was an easy one to make. My former team will do exceptionally well from this deal. I don't do so bad out of it myself. It was the right decision for me, leaving England.

Lunch is a quiet affair. Logan doesn't mention Jess and neither do I. I certainly don't mention that I could be seeing her soon, because if I know him, he would change his plans just to come along and check her out. And there's no way I want him checking her out.

"Let me know how you get on this afternoon," Logan says as we part ways.

"Will do."

Now, please let it be Jess who's waiting to meet me.

Chapter TEN

Jessica

EVERYTHING IS SO DIFFERENT WITHIN the apartment building. All the finishing touches are taking shape. It looks so good in here now. I can't wait to see what the penthouse looks like. I make my way toward the lift; there are people coming and going in all directions. With a quick glance at my watch, I see I have time to spare. Time for me to have a look around the penthouse.

The designer that has worked on this project is a fairly new designer, Matt, and he has some fantastic original ideas. The guy has talent. If I ever need an interior designer, I'll be using him.

I exit the lift and the first thing that hits me is the colour. Lots and lots of colour. Already I know this isn't going to be a bland apartment with creams and whites. No, this penthouse has been designed with someone young and funky in mind; it's ultra-modern. The entrance hallway is bright orange and white, but it's not an in-your-face colour. I love it.

I wander through the apartment, taking everything in. This apartment has a very American feel to it. I think this is the first of its kind in Glasgow. Yes, there are apartments along the banks of the Clyde, but nothing as luxurious as this. There is nothing I don't like about it. Well, maybe there is. I'm not so keen on the canvas picture that hangs in the office. It's a strange painting of a man, with a modern twist. It matches the colour of the room; bright green, but the painting itself is kind of sickly.

The lounge is amazing and has floor to ceiling windows along two walls, and doors that open out onto a large decked sitting area. I would never get any work done staying here. The view, what can I say about that? For me, the views are going to sell this apartment. I can't wait to do a night time viewing to see the riverbank all lit up.

In the kitchen, I find milk and bottled water in the fridge, and some biscuits in one of the cupboards, so I put the kettle on. I can at least offer the viewer a cup of tea or coffee.

Lee has been busy; she's sorted out all the promotional material. A job I was meant to do. If it hadn't been for her these last few weeks, I don't know what I would've done. She has done an amazing job of keeping the business ticking over when I couldn't.

Shivers run down my spine at my thoughts.

Today hasn't been as hard as I thought so far. Maybe that's because I've been so busy. But I find myself thinking about Scott and everything that's happened. Lee has put my house up for sale, and with the price it's on the market for, I'm sure it won't be on the market for long. I'm going to have to go there soon to get anything I want to keep, and I'm not sure if I'm ready yet.

The buzzing of the intercom distracts my thoughts. My viewer or viewers are here. There will be permanent staff downstairs when there are residents staying here, but for now, my viewer is being brought up in the lift by one of the workers.

I take a deep breath, walk back out to the hallway, and ready myself for whoever is about to exit the lift.

The lift door opens and I hear his voice thanking whoever brought him up. The very same voice that made me smile this morning. I lift my eyes to see Fletcher.

I stand in the hallway, staring at him in total surprise, unable to do or say anything. He's changed out of the gym gear he was wearing this morning. Now he's wearing a dark shirt, sleeves rolled up casually, and light grey trousers.

He walks toward me slowly, with a goofy grin on his face. And if I thought he looked good this morning, that was nothing compared to how he looks now, as I take in his impressive figure. He looks pretty perfect.

Has that thought really just crossed my mind?

Those blue eyes are watching me and suddenly I feel out of sorts, almost irritable and angry with myself for allowing those thoughts about him to enter my mind.

"Fancy meeting you again," he finally says, stopping in front of me, smiling.

God, he has a lovely smile. Lee told me the viewer was a footballer. Fletcher is a footballer? So I was right about him being a player, and at a guess, I bet he's as much a player off the pitch as he is on it.

He's been staying in his gran's house next door to my parents, spending time with my dad, and here's me knowing absolutely nothing about this man. This man who carried me in his arms into my parents' house. I find him intriguing. But I shouldn't, especially after everything that's happened. I've lost my baby and here I am thinking about a man. This is wrong. So wrong.

"Hey, are you okay?" he asks, reaching out and clasping my shoulders.

"Sorry, yes. I was a million miles away."

"Are you sure?"

"Yes, of course." I snap myself out of whatever has come across me. Focus. I need to focus. "Come on through and I can tell you a bit about the apartments in this block."

He lets go of my shoulders and I turn and walk toward to the kitchen. I know he's following, I can hear his footsteps behind me.

"So, you're a footballer?" I ask, turning to face him.

"Yes. I thought you knew, or at least that your dad would've mentioned it," he says, walking over to the windows. The kitchen has windows facing the buildings behind. Why the hell did I come in here first? I'm not thinking straight, he's distracted me. I should've taken him straight into the lounge so the first thing he saw was the view.

"Can I get you a drink before showing you around?"

"No, I'm good. Let's see what you have to offer me," he says, his gaze never leaving me. I stand, speechless again. This really is becoming a habit. "Jess . . ."

"Sorry." I shake my head. "Let's go through to the lounge." I lead the way. "What do you think of the colour scheme?"

"I love it. Very me."

Now I know he's a footballer, why doesn't that surprise me?

"Bloody hell! What a fantastic view." I can only nod my head in agreement with him as he walks over to the windows. "Can I?" he asks, gripping the door handle.

"Of course," I answer with a smile.

Yes, this is the room I should've brought him to first. Too busy being distracted by his good looks to concentrate on my job. He opens the doors, wanders out, and stops, leaning his hands on the railings with his back to me, and looks out across the river.

"It's a great view," I say, joining him.

"God, it is. Until now, I hadn't realised how much I've missed this city. For the first time in my life I feel as though I'm home." I can hear the sadness in his voice. "This is where I belong."

"I'm sorry," I say softly, looking across the river.

I can feel him turn toward me, but I'm scared to look at him. "You have nothing to be sorry about." He reaches out, takes hold of my shoulders, and turns me to face him. "Jess . . ."

There's something about the way he says my name. I can't put my finger on it, but I like it. His eyes are studying me. "Are you sure you should be working?"

His question surprises me, although I'm not sure why. "Yes. I had to do it at some point."

"Sorry, I shouldn't be questioning you." He stands before me, repeatedly rubbing his face before dropping his hands. Drawing his eyebrows together, he watches me, looking almost concerned. Is his concern for me? "What's the asking price?" he finally asks after a few moments of the two of us just looking into each other's eyes.

"Prices start at four-hundred-and-twenty-five-thousand," I tell him.

"No, what's the price for this? The penthouse."

Oh, I should've realised. Of course, if he was to move here, he would want this one.

"This one is sold as seen and . . ."

"Jess, just tell me how much."

"Six-hundred-and fifty-five-thousand."

"That sounds reasonable."

Reasonable. If he says so. I wouldn't pay that for an apartment. A house—that would be a different matter.

"Do you want to go and look around on your own?"

"No. I want you to join me and tell me everything I need to know."

I'm not sure I'm capable of telling him everything I'm meant to. Around him, I seem to be lost for words.

"Well?" He holds his arm out, indicating for me to go first. I smile politely at him and walk on.

"Well, you've seen the kitchen and the lounge, so the office and bedrooms, then," I say casually over my shoulder.

"That's what I'm here for," he says with an air of smugness.

"Of course it is."

He smiles broadly and he seems so laid back. We enter the home office first, and it's a great sized room, with views across the Clyde. It's well kitted out, and again, the colours are striking, but I hope he doesn't focus on the artwork that I've taken a dislike to. I'm really loving all the bright and bold colours, but when I see Matt, I'm going to ask him about that awful artwork in the most tactful way I can.

"This I like," he says with a wide grin, looking at the picture.

"Do you? I'm not sure I do, but each to their own, I suppose."

From the wide grin, I'm not sure if he's being serious or not. I want to go with the latter and give him credit for having good taste. We look in on the dining room next. Fletcher says he might consider changing this room. Next is the second bedroom. He seems happy with everything he's seen so far and asks lots of questions, which, of course, I answer. It seems easier now I've settled into my role of agent.

"The master bedroom," I say, holding the door open for him.

"Wow!" The king-size bed faces the floor to ceiling windows, with the same unobstructed views across the Clyde as the lounge has. He walks over to the windows and looks out. I wonder what he's thinking about. I leave him on his own with his thoughts and go into the en-suite. This is THE most amazing bathroom I've ever stepped foot in. Everything about it screams ultra modern but comfortable. The whole apartment is comfortable.

"So, that bath looks as though it could fit two." I jump back. "Sorry. I didn't mean to startle you."

I turn to face him. Who else was it going to be?

"It's fine," I try to say with confidence. "And yes, I'm sure the bath could fit two." I watch with amusement as he slips his shoes off, steps into the bathtub, and sits down. "What are you doing?"

"Trying it out. Join me." He laughs. "I need to know if it fits two."

He holds his hand out to me, but I shake my head. *He's insane.* Why the hell would he need to know if it fits two? Anyone can see from the size of the bathtub that it's more than likely to fit more than one person. He doesn't need me to climb in there with him. And for me to do so, would be unprofessional.

"No."

"Go on. Please . . ." His sparkling blue eyes plead with me. I continue to shake my head at him. "Go on."

Oh, what the hell. He's not going to stop asking until I do. I slip my shoes off and take his hand as I step into the bath and sit opposite him.

"See, it wasn't so bad," he says, smiling.

"As you can see, it does, in fact, fit two. So what do you think about the apartment?" I try to avoid his gaze, but it's hard sitting opposite him when I can feel his blue eyes are on me.

"It's perfect. I can see myself staying here. Has anyone else shown any interest?"

"You're the first person who has viewed it, so no, not yet, although Friday is the launch of the entire block. Will you be able to come along?"

"I'm sure it could be arranged." He smirks at me. "So, I have a few days to think about it before making an offer?"

"Yes," I tell him, surprised he's even considering putting in an offer. I was under the impression he was settled in his gran's house. I've obviously got my wires crossed.

He seems deep in thought. I close my eyes and think how silly we must look sitting in a bathtub, fully clothed. Opening my eyes, I find his gaze upon me, and he's smiling. He does have an infectious smile. I watch as he climbs out of the bath, and he turns, holding out his hand to me.

I take his hand and feel a quiver in my stomach. The hairs

on the back of my neck stand on end. Shakily, I stand up as he helps me out. I stand before him and a curious look crosses his face. Something passes between us as he keeps my hand in his.

"Jess . . ." I remove my hand from his first and pull at my clothing. "Thank you for today." He studies me for a few moments. "Where are you going now?"

I look at the time; there's no point in going back to the office.

"Back to my parents'."

"Funny, that's the same direction as me. You want a lift?"

"Okay." The word is out of my mouth before I think about it. I'm not sure this is a good idea.

Chapter ELEVEN

Fletcher

I MUST BE MAD, ON the verge of going insane. Although I'm pretty sure others will say I'm already insane. Why the hell am I putting myself through all this torture? I should be avoiding Jessica Taylor at all costs, not trying to spend more time with her.

Nothing can happen with us. But I want it to.

I've watched her as we've moved around this apartment; she is as much affected by me as I am by her. What the hell was I playing at? Asking her to join me in the bath? I smirk at how we must have looked, sitting fully clothed in the bath. But it was fun watching her expression change. She was initially horrified at my proposal. I still can't believe she humoured me. She let her guard down, if only for a few moments. I got a chance to see a small glimpse of the woman she really is, and that is someone who is fun, warm, loving and most of all, sincere.

Maybe those characteristics will eventually come back to her and be with her all the time, instead of the pain and sadness I see when I look into her eyes. That look breaks my heart in two.

I know it will take time, but I'd like to be the one to help her through this. Be the one to bring a smile to her face. The one to bring her back to life.

How the hell can I feel the way I do about someone I've only just met?

I wait patiently in the hallway as she wanders from room to room, ensuring everything is off and that there isn't so much as a cushion out of place.

Credit where credit's due; she looked shocked when the lift door opened and she saw me standing before her, but quickly re-gained her composure then proceeded to be professional throughout the viewing.

There are many sides to Jessica Taylor and I want to get to know them all, especially the closely guarded personal side of her.

Chapter TWELVE

Jessica

THE DRIVE BACK TO MY parents' is . . . how shall I put it? A bit uncomfortable, on my part, at least. Fletcher has been very talkative and charming, yet also seems as distant as I am. He pulls the car into his gran's driveway.

"Well, we're home sweet home," he says as the car stops.

"I'm afraid it doesn't feel like home to me." I stare ahead, looking at his gran's house.

"Jess. Jess?" He repeatedly calls my name, pulling me from my trance-like state.

"Sorry."

Maybe I'm not ready to be back at work. My morning went well enough, and lunch with Lee was good, but I've been out of sorts since Fletcher walked out of the lift and into the entrance of the penthouse.

Why? Is it because I find him attractive and he intrigues me? Or is it because the feelings I had around him today scare me? It's all of it.

I turn to face him; the bright blue of his eyes has darkened and he has wrinkles on his forehead as he frowns at me.

"I don't want you to keep apologising to me. You haven't done anything wrong. So, where is home?" he asks, with tenderness in his voice.

"That's a very good question. I wish I knew the answer to that."

It's something I should really think about; I can't stay with my parents forever. I thought I would only be here a few days, now I have no idea when I'll leave or where I'll go. I love them both dearly, but it's only a matter of time before we start getting on each other's nerves. "I should think about going to my house and packing up all my belongings for storage before it's sold."

"You're selling?" he asks.

"Yes. I can't stay there after everything."

"No, I don't suppose you can."

"What are you going to do with your gran's house?" I ask, trying to change the subject from me because I now feel more uncomfortable than I already did, and I'm scared what he might ask me next.

"I'm unsure. I loved this place as a small boy, but it's a family home. It's not right for me. To be honest, I'm in two minds. Part of me wants to keep it, but the other part says I should sell it, let go of the past." He swallows hard with a slight shake of his head and glances around. I can hear the reluctance in his voice. If I were to put this on the market, I know we would have a buyer within days. This is a sought after area of Glasgow.

"A guy like you would probably prefer to be closer to the city centre and the nightlife. You could always keep it and rent it out for a while."

"Nightlife. No, I should stay away from the nightlife, that way I won't get myself into trouble." I'm more than intrigued about what trouble he's been into in the past. My assumption on him being a bad boy was correct. "I do love the penthouse," he adds.

"Could I come and have a look around at some point? Give you some indication of what you could get both selling it and renting it out? It would give you something to think about."

"Yeah. Now would work for me." He smiles.

Do I want to do this now? I glance across the driveway and see my dad's car isn't there. Now I remember they had somewhere to go. I sigh.

"Go on then. I've nothing better to do," I say with a smile. "I forgot my parents are out and I'm fending for myself."

"Well, in that case, come on. What are we waiting for? But you'll have to excuse the mess. I've started going through some of Gran's things."

"I'm sure I've seen worse." You would be surprised at some of the sights I've seen in houses; some people just don't seem to care or have any pride.

He exits the car and rushes around to open my door. Oh, such a gentleman and old-fashioned; there's not many men who still open doors. I know my dad does, but he's from a different generation. If he's trying to impress me, it might be working. Fletcher takes my hand, helps me out slowly, and closes the door behind me. He keeps my hand in his as we walk hurriedly toward the house. Why won't he let my hand go? It's clammy in his grip.

Wrong!

My hand in his should feel wrong, but I'm not sure it does. I don't do holding hands with *anyone*. So why am I letting him? I can't answer my own bloody question. There's no reasonable explanation for my hand to be in his, but it feels nice. He's just trying to be friendly; that's what I'm going to keep telling myself.

He opens the door, finally letting go of my hand, and indicates for me to go first. This house is identical to my parents', although it does need some modernisation, which should he choose to sell it, would have to be reflected in the asking price. But if he decides that's what he wants to do, we can discuss it at a later date.

We go into the living room first, and he wasn't kidding when he said excuse the mess; he has boxes everywhere, but I have seen worse and I know it must be hard on him, going through his gran's belongings.

"Sorry," he says, clearing a pathway through to the dining room. The dining table is covered in newspaper cuttings and more boxes. I pick up one of the cuttings and smile when I realise it's a younger Fletcher in a Scotland strip. So, he's not just any player, he plays for the national team as well. His gran has kept everything that has been printed in the news about him. I put the paper down and pick up another. The article in my hand is from two years ago, when he signed a deal with one of the biggest clubs in the UK. She must've been so proud of him. Not many people can boast that a relative has played with the biggest football club in the country, or the national team. I might not be a football fan, but even I know the team.

"Well, are you any good?" I ask, holding the paper up.

He laughs. "I do okay. Do you follow football?"

"Me? No. Scott did, but he said it was a man's sport when I asked a question."

"He sounds like a fucking arsehole. There are many women that not only enjoy watching the sport, but play as well."

"Well, I think we can both agree on him being an arsehole." I can hear the pang of sadness in my own voice, and I wonder if Fletcher notices it. "My dad is a huge football fan," I quickly add.

"Yeah, I know." He pauses and watches me for a second. "I've enjoyed the time I've spent with your dad these last few weeks. He's helped me work on some stuff. I thought coming home to Glasgow, I only had to choose which team I was going to play for this coming season, but all this means I have a lot to think about."

"Dad is always available with words of wisdom and support."

"Yes, and I think talking to me has helped him with how he feels about you and this Scott."

He has my full attention. I sit down at the table. "What do you mean?"

"I don't want to speak out of turn, but I saw how bad you looked a week after the incident; you looked bloody awful. Your dad was there in the hospital after the incident. I think, and this is only my opinion, that he's struggling with everything that happened to you."

I'm not sure how to take his words. I suppose I never really gave any thought to how this would affect my parents.

"From our conversations, you mean the world to him, his only daughter, and he couldn't protect you from what Scott did to you."

"There was nothing he or anyone else could've done." I feel my tears building.

"Maybe not, but it doesn't make it any easier for your dad. He still wants to kill him and I think if their paths cross, Scott would be fighting a losing battle."

My tears, that I've so desperately been trying to stop, now fall. I can only imagine how my parents feel. My dad has old fashioned family values; he believes it's his job to not only provide but protect his family. Of course they're both going to be hurting. I know if anyone hurt either of them I would be angry, but I don't want my dad to do anything stupid.

I just don't see my situation getting any better. I don't see how my life is going to get better. All this pain and suffering, and for what?

"Oh, shit. I didn't mean to upset you." He moves toward me but I can't bring myself to look at him. Fletcher kneels down in front of me and wraps his arms around me.

I jump and push him away. "Don't touch me," I shout, and rise from the chair, shaken. I wrap my arms protectively around my body. I close my eyes as fear floods through my mind. For weeks, Scott and I had been having small, silly arguments. After each one, he would wrap his arms around me, telling me he was sorry for upsetting me. Fletcher's arms around me took me back to a place and time I want to forget about.

Every muscle in my body tightens, I open my eyes and glance around the room, looking for the quickest exit.

"FUCK! Jess, I'm sorry. I didn't think. I would never hurt you." He stands, shaking his head and slips his hands into his pockets. I look into his eyes and all I see is pain. He draws in a deep breath and stares. I want to run but something is stopping me. "Fuck. Your dad isn't the only one who wants to kill Scott." I look at him and my face falls. Here I am in a complete stranger's house, and he feels the need to kill my ex. "Jess . . . please. I'm sorry, I never thought." He shifts from one foot to the other, and now I feel bad because I've made him uncomfortable in what is his home for the time being.

I need to get out of here. I can't be around him. What the hell must he think of me?

Turning my back to him, I need to be on my own.

I move quickly the way we came, but there are so many bloody boxes to navigate. Just when I think I'm on the home straight, I trip over the last box. My tears fall uncontrollably as I feel myself falling to the floor in slow motion. I don't hit the floor, though. Two strong arms catch me, breaking my fall.

"Jess, let me help you. I promise I'm not going to hurt you." I'm sure he can see straight through me. "Please . . ." I close my eyes as he lifts my chin. I nod my head. He pulls my body tight to his and holds me whilst my tears continue to fall.

"I should go next door," I finally say after what seems like an eternity. "You don't need some emotional woman cramping your style. I'm sure you must have things to do." I let out a light-hearted laugh.

"You. Are. Not. Cramping my style. I'll walk you next door and I'm staying with you until your parents come home."

"Thank you."

He helps me to my feet and keeps his arm around me, supporting me. If I'm truthful, I don't think I would make the short distance on my own. My legs feel weak and my body is shaking. I hear the front door closing behind us; I hadn't even realised we were moving. We cross the grass between the houses instead of walking down the footpath and up the other side.

"Jess, do you have a key?" I hand him my bag, unable to look through it. He spends a minute searching before finding it and opening the front door.

Fletcher leads me into the living room and sits me down on the couch. He hovers around as I get settled before leaving and making his way into the kitchen, I think. I hear his voice.

"No, it's fine, honestly . . . I just wanted to let you know . . . I'm going to stay with her . . . To be honest, she looks shattered . . . I would make her something to eat but I don't think she would take any . . . Do you have any brandy . . . Okay, I'll be here when you get home."

My dad. He's called my parents.

I can hear him moving about in the kitchen, cupboard doors opening and closing. What the hell is he looking for? If I really cared, I would go and help, but I don't care. Closing my eyes, I rest my head on the back of the couch.

Forget.

I just want to forget everything that's happened. But I know that's not going to happen. Will I ever escape from this nightmare I'm living in?

"Jess." I open my eyes to see Fletcher standing in front of me with a glass, and after hearing his half of the conversation on the telephone, I can only presume it's brandy. "Take a drink." I shake my head. "Please. Then you can close your eyes and fall asleep."

My phone ringing in my handbag distracts him. He takes the phone out of my bag just as it stops, but then starts again. "Someone called Lee," he says.

"I'm not ready to speak to her but I know she'll continue to call until I answer." One thing about my best friend is, she's persistent.

"Hello, Lee . . . She's resting at the moment. Can I take a message and pass it on? . . . What do you mean, who the fuck am I? . . . A family friend . . ." I can hear Lee's raised voice but I can't make out what she's saying to him. Poor Fletcher. Bet this isn't how he saw his day panning out. "Look, Lee, why don't you pop by in the morning and see her for yourself before you go into the office . . . I'm certain she's overdone it today . . . I'll pass it on." He sighs with relief, ending the call. "Bloody hell! She has some fucking mouth on her." I smile. "That's more like it. You need to smile more often."

"I'm not sure what there is to smile about. Sorry I left you dealing with her." I know Lee and she will be desperate to find out who answered my phone.

"Don't be. She'll get over it. She says she'll come over in the morning, but . . ."

"She might come over tonight." I finish his sentence. "I should drop her a text, just to let her know I'm fine."

"You could be onto something."

I take the brandy glass from him and take a drink. It tastes fucking awful. Pushing the glass back into his hand, I want to close my eyes, but I don't want to be alone. I want him to stay with me. I believe him when he says he wouldn't hurt me, and right now, I want to feel safe. Safe from the fears that haunt me. Do I trust him? He's not done anything to make me doubt him. I have to learn to trust again.

He turns away from me and walks toward the kitchen.

"Fletcher?" He turns back to me. "Stay."

"Of course I will."

He's back within a few minutes and sits down on the couch beside me. I close my eyes as I feel his arm around me, holding me tight. Protecting me.

Chapter THIRTEEN

Fletcher

NEVER DID I THINK FOR one minute when my day started, I would end it sitting here with Jessica Taylor in my arms. No, I had hoped that one day I would have her in my arms, just the same as I've dreamed of kissing her. I know it's not happened the way I've dreamt of, but if this is the only way I can be close to her, I'll take it. My grip on her tightens as she snuggles into me, and I have to admit, I like this feeling. She fits perfectly into my side, as though it's where she belongs, but I know it's not, even though it's where I want her. I have an overwhelming sense to keep her safe, to protect her. It's not my job yet. Do I want it to be? I have no idea. The first guy that had the job of protecting her well and truly fucked up when he lifted his fucking hand and beat her up.

How could he? What the hell was going through his mind? She was six months pregnant with his child.

I need to lose these thoughts because it makes me so fucking mad.

I don't do proper relationships. Never have and not sure I ever will. All that having to stay faithful to one person; I'm not sure I'm capable of doing that.

It's hard to think about anything else but Jess right now, so I grab the TV remote and turn it on, turning the volume down. I get the feeling Jess has been struggling to sleep, and at the moment, she's settled; I don't want the noise of the TV to wake her. Jim said she's still having nightmares. I'll never forget the day I heard her scream; it's haunted me since.

I flick through the channels until I get to the sports news—I don't know why I still do that when I know that's all I'm going to watch and listen to anyway. The presenter is talking about all the transfer news, who's signed with who, and who is on their way out the doors of various clubs up and down the country. It makes me realise how lucky I've been over the years. Yes, I have been a complete dickhead at times, but I'm still a lucky one.

My career has been interesting since the day of my fourteenth birthday when I first signed a contract for one of the lower league teams down south. It doesn't matter who I've played with over the years, I've always given one hundred and ten percent on the pitch, although my personal life has let me down over the years.

When girls find out you're a footballer, they throw themselves at you. The more well-known I became, the more interest was shown my way. From a young hormonal teen, girls have always been a means to an end. My problem was, I never had any respect for the opposite sex.

I've been lucky that my personal life has never really interfered with playing the game. I've also had the opportunity to play with some of the best teams around the world. Playing in Italy and Spain has to be up there for me.

Every move I've made over the years has been calculated and has earned me good money. But what good is money when you have no family to share it with? So what do most guys in my position do? Yes, bloody squander it. Not all of it, but I have wasted a lot over the years. However, there is still plenty in my account for a rainy day.

My phone rings and I answer it straight away.

"Hey, Fletch. Thought you were going to let me know how today went," Logan says.

"Oh, shit. Something came up," I say.

"Why are you whispering?"

"Because Jess is sleeping." Why the fuck did I say that? He's going to jump the gun about this.

"As in Jess your neighbour?"

"Yes, so please stop shouting. I don't want to wake her."

"You moved fast. I didn't think you would take her on a date."

"Look, we haven't been on a date."

"I think you have some explaining to do, don't you?"

I tell him about today and tonight. He listens quietly without interruptions, even though I can sense he has an opinion on it all. As I speak, Jess moves in my arms, but she's still sleeping. I stroke the side of her face.

"As I've said before, too much baggage," he says when I finally stop speaking. "Fletch, you're my friend, but for fuck's sake, don't get involved. So you're still with her?"

"Yes."

"Why? Go home, or better still, do what I said earlier and go out and fuck someone's brains out and forget about Jess."

"Logan, I'll talk to you tomorrow."

"Yeah, and whatever you do or don't do tonight, just make sure you're not fucking late for the boss. Because if you are, you'll start the season off in his bad books, and you need to make the right impression."

"I hear you."

I end the call and I know he's right, but Jess needs friends who can support and care for her. I know I'm not even her friend, yet, but I want to be. I just want to be there for her, be part of her life and protect her from anymore harm. Would I like more? Of course I would, but I'd settle for being her friend.

Leaning back on the couch, I close my eyes because I can't sit here and stare at her all night. Even I know that would make me look like a creep.

I'm not sure how long I've slept when I hear the front door open. I keep my eyes closed; I'm not ready to leave her yet.

"Jim," says Elaine in a soft voice. "Shall I wake him?"

"No, leave them both. From what Fletcher said, she was exhausted. I'm glad he was here."

"Hmmm. You might be, but I'm not sure. I know his type and I know all about him."

"Elaine, sweetheart, sometimes you have to give people the benefit of the doubt. In my opinion, for what it's worth, he's nice enough."

"But what about all that stuff in the news?"

"Elaine, give the boy a chance. All he's been to us so far is kind and helpful. He's not done anything wrong."

I hear their footsteps leaving the room. Elaine might have a point. My reputation isn't great. I wish it didn't follow me around, but I have no one to blame but myself. Others are always bound to use my past against me, but hearing what she's said fucking hurts. Doesn't everyone deserve the benefit of the doubt?

I should leave. Go back next door into the bed I've slept in these last few weeks, but this is the comfiest I've felt in a long time, and I'm in no hurry to leave. So I do what I want to do, which is stay right where I am.

Chapter FOURTEEN

Jessica

"MORNING, FLETCHER," I HEAR MY dad say.

Morning.

Oh, God. I'm not sure I want to open my eyes. Why is Fletcher here? I try and think back to yesterday; everything is clear up until I left the penthouse with Fletcher. After that, it's all jumbled up.

I try to think. There must be more.

We were in his gran's house. The newspaper cuttings his gran had kept. Me upset. His arms around me. Pushing him away. Me shouting at him. The hurt in his eyes. Oh, God. I remember it all. I've made a complete fool of myself in front of a handsome stranger.

I want to fall back asleep until everyone leaves.

"Morning, Jim," he replies to my dad in his husky voice.

"Can I get you a coffee? You didn't have to stay. Don't you have somewhere to be this morning?"

Oh, no. My meltdown last night is interfering in his life.

"No. I don't have to be at the stadium until eleven, then the press conference is at two p.m. So, yeah, a coffee would be good. Then I'll get out of your way and go home and shower," says Fletcher.

"I'm sorry we didn't get back before you fell asleep. I didn't mention all the details about what happened to Elaine, and I think I'll leave it at that."

"It's fine. Don't worry about it. I'm just glad I was here."

It feels strange listening to their conversation.

"Did she have any nightmares?" Dad asks him.

I'm curious to hear the answer as well, but I don't think I did. I'm sure I would remember waking up screaming and sweating.

"She didn't wake up, although she was crying in her sleep," Fletcher says. There's a moment's silence and I can hear Dad's footsteps leave the room, so I shift myself on the couch and open my eyes. "How much of that conversation did you hear? And don't pretend you've just woken up."

"Oh, most of it," I say with a yawn. "So, you stayed?"

"Yes. You asked me to stay with you. How are you feeling?"

"Better than I should. I'm sorry if I interrupted any plans you had for last night."

"The only plans I had for last night were going through some more of Gran's things and a microwave dinner for one."

"Oh, God. You never had dinner."

"No, and neither did you, and you need it more than me. I sat down with you and watched you until you fell into a deep sleep, then I closed my eyes and fell asleep too."

"Sorry." I sit up, pulling the cover up around me. "What time is it?"

"Just going on eight, sweetheart," my dad says as he hands Fletcher a mug. "Can I get you anything?"

"No. I should go and grab a shower before going to work." They both stare at me like I have horns. "What?"

"Take the day off. Lee can run things." Dad's focus shifts from me to outside in the driveway. "And I'm sure, now she's here, she will say the same thing."

This is going to be interesting. My gaze shifts from Fletcher to the cover that's over us. God, what is she going to think? The front door opens.

"Please tell me that is coffee I smell?" Lee calls out. I smirk, knowing my dear friend needs several cups of coffee before starting the working day. Dad leaves the room; he knows Lee as well as I do. "Good morn . . ." Lee's voice trails off as she looks at Fletcher then at me then back to Fletcher and the cover over us both. "Sooo, you're Fletcher Adams."

"Last time I checked," he says with a hint of amusement in his voice. I'm sure he must get this all the time, women recognising him. Except me. I had no idea who he was, and maybe I still don't.

"As in the Scotland striker? Who is currently on the transfer market and been linked with the two big clubs here in Glasgow? What are you doing here?" she asks him.

"Yes, that's me, and I'm here looking after a friend," he replies, although his eyes are firmly on me. I smile. "I'm going to finish this in the kitchen then I should go."

"Don't leave on my account," Lee says almost breathlessly as he stands up.

"I'm not, but I do have a busy day ahead. Jess, I'll let you know about the penthouse and the launch in the next day or so. Is that okay?"

"Yes. And, Fletcher, again, I'm sorry about last night."

"I've told you, stop apologising."

He leaves the living room and I don't allow my eyes to follow him. Okay, maybe they do. Lee sits down next to me and I await her barrage of questions because I know she has a lot to ask.

"How the hell do you two know each other, and why am I only finding out this now?" she asks, facing me. Dad brings her in a cup of coffee. "Thanks, Jim. Now, where were we?"

"Fletcher was my appointment at the penthouse yesterday."

"And . . . what? You just decided to bring him home with you?" I laugh at how silly that sounds. "Don't laugh at me. I'm serious, even though it's nice seeing you laugh."

"I'll start at the beginning."

"Go ahead. We have all the time in the world."

"The day my parents came to the hospital, Dad's car wouldn't start, and it was Fletcher who drove them. Fletcher is Mrs Adams from next door's grandson. Dad obviously told him what had happened with Scott. Well, on the day I came home from hospital I was a little uneasy when I got out of the car. Fletcher came to my rescue and carried me into the house and straight to the bedroom."

"I bet he did!" She smirks.

"I slept for the whole day and night, and when I woke up, he was here speaking to my dad. To cut a long story short, I wasn't feeling good, and he helped me again."

"Really? A real knight helping a damsel in distress." She laughs. "Fletcher Adams only helps someone when he hopes to gain something for himself. Mr Bad Boy of Football who has a string of women everywhere he goes, who has been on the wrong side of the law on more than one occasion. You're expecting me to believe he's just a friend?"

"I don't know what he is, Lee. Christ, I didn't know who he was until he walked out of the lift yesterday. I had no clue he's a footballer. You know me, I know nothing about the sport."

"Well, your hot friend has to introduce me to some of his hot friends. A night out. That's what we both need."

"Lee, I don't think I'm ready for a night out."

I've not had a drink in months. Five months, to be exact. As soon as I found out I was pregnant, alcohol never passed my lips.

"Oh, go on. We could go out on Friday night after the launch, grab some dinner, a few drinks, and none of us have to work Saturday. You could stay with me and we can chill like we used to." The thought of doing something so normal both appeals and scares me. We would need to go somewhere no one knows me because I wouldn't want anyone to judge me. "Go on. What do you say?"

"Okay. Anything for a peaceful life. Now, I'm going for a shower and we can go to work together."

"Take the day off. I can cope," Lee says.

"No. I can't stay here. Please. I can find something to do in the office."

"Alright, if you insist. On the way, you can tell me more about your hunky friend."

I shake my head as I leave the room. She is going to be impossible today but talking to her about my hunky friend has put a smile on my face.

Lee hasn't stopped talking about Fletcher the whole morning. She seems obsessed with him. Well, she seems obsessed with me and Fletcher. She has made me laugh on more than one occasion, and this feels good. Lee has been busy sorting out the guest list for the launch on Friday, and I've spent the morning organising viewings for not just the apartments on the Clyde, but a few of our other properties. It's only Tuesday, and already I have a good feeling about how busy I'm going to be this week. Which now leads to another problem; I'm going to have to go and get my car and a few more work outfits.

"Lee?"

"What's wrong?" She lifts her head away from the computer screen in front of her.

"Would you be able to take me over to my house tonight? I need to pick up a few things, including my car."

"I can, but I don't think you should be driving yet."

"I'm not in any pain or on any medication so I don't see what the problem is."

She pushes her hair away from her face, tilting her head from side to side as only Lee does when she's unhappy with me or something I've said, but doesn't engage in any further conversation on the subject. My friend knows when I mean something.

We work through lunch without taking a break, and I feel so much better working today than I did yesterday. I suppose a lot of that would be down to nerves.

"Right, we need to eat," Lee says, grabbing my attention. "Some of us more than others. I'm going to nip out and get us a sandwich."

"Could you get me some chocolate as well?" I ask.

"Yip, I sure can. I won't be long." She takes her purse and leaves the office.

I'm sorting through my work diary for the next few weeks. Both Lee and I are going to be busy; lots of footballers on the lookout to sell up and new players looking to buy. It's always like this at this time of year, although I never know who any of them are. Lee always has to keep me updated on the comings and goings. I remember last year, she got her knickers in a twist over a certain manager, only to meet his wife at the viewing. She was so disappointed when she came back to the office. I couldn't help but laugh when she told me all about it.

The door opens and Lee rushes in. "Put a news channel on," she says in a hurry.

"Why?"

"Because Mr Hot Hunky Friend is on it."

I do as she asks and open the news channel on the internet, and there he is, clear as day, doing a press conference. Now, I'm not the brightest when it comes to football, but even I know he's signed for one of the biggest football teams in Scotland. I gasp when I hear the amount the club has paid for him.

"Bloody hell," I say. "And they paid that amount to his former club?"

"Yip, but they haven't revealed how much he will get paid, so will you be quiet?"

It has to be said, he looks just as good in front of the camera as he does in real life. He's being asked lots of questions that he answers exceptionally well. He says he's looking forward to settling back home in Scotland after being in England for so long. He talks about his passion for the game. A reporter passes a remark on him having the same jersey number for club and country. His reply is that he is honoured and lucky, and he will wear both shirts with pride.

"So, can we expect just as much drama off the pitch as we get on the pitch?" a reporter asks him.

He shifts and looks at his manager before answering. "No. I'm all about the quiet life now, but on the park, well, that's an entirely different ball game. And after all, that's what I'm here to do. Play football and hopefully score some goals along the way for the manager who has shown faith in me."

"Bloody hell, Jess. I think I'm in love. Look at those muscles in his arms. I bet the rest of him looks just as good. He can exercise with me any day or night."

She's right. He does look great.

"I need to get a man like him. He is perfection on a plate with a strawberry on top."

I laugh at her assessment of him. "Lee, I'm sure we just need to get you any man."

"Hey, I might be going through a bit of a dry spell, so to speak, but I'm certainly not settling on some complete arse. Especially not when I've seen some of the goods on offer."

"No, I would never expect you to settle for anything less than the best," I say, mocking her.

"Oh, I don't know. After seeing Fletcher in person, all other men will pale in comparison."

"Let's get on with some work," I say, switching the press

conference off.

As much as it appeals to sit and drool over Fletcher Adams, I have work to do.

God, has that thought really crossed my mind? This can't be right. I shouldn't be thinking of him like this. There must be something wrong with me. This must be my grief playing tricks with my mind. If I mention all this to the counsellor when I see him, I'm sure he'll have a field day. An hour's session might not be long enough. I do know I need to speak to someone about how I feel.

Chapter FIFTEEN

Fletcher

"WELL, THAT WENT WELL," PETER, the manager, says. We sit in the calm of his office after an interesting press conference. "Really well. No regrets, son."

I have to agree with him; it wasn't so bad. In England, whenever I did a press conference, all they seemed to focus on was my personal life, not the football. Not today, though. It was all about the football and my ability to help the club achieve its goals. The boss is being ambitious in his first season; he wants all three domestic trophies. He would also love for us to do well in Europe, but his priority is building the team he wants. A team for not just today, but the future.

"None whatsoever. I'm back in the city I belong, and playing for my childhood heroes. Life is pretty perfect at the moment." I smile, and it's not just because of the football or the wages I'll receive; I've taken a pay cut to play here. Money isn't what drives me. Yes, I was paid ridiculous wages when I played in Manchester, but I also did the job I was paid to do.

Now, though, I would play for free, but I won't be telling the boss that anytime soon. He might just take me up on it.

"So, Fletcher, tell me what is it you're smiling about, and don't tell me it's the football. A smile like that can only mean one thing; a special someone."

"There might be," I answer coyly. In my eyes, she is someone very special.

"Well, if there is a special someone, it's time for changes in your life."

Oh, fuck. Don't I know it. "I started to make changes when I asked for a transfer. Being here in Scotland and playing football is more than enough for me at the moment. Anything else is an added bonus."

"Fletcher, you know I've followed your career for a number of years, and I'll be truthful. If I wasn't sitting in front of you now, I might not believe the words you've just spoken. But something about your words and the way you've conducted yourself today tells me you mean everything you say."

"I do. I want and need to put my past behind me. Even though I know it's going to be hard. It has a way of following me around like a bad fucking smell."

"Even with all the off-field crap you've been up to over the years, and let's face it, there has been a lot, your football never suffered. Not once. Now that we have all the formalities out of the way, all the lads should be on the training ground. Are you ready to meet everyone?"

"Yes. Let's do this."

We leave his office and wander through the building. Peter introduces me to each person that passes us, even the poor cleaner who got a fright as he switched off the hoover. I've been in and out of this building over the last few days, and each time, I feel at home. Everyone has made me feel welcome. I'm finally where I belong.

Peter blows a whistle when we get outside. The lads stop what they're doing and a loud cheer erupts. I can only presume they're happy about my signing. Logan and Jackson are the first to reach us, shaking my hands and slapping me on the back, but they already knew. They were influential in my decision.

I spend some time being introduced to each player and all the background staff, some of whom I've already met. Peter has worked with the same background staff at each club he's managed, so there are more than a few familiar faces.

"As training is almost done, why don't you all have a kick about?" Peter shouts out above every other voice on the pitch. Some of the lads look a little surprised by his words. "Go on," he says. "Only thirty minutes and no tackling. I don't need any injuries before our first game. Fletcher, go and join them."

Peter and his staff stand at the sidelines and watch. We split up into two teams and play a fun game of football, with everyone enjoying it and taking part. It reminds me of playing in the school playground; there it was always about playing the game and having fun, and if your team won, it was a bonus.

Chapter SIXTEEN

Jessica

"ARE YOU SURE YOU WANT to do this?" Lee asks as we sit in her car outside my house. I'm not sure now we're here, but I know it has to be done. And now is as good a time as any.

"Yes, come on. I only want to grab some clothes and my car keys."

We exit the car, and I wrap my arms protectively around my body. My chest tightens and my breathing starts to accelerate. There is a churning deep in my stomach and I think I might be sick. This is the first time I've been here since Scott attacked me. I know he isn't here because Dad has made sure he hasn't got the new keys, but as we walk toward the door, I look over my shoulder. Shivers run down my spine and I'm not sure why, but I don't have a good feeling about this. Something just doesn't feel right.

"Jess, it's fine," Lee says, trying to comfort me, obviously sensing how I'm feeling. "The sooner we get inside, the quicker we can leave."

I nod, still distracted at being here.

Handing her the new keys, I let Lee open the door and we step inside. I've seen a few of my neighbours at their windows; I'm just hoping I don't need to speak to any of them. I'm pretty sure they've all been gossiping about what happened in my house that night.

It's cold as I stop in the hallway and look around; everything feels so . . . different. A few weeks ago, this felt like home, but now . . . nothing. I make my way slowly to the bedroom I shared with Scott—the room where he attacked me. The cleaners Dad organised have done a great job because you would never know what took place that night. Yes, there are a few things missing. I remember ornaments and vases being smashed in a rage, but there's no sign of broken glass anywhere. I pause at the bed and close my eyes, memories of what he did to me flooding my mind.

My body starts to tremble. I feel lost. Everything I wanted and loved was taken away from me in this very room.

I hate him. I hate Scott Stevens.

"Jess, it's too soon for you to be here." Lee's voice echoes in the room.

"I need some clothes, but more than anything, I want and need closure. There's nothing I can do to change my past. I can't have my baby in my arms. But I can try and live my life. Make new memories. I don't want to erase all my memories, just replace them with better ones."

"I get it. I do," she says with a deep sigh.

I take a large suitcase from the wardrobe, open it, and sit it on the bed. Lee takes another suitcase and starts emptying the drawers with my things into it. I start with the clothes on hangers. We work quietly and quickly. It's a job that needs to be done, but neither of us wants to be here longer than we need to be.

There are loads of things I need to get at a later date. Some framed pictures of my parents, and some of Lee and me; those I want to keep. The ones with me and Scott, well, those can all go in a bin for all I care.

There is one thing I pick up from the bedside table at my

side of the bed; the first scan picture of James when I was only twelve weeks gone. It sits in a beautiful silver frame with dates engraved. I stare at it for a moment before tucking it into the side of the suitcase. I don't have to look at Lee to know she's watching me; I feel her eyes on me.

Bang . . . Bang . . . Bang.

We both jump, startled with the banging at the front door. I stand, rooted firmly to the spot.

"Jess! Jess! I know you're in there. Please. I need to see you." I would know that voice anywhere. Scott.

Fear creeps through my body. My pulse races for all the wrong reasons. There's a thumping pain in my ears, but it's not drowning out the noise. The sound of his voice has my stomach churning. I push my hand over my mouth in an attempt not to be sick.

"Jess, I'm going to call your dad, then I'm going out and I'll deal with him, okay?" I can't answer her. There are no words to say.

As I stare blankly into space, I know Lee is on the phone, but I can't hear what she says. My mind is running in all directions, and none of them lead me to a destination I want to be.

I can't face him. He's caused me too much hurt.

Just hearing his voice has sent me into a panic. Never in a million years did I think I would become a victim. All my words from moments ago about creating new memories have faded into the background as fear and panic take me hostage.

"Jess . . . Bloody . . . Hell. Let me in," he shouts, banging on the door furiously. "I'm not leaving until you see me. We need to talk." How does he know I'm here? He wouldn't recognise Lee's car because it's brand new.

Bang . . . Bang . . . Bang.

Lee stands in front of me. She speaks but I don't hear her. My focus is on trying to block out Scott's voice and the constant thumping on the front door. The neighbours are going to have a field day with this; something else for them to gossip about.

"Jess, snap out of it." Lee takes hold of my shoulders, guides me over to the bed, and sits me down. "Stay here. I'll deal with this arsehole."

She leaves the bedroom and now I'm alone with only my thoughts. *Dark* thoughts. I wish he were dead.

"What the hell do you want?" Lee shouts after opening the door.

"I should've known you would be here. Get out of my way. I need to see Jess."

"She doesn't want to see you."

"Lee, please. I need to see how she is. I need to apologise for my behaviour," he says more quietly.

"I can't let you see her. You really have no idea what you've done to her, have you? She's a mess. You've taken everything away from her. I'm still struggling to get my head around what you've done. I never had you down for a bully, someone who hits women."

"Oh, for fuck's sake! I love her with all my heart . . ."

"Love? You don't know the meaning of the word."

"Lee, I want to see her and not even you will be able to stand in my way!" I hear a crash. My tears fall.

"Get out of here."

"No. Get out of my fucking way!"

There's a loud bang and I jump up from the bed. I don't think I'm strong enough to face him, but I can't sit here and let Lee get hurt. After what he did to me, I wouldn't put it past him to lash out again. She's my friend, and if he hurts her, it's because of me. I can't sit here and do nothing.

I take several deep breaths and try to pull myself together as I brace myself to leave the bedroom. Walking out of the room, I take in the scene at the front door. Scott has Lee pinned up against the wall, his hand on her neck. My anger towards him builds as I see him and I use that against him.

"Take your hands off her. NOW!" I shout, using all the strength I can. They both turn and look at me.

"Jess." My name rolls off his lips. I used to love the way he said my name, but not now. He lets go of Lee and her body relaxes. "Can we talk in private?"

"No. Lee isn't leaving."

"But we need to talk."

"I have nothing I want to say to you."

"How are you?" he asks, taking me by surprise.

"How the fuck do you think she is?" Lee spits the words out. "She's lost the baby she longed for, all because the man she thought loved her turned into a violent thug."

"I swear to God, Lee. Fucking keep your nose out of our business."

"Why? You going to inflict the same pain on me? I don't think so."

He turns and grabs her by the throat. Everything happens in slow motion. She's shouting for him to let go, but he doesn't. I can see his grip get tighter, and Lee is struggling to breathe. I rush toward him and pull at his arm.

"Let her go, you bastard!"

He turns, and when I see his bulging eyes, I'm scared. So fucking scared. They're wild and dark. "You just don't do a thing you're fucking told, do you?" he hisses, pulling one hand off Lee. Before I can do anything to stop him, he lashes out at me, belting me hard across the face. My body isn't strong enough and I fall to the floor. Pain echoes through my face and I feel wetness dripping down my check. I know I'm not crying, so it can only be blood.

I'm ready for darkness to take me now. There is nothing more Scott can take from me. My mind is racing in so many directions, I just want it to stop. I need the pain to go away.

Scared.

Dizzy.

Darkness.

"Jess!" Lee calls out. I open my eyes. She pushes him quickly and does the only thing she can. She lifts her leg and knees him in the balls. He cries out in pain and doubles over. She passes him and is beside me on the floor, holding me, rocking me in her arms

"Jessica," she says softly. "Are you . . . ?"

"You will pay for that, bitch!"

I hold onto Lee tightly as he lunges toward us. I want to close my eyes.

"No one is paying for anything," a deep voice shouts. I look toward the door to find Fletcher pulling Scott away from us, and he punches him. My dad is just behind him. "You think you can just do what you want?" He hits him again, and Scott's body sags against the wall. Fletcher pulls him back to his feet and holds him roughly by his arms.

There is suddenly a lot of activity and voices I don't recognise.

"We'll take it from here," a loud voice says over the noise. A police officer takes Scott from Fletcher's arms. Dad and Fletcher rush over to Lee and me. Lee stands, turning her attention to Fletcher. He puts one arm around her for support. Dad holds out his hands and helps me to my feet. I wrap my arms around him and he holds me tight.

"Jessica, it's alright, sweetheart. He can't hurt you now. I'm here," Dad says, trying to reassure me. I lift my head from his shoulder slightly and I'm met with Fletcher's worried eyes. He's talking to Lee but his eyes are firmly on me.

A pang of jealousy hits me. Why is it all of a sudden I want Fletcher's arms to be around me, holding *me* close, not Lee?

"Come on, let's get what you came for and get out of here," Dad says softly. I let go of Dad and see his shirt is stained with my blood. He looks at me and frowns. "We might need a trip to the hospital, sweetheart. I think you might need stitches."

"Before any of you do anything, we need a statement," one of the police officers says.

"Of course you do," says Dad. "Sweetheart, you have to." His voice and eyes plead with me. Maybe if I had done this a few weeks ago, this wouldn't have happened tonight.

"I know."

I lose track of time. All the comings and goings at my house are making me dizzy. Sleep, that's what I need. Dad and Fletcher's statements were brief. There wasn't a lot they could tell them, but I feel as though I've been getting grilled for hours. Dad and Fletcher have been packing up my belongings as Lee and I speak with the officer in charge. Dad doesn't want me to come back here for anything now. Lee and I had most of my clothes packed.

Dad asked if there's anything I really want. I told him about the pictures and a few other things. He also asked what I was doing with my furniture. My reply was, "Burn it for all I care. I don't want anything that Scott and I shared. It can all go to charity."

From tonight onwards, I start a new life, just for me, and when I decide where I want to stay, I'm more than happy to start from scratch.

Chapter SEVENTEEN

Fletcher

I WAS ARRIVING HOME WHEN Jim rushed from his house. When he told me why, of course I was going to come here with him. On the drive over, he called the police, even though I know he would've much rather taken care of Scott himself. Shit, when I saw Jess on the floor with blood running down her face, I couldn't help myself. He was lucky I only punched him, because if it hadn't been for the police, I'm sure I would've done a lot more to him.

It's after ten p.m. and we're finally leaving her house. Everything she wants is in the back of my car. Jim has tidied up the broken glass as Lee said the house is ready to be sold, and Jess doesn't need to come back here. I'm standing by the car with Lee; we wanted to give Jess a few minutes with her dad.

"So, Mr Hot Hunky Friend, what are you really doing here?" Lee questions me with a stern look.

"What do you mean? Jim was rushing out of his house when I arrived home, so I brought him here."

"That's not what I meant and you know it. So come on, explain yourself, because I'm not blind nor stupid. I've seen how you look at her."

Shit! How do I explain this? It doesn't matter what I say, because if I tell Lee a lie, she's going to see right through me.

"Mr and Mrs Taylor have been good to my gran in the past, and if I can help them in any way, I will."

She shakes her head, smirking at me. "Okay, we'll play it your way, handsome. Jess might not see it but I do. If you hurt her, you will have me to answer to. In my opinion, she shouldn't have someone like you in her life, even as a *friend*. She might not be aware of your past, but I am."

"You never heard of don't judge a book by its cover?"

"Oh, I know, but in your case I'm not sure I can make an exception. She's my best friend in the whole world and you have no idea what she's really been through these last few weeks. No one but me really knows. Yes, you know about the beating and the baby, but you have no idea the strength that girl uses just to get out of bed each morning."

Lee doesn't have to elaborate on what she means. I feel as though I've just been punched in the gut with her words. I know what she means.

Our conversation is interrupted as the front door closes. We turn to see Jim helping Jess down the path. I'm sure Lee is thinking about tonight being a setback for Jess, and she's probably right. But Lee's words have got me thinking. I'm the last thing Jess needs in her life right now. She needs to get well; that's what Lee implied, and I should try to concentrate on football. Obviously, me being around Jess isn't going to help her get better.

"Jess, honey," Lee says quietly. "How are you?"

"I'm going to be fine," she says, with an air of confidence I don't expect. Lee looks puzzled at her answer, or rather the way she said it. "Honestly, don't worry about me." She walks over to Lee and gives her a kiss and cuddle. "Now, I think we should both take the morning off."

"I don't know. I have a few things to do," Lee tells her, shaking her head. "Are you going to the hospital?"

"Yes, but only to keep Dad happy." Jess smiles at him. "Can

you drop us there?" she asks me. "That way Lee can get home."

"I don't mind," Lee says.

"I know you don't, but go home, have a bath, pour yourself a drink, and relax." Lee looks at me and then back to Jess, eyes wide and mouth slack. I don't think any of us were expecting Jess to be so . . . carefree.

"Of course I can," I reply.

I offer to take Lee home, but she insists on driving herself. The girls say goodbye and Jess tells her she will be in work for lunchtime because she has an appointment with a developer. Jim climbs into the back of my car beside his daughter and I smile when she rests her head against him and closes her eyes.

It makes me think; I've never had that close a relationship with one member of my family. My grandparents when I was a small boy, yes. But nothing like the closeness between father and daughter. My vision blurs at my own thoughts. There is a heaviness in my heart as I think of what I've missed out on growing up. With a shake of my head, I move my eyes to the road ahead and don't take another glance in the rear view mirror.

The journey to the hospital is short and quiet. When we arrive, I offer to stay to bring them back home but Jim says I should get home. He knows about my early start tomorrow. I get out of the car.

"If you can't get a taxi when you're leaving, please call me," I say. Jim thanks me for what I've done tonight and walks on.

"Fletcher." Jess says my name softly and it sends shivers down my spine. I take her hand in mine and a charge of electricity runs through my body. We stare at each other and something deep inside me clicks and connects with her. I watch as she draws in a deep breath. Has she felt it too? "Thank you for tonight. I'm sorry you've been dragged into my mess of a life."

"You don't have to thank me. I just wish you hadn't suffered at his hands."

I let go of her hand and watch as she walks toward her dad, who, thankfully, hasn't witnessed our conversation. I stand for a few minutes to calm my racing heart before turning away and getting back into my car.

I've tried to sleep, but it's not working. So now, here I sit at two-thirty a.m. watching the movie channel on Sky. This Bond movie, I've lost count of how many times I've watched it, but I like it and it's the only thing worth watching.

Light knocking on the front door startles me. Who the hell is it at this time of the morning? It had better not be Logan, pissed. He did say he was going for a few drinks. I stand and go to the door, opening it without even looking to see who it is.

"Jessica!"

"Can I come in?"

I nod and feel her eyes travel down my body. *Shit.* I'm standing in only a pair of boxers. She smiles as she passes me, her eyes approving.

"Give me a sec," I call out, closing the door. I grab a t-shirt from the bedroom before joining her in the living room.

She's pacing the floor. I stop, lean against the doorframe and just look at her, wondering why she's standing in my living room at this time of the morning.

"I know you're there," she says without turning around. I have an urge to walk towards her, slip my hands around her waist, and kiss her softly on her neck.

"Can I get you anything? A drink, perhaps?" I ask.

"No, thank you. I saw the light on and just wanted to come in and thank you again," she says, turning. Now I have a clear view of her face. I walk toward her, and without thinking, I reach out and run my fingers under the cut that now has stitches in it. She freezes under my touch, but doesn't shout at me. If she did, I would draw back and give her space.

"Is it sore?" I ask.

"Compared to what I've been through lately, no. But it stung like a bitch when the nurse cleaned it." I laugh and can't seem to stop. "What's so funny?"

"The way you said it. Sorry, I shouldn't laugh. Are you okay?"

"Yeah, I'm fine." I frown at her. "Don't you look at me like that too. I have enough with everyone else."

"Like what?"

"Worried that I'm not okay, that I might do something stupid. Or the look I've seen a million times these last few weeks. That you feel sorry for me."

Both statements take me by surprise.

"Sorry." I try to avoid eye contact with her because if she sees through me then she's going to see a lot more than I'm prepared to admit, even to myself.

"Now who's the one apologising?" she says, and I lift my head and meet her gaze.

Fuck, she's beautiful.

"Okay, how's this . . . neither of us is allowed to say sorry."

"Deal," she says, smirking. "I should go and let you sleep. Dad tells me you have a busy day ahead. He also said I shouldn't be bothering you at this time, but hey, I didn't listen."

"I'm glad you came in. I've been worried about you. That's one of the reasons I couldn't sleep."

"Me too," she says with a smile. "Although I'm not sure I'm happy about you worrying about me."

"Of course I was worried. I wish you had let me stay at the hospital with you. So tell me, how many stitches?"

"Just four. I'm hoping they've made a good job of it and I'm not left with too bad a scar."

"A scar wouldn't change how you look. In my eyes, you'll

still be beautiful."

She looks away quickly, embarrassed. I can't believe I've said the words out loud. I'm so fucking stupid.

She turns back to me. I want to say sorry, but we've both agreed not to say it. But then again, why should I say sorry for stating facts? She is beautiful with or without the scar.

"Fletcher, I . . . don't know what to say." She gazes at me, and if I'm not mistaken, I see a longing in her eyes.

"Don't say anything, but understand this . . . I do mean it. A small scar is never going to change how beautiful you look."

Slowly she leans toward me. I keep watching her eyes for the slightest change, for an indication that she doesn't want to kiss me, but all I see is a pool of desire. Slowly, she wraps her arms around my neck and pulls me closer.

"Jess . . ." I say in a low voice.

Her lips part and she tilts her head. She presses her lips to mine. I try not to think about what this means. She can't be thinking straight because I'm sure if she was, this wouldn't be happening. I pull back because I need to know she wants this kiss, and as I look at her, I see hurt in her eyes. Hurt I'm causing by pulling away. I thread my fingers through her hair and pull her back to me. We shouldn't do this, but there is no way I want her to feel rejected by me. Not tonight.

A small smile plays on her lips and her hands slide across my shoulders, gripping me tight. This time I press my lips to hers and wait a moment to see if she's going to pull away. She doesn't.

If this is the only kiss we're going to share, I want to enjoy every last second of it. Her lips are soft and sweet, just how I imagined they would be. She slides her tongue inside my mouth and it brushes against mine. I moan against her. She pulls me closer and grips onto my neck as our kiss deepens. If I was any sort of good man, I would stop this now before it gets out of hand. Because if this goes any further, I won't be able to stop myself.

I know I shouldn't, but I want her.

Realisation dawns on me that one kiss . . . this one kiss is never going to be enough. It's never going to satisfy my burning desire for her.

She finally pulls her lips from mine, and I miss them.

"I need to go and let you get some sleep."

"Okay," is all I can say, because I want her to stay. Standing in the middle of the living room, I watch as she walks away and returns to her parents'.

Fuck knows how I'm going to concentrate on training now. One taste, one kiss, is never enough.

No. I need and want more of Jessica Taylor.

Chapter EIGHTEEN

Jessica

IT'S FRIDAY, FINALLY. THE END of a very long week, and I'd love to go straight home and soak in a hot bubble bath. But, no, Lee has other plans after we finish up at the apartment launch. She wants to go out. I know we spoke about it. Well, she spoke about it and I just listened, but that was before the incident with Scott at my house on Tuesday night.

Tuesday night was a turning point for me. Lee has been surprised at how well I'm dealing with it all. But I only had two choices; deal with it the best I can and move on with my life, or go back to how I was a few short weeks ago.

My choice was easy; move on and live my life. I don't ever want to go back to the darkness I was in.

The police came to see me on Wednesday morning, and this time I pressed charges, for not just what happened on Tuesday, but what took place weeks ago. After speaking with the police, and also my solicitor, it was decided I should take out an injunction against Scott.

He pleaded guilty, sparing me the ordeal of having to testify. His solicitor made an appeal for Scott not to be held in custody as they awaited reports to be prepared by the probation service. So, at the moment, he's out on bail with conditions attached. If he tries to contact me in any way, he will be arrested. For the last few days, I've really tried to focus on good things going on in my life.

And then there's Fletcher. I've not seen him since I left his house in the wee small hours the other night—or morning. I've not purposely been avoiding him. I'm sure he's been just as busy as I have the last few days. His car has been gone early each morning and back late. I'm sure Dad has spoken with him, but I've not asked him outright.

I still don't know what I was thinking when I leaned closer to kiss him, and I still don't know why I did it. I've played it over and over in my head a million times since it happened. He's good-looking, sexy, and also easy to be around. I do like him, but it's too soon for me to be thinking about another man, never mind kissing him.

Yesterday I saw the counsellor, Doctor Harry Fieldman. He's an older man with a receding hairline. I felt comfortable with him. He asked a few questions and I answered, but I spoke at length about Fletcher. I decided before I went in that I wasn't going to mention him, but I found it so easy to talk to him. Well, that is his job, after all; getting people to open up about their fears and feelings. If I wasn't talking, I was crying. By the time I left the hospital, I was an emotional mess, but things did seem clearer.

Scott also came up in our conversation after Harry asked what happened to my face. He asked how I felt about him, which was a very good question. I don't love Scott, and I don't think I have for a long time. Me falling pregnant probably delayed me turning my back on a relationship that wasn't working. I'm angry for allowing myself to be a victim because I've always thought of myself as a strong woman. I'm past the stage of being angry toward Scott. I almost feel sorry for him because he has to live with himself for what he's done and what he's taken from both of us.

Our baby.

I told him how bad I felt a few weeks ago. That I couldn't see light ahead and that I was more than happy for the darkness to take me. To take me away from all the pain. I suppose this was when he took the most notes as I tried to explain how I felt just after losing my baby. But how can you explain that to someone when you have no idea what it means? I told him Lee has been my rock. Yes, I've had the support of my parents, but Lee has listened when things got so bad I wasn't sure I wanted to be here anymore. That alone has been hard to admit. He smiled when I told him I was back at work and trying to do normal things.

So that brings me back to Fletcher, and I'm not sure what Harry made of my feelings toward him, and the kiss we shared. A kiss I instigated. He said we can talk more about it next time. Before I left, he asked if I wanted any medication to help. I refused because I want to try and get through this without it. That was something else he said would be discussed next time.

Fletcher . . . in a short time I'm going to see him at the penthouse. Or rather, I hope I'm still going to see him. Worries and self-blame come to mind when I think about the last time I saw him. My foot is bouncing on the floor.

"Right, are you ready to leave?" Lee asks me.

I switch off the computer and stand, brushing down the front of my dress. When Lee said we were going out tonight, I decided to wear a dress, something suitable for work, but yet still good enough to go out in tonight.

"It has to be said, I have one sexy friend," she says with a smile. "I think everyone you speak to will want to buy an apartment from you."

"Nonsense."

"Oh, I don't know. With your looks and my charm, I'm sure

we'll have them eating out of our hands."

"Everyone is coming to see the apartments, not me and you."

"That may be so, but we are an added bonus." She laughs.

We gather our bags and the paperwork that we need for today.

The drive through town is pretty painless considering Lee is driving, and we arrive at the apartments with plenty of time to spare. There's not as many workmen wandering the building as we enter, which means most of the work is complete, although I'm sure a few snagging problems will come up as new buyers move into their homes. It's only to be expected, but I don't anticipate any major problems with this development. The developer is too professional. We make our way to the lift and straight up to the penthouse.

"Everything is perfect," Lee says as we walk towards the living room. This is the first time she's seen it complete, with all the fixtures and fittings in place. I have to agree with her. No expense has been spared when it comes to the finishing touches inside each apartment. We've hired a local company to do some food and drinks for today, so they're busy getting ready. Everything about today will be perfect, and hopefully we will have a few reservations.

"Right, we don't have time to stand here admiring the view, we have just under an hour before people start arriving," I tell her. We will have approximately one hundred people coming through here over the course of the afternoon, so we're going to be busy. Roll on five o'clock.

"Okay, let's get organised."

It's not long before Dale, the developer, and Matt, the designer, arrive, looking pleased with themselves. I spend a few minutes going over protocol with them for this afternoon. We have one of the country's leading newspapers coming out to do a feature on the development. This is a fantastic opportunity for Matt to have his work seen.

Lee hands us a glass of champagne each, and I eye her curiously.

"A toast," Dale says. "To success, and to the two beautiful women who have made this man very happy. All going well, we will all make a lot of money from this development. Here's to a prosperous future."

Dale is a charmer, a very wealthy charmer, and Lee looks smitten at his words. But then again, that's Lee. She always loves a charmer.

"Cheers!"

Lee and I spend the next few hours doing what we're getting paid to do, and that is talk to everyone who walks through the apartment. I spend a lot of time with Dale. Some of the clients are very interested in meeting and talking to him. And as for Matt, the journalist and photographer were the first to arrive. I'm sure the article is going to be amazing, a great start for a very promising career.

Lee and I work well together, although I should've left her charming clients whilst I got to sit down for the afternoon doing paperwork. I never thought this through when I picked out these shoes for today. Four-inch heels aren't very practical for being on my feet all afternoon.

I stop for the first time, and as I've spoken with everyone in the room, I head outside for a few minutes. Needing some fresh air, I draw in a deep breath as I look out across the river. I hear footsteps and turn to find Dale holding two glasses of champagne.

"How do you think it's going?" he asks, handing a glass to me.

"Really well. I've just spoken with Lee and we have ten reservations so far."

"Fantastic. I wasn't sure how today would go. Saturday and Sunday are busy days for buying houses."

"Remember you also have what, five that bought from the plans? I'm seeing each of those clients on Monday so I can show them around the apartments they're buying."

"Jess, while we're alone, I just want to thank you for everything," he says with a warm smile. I like Dale; he's really easy to get along with. He reminds me of a younger version of my dad; laid back but completely focused on his business. Dale is in his early forties, and still has all his dark hair that I've never seen out of place. It has to be said, he is an attractive man and does have a certain amount of sex appeal, and he knows it.

"No need. This is my job."

"I know, but with everything going on in your own life." He pauses. "I think you are an amazing, strong woman. Not sure if I could carry on with the strength and determination you've shown."

God, if he only knew how much I've struggled with everything.

"What other option do I have?"

"You always have options. I'm just glad to see you looking well, especially after the other night." He moves my hair and studies the cut on my face. "It doesn't look so bad."

"It's not. I thought it would look a lot worse than it is. The doctor said it should heal nicely."

"Come on. Let's get back inside before word gets back to my wife that I'm standing outside alone with a very beautiful young woman."

I smile. Dale's wife is stunning. If I look even half that good when I'm in my forties, I'll be very happy. I went for dinner with them both when Dale first came to me with his proposal for these apartments. They wanted to work with a young local company with drive and ambition, so here we are, all working together. She was meant to be here today, but one of their boys has chicken pox, so she's at home.

Dale holds the door open. I walk through the doors and instantly stop when I see *him* standing in the middle of the living room, talking to someone. He's casually dressed in jeans and a white shirt that's rolled up at the sleeves, as is the guy he's talking to; not like everyone else who has passed through the doors today. They've all been suited and booted. Poor Dale walks straight into the back of me and almost knocks me over.

"Shit! Sorry, Jess. Are you okay?" Dale asks, grabbing me and holding me steady. The glass wobbles in my hand until he takes it from me and hands it to a member of staff that approaches us.

"Yeah, I'm fine," I say without turning to face him. I move slightly out of the way of the doorway.

As if sensing me watching him, he looks up and our eyes meet. The guy he's with looks between Fletcher and me, and grins. He tries to get Fletcher's attention back, but he's too busy staring at me. Suddenly, I feel embarrassed by my actions the last time I saw him. I try to pull my eyes from his, but I can't; they're holding me hostage.

"Oh, do you know Fletcher Adams?" Dale asks as he moves to see what's keeping me from moving.

"You could say that. He was here on Monday afternoon for a viewing."

"Was he? Why didn't you say something?"

"I wasn't aware you wanted to know every possible buyer that comes through the doors. He's also a neighbour. He's currently staying next door to my parents, in his gran's house."

It's late; I hadn't realised what time it is because it's been so busy. I was beginning to think Fletcher wasn't going to show up. Dale grabs my hand and walks toward him.

"Mr Adams," Dale greets him. "How are you?"

"I'm good, and please, it's Fletcher, or Fletch to my friends," he states, eyes on me.

"Fletcher, this is Dale, the developer," I say. He smiles.

"Dale, this is Logan," he says introducing his friend. "Logan this is . . . Jess."

"Dale?" Lee shouts. I turn to see her looking flustered, but I catch the smug look on her face when she sees Fletcher. Oh, boy.

"Excuse me a moment," Dale says, rushing off. I should go and find out what's wrong instead of standing here not knowing what to say to Fletcher in company.

"Now I understand what all the fuss is about." I turn back to the two men in front of me, just in time to see Fletcher slapping Logan on his arm. "Jess, it's good to finally meet you," he says, taking my hand and lifting it to his mouth. "I've heard a lot about you."

"Logan . . ." Fletcher raises his eyebrows and stares at his friend in a warning, although I'm not sure why. Logan lets out a laugh. "Jess, ignore him."

"Okay, I'll try. Have you had a look around?" I ask, glancing at the time.

"Yeah. Sorry, are we holding you back? I know we're later than I expected."

"No, don't be silly. I'm just glad you made it along. Have you given any thought to the apartment?"

"Lots, but I've not made any decision. I would like a chance to talk to you about Gran's house, though."

"There's no rush, and of course," I say as Lee joins us. I'm not even going to ask what the problem was. I'm sure she has sorted it. I look around the room, which is almost empty, and I can see Dale saying goodbye to someone. I smile, thinking this afternoon has been a huge success.

"Hi, Fletch," she says. "Jess, we just have a few more clients including these two then we're done for the night. And I'm ready for a proper drink."

"Are you going out?" he asks.

"Yes, why don't you join us?" Lee says without looking at me, because she must know how I'll react. "We're going for dinner and a few drinks."

Bloody bitch. I could kill her for this.

Chapter NINETEEN

Fletcher

"YEAH, WE COULD JOIN YOU," Logan says, flashing Lee his trademark smile and winking. *What?* He can't just accept like that. But he already has.

This should be interesting if he's in the mood to flirt. I already know how this might end up. He can be pretty relentless in his pursuit of a woman, although from the smile on Lee's face, she's flattered by his attention.

Jess shifts from one foot to the other. She's rubbing her hands together over and over and biting down on the corner of her lip. Christ. She smiles politely but I can tell she's nervous. If I'm not mistaken, she still has our kiss firmly on her mind, and she's not the only one. I don't want Jess to be ashamed about it. Fuck, I'm not, and if it's the only kiss we ever share, I will treasure it. I can still feel her lips against me. The tingling sensation as her lips touched mine. The taste of her.

Fucking heaven.

Jess looks everywhere around the room to avoid looking at me. That hurts.

Neither Logan nor Lee have even noticed, they're too busy flirting with each other. Jess looks at Lee and shakes her head, only slightly, but I notice. She takes a deep breath and slowly releases it. Jess is pissed off with Lee, and I don't blame her. Yes,

I want to spend time with her, but not when she's being pressurised into it.

Jess grabs Lee by the hand, interrupting the flirting and laughing between her and Logan, and rushes off into the kitchen.

"Let's not go out with them," I say, turning toward Logan.

He studies me, almost searching for the reason behind my words. "Not happening," he calmly tells me. "Something is going on with you two and I want to know what it is."

"Nothing's going on." But I wish to *fuck* it was.

Chapter TWENTY

Jessica

"WHAT THE HELL DO YOU think you're playing at?" I shout at Lee as we enter the kitchen.

"What? Oh, please. Don't tell me you don't want to be around him. Because, girly, your body language tells me you do. There is chemistry between the both of you. And by chemistry, I mean off the charts. You are both young, free, and single. Let your hair down."

"Bloody hell, Lee. You make it sound so easy." *If only.*

"It doesn't have to be hard."

My life is complicated enough without adding a man like Fletcher into my life. The only problem with that is . . . I've already let him in.

"We kissed."

She takes a step back in shock. "When? And why haven't you said before now?"

"I would've told you tonight, whilst we were alone, but now you'll just have to wait. Maybe I'll get around to it over the weekend, but let's get out of here because if nothing else, I'm hungry."

I walk away from her, not giving her the chance to say anything else. Logan and Fletcher are standing in the entrance hallway, talking, and they stop when they see me. Why do I think I was the topic of conversation? Fletcher shifts on his feet, looking as uncomfortable as I feel. I'm such I fool. Why the hell did I have to kiss him?

"Let's go," Lee calls out, strutting toward us. "What are we waiting for?"

"Funny, we're waiting on you." I laugh. The last of the clients have left and we say goodbye to Dale, leaving him to lock up.

When we pull up outside the restaurant, I'm glad I took some time thinking about what to wear today; it's one of the best restaurants in the city. I've been a few times and the food is excellent. The four of us have travelled in Fletcher's car after he insisted, and Lee left hers in the secure car park back at the apartments.

Fletcher gets out of the car and quickly opens the door for me, holding his hand for me to take, which I do. "Jess, we need to talk."

"Maybe we don't. Why don't we forget about the other night?" I say, trying to ease the strain around us. I don't want this to be difficult between us.

"Is that really what you want to do?"

It should be, but I can't seem to get him out of my mind.

"Yes . . . No . . . Christ, I'm not sure."

"Can you two hurry up?" Logan shouts.

"Yeah. Jess, we'll talk. Let me drive you home tonight."

"I'm staying at Lee's tonight."

"Okay." He sounds almost deflated. He quickly takes my hand and walks toward the entrance. I like the feel of his hand in mine, but I'm not sure about holding his hand in public. I wouldn't want anyone getting the wrong idea. My pace is a little slower than his, and he glances over his shoulder, smiles at me, and my heart melts.

What the hell am I playing at? I lower my head and press

my lips together tightly. I'm disappointed with myself for my actions.

As we wait to be seated, Lee smiles, looking at my hand locked in Fletcher's. God, she is going to spend the night grilling me when we get back to her house. Nothing in my life is simple.

We're shown to a table in the far corner of the restaurant. Fletcher holds out a chair for me, and I'm not blind, I catch the smirk of amusement on Logan's face as I sit down beside Lee. Fletcher takes the seat opposite me. We order drinks first. Lee and I opt for a bottle of Prosecco, Logan orders beer, and Fletcher surprises me and only orders water. I must have a surprised look on my face. "I'm not leaving my car in town," he states matter-of-factly.

If I had his car, I wouldn't leave it either.

We all sit quietly reading the menu, and I notice the silent conversation going on between Fletcher and Logan. Right now, I want to kill my best friend for putting me in such an awkward position, because there is no other way to describe this situation.

"So, Jessica." I close the menu and turn slightly to face Logan. "It seems my boy here is a real life knight." I can hear the humour in his voice. Looking at Fletcher, I wonder what he's told his friend. As if reading my mind, he answers.

"I was in the right place at the right time."

"Yes, you were, and I'm sure Lee is just as grateful for that as I am," I say not adding anything else to conversation.

The waiter comes back to the table and we order. I wasn't going to bother with a starter, but Lee being Lee and acting like mother hen insisted, and Fletcher agreed with her. These two are worse than my parents. So a sharing starter has been ordered for the four of us.

"So, Fletcher, what's putting you off the penthouse?" I ask, breaking the silence that's descended on our table.

"Surely it's not the price tag?" Lee asks with a smirk.

Yes, she knows just how much he earns in a week. Christ, some people struggle to make that in a year.

"No, it's not the price tag," he tells her. "I love my gran's house and I'm considering renovating it and staying there."

"Are you?" Logan questions him with a glare.

"What? We've spoken about this."

"Yes, but I thought you said it was a family home?"

"I still consider it a family home, but it's the only place in the world where I feel I belong," Fletcher says. "If anyone shows interest in the penthouse, though, can you let me know?"

"Yes."

"If you're looking for a designer, I'm sure Jess can recommend one or two," Lee says.

"I'm sure I can help," I say at the same time, glaring at my friend, who for whatever reason, seems to be doing her best to push Fletcher and me together.

"I'm sure you can," says Logan quietly.

"Enough," Fletcher says sharply.

Oh no. This is going to be a long night. I really want to make my excuses, head on home, and forget about going back to Lee's. The waiter brings over our starters and tops up our wine glasses. Logan also orders another round of drinks, including more wine.

The atmosphere at the table has shifted and I have Lee to thank for that because she seems to sense how I'm feeling. She spends time asking the guys questions about football, and Logan seems impressed with her knowledge of the game. I'm more than happy to sit and listen to their conversation.

"Jess, are you okay?" Fletcher asks with concern.

"Yes, but as you already know, I'm not a football fan."

"Oh, Fletch. We have to change that," says Logan. "Why don't we get the girls some tickets for our first pre-season game?"

"Oh. My. God. I would love that," Lee almost screams with excitement, causing a few people at tables around us to look in our direction. "Jess, we have to go."

"It's up to you. I have tickets for the game." Fletcher gives me a warm smile.

"We'll see." Would I enjoy a football game? Who knows, but watching Fletcher run around a football pitch for ninety minutes does have a certain appeal to it. He's staring at me with a glint in his blue eyes. Oh God, he knows what I'm thinking. Is it really so obvious? To him it must be. My eyes glance across to Lee who is deep in conversation with Logan about the pre-season game.

I excuse myself from the table when our starters are cleared. Lee is too busy talking to notice, and I'm glad. I could do with a few minutes on my own. I make a mental note to order some water because the alcohol is going straight to my head. It's only to be expected after the length of time I've not had any, but I am enjoying the buzz flowing through my veins.

Now the question I should ask myself; is that the alcohol or Fletcher?

I'm washing my hands at the sink in the ladies' room when the door opens. I lift my head to see Fletcher standing beside me.

"What are you doing in here?" I ask, aware I'm alone in the ladies' bathroom with a man I find very attractive. I turn off the taps and face him, my back against the sink.

"I wanted a moment alone with you."

"Why?" My breathing quickens and I want to run, but he's standing between me and the exit.

"Because I haven't been able to stop thinking about you since our kiss the other night and I know I shouldn't want more, but I do. But the thing is, you also want more. I can see it in the way you look at me. There's something between us. You can try and deny it, but you and I both know you would only be lying to yourself." He moves closer, resting his hands on the sink behind me. My breath catches.

We each hold the other's gaze for a few long, drawn out moments. He's within reach, and I could so easily wrap my arms around his neck and let my body melt into the comfort I know he can provide. But I'm not stupid. I know I would only be some fun until the next girl comes along.

Maybe some fun is just what I need.

I shouldn't be thinking like this.

"We need to go back out."

"We do." He sighs. "But I want to give you something to think about."

"What's that?"

"This." He leans forward. I close my eyes in anticipation. His lips meet mine. I don't think about it and kiss him back. He moves his hands from the sink, and one caresses my back whilst the other has a tight grip on my backside. I wrap my arms around his waist. This kiss is different from the one we've already shared. He's taking whatever I offer him. Our lips mould perfectly to the other's. His tongue flicks against mine and my stomach muscles clench. I want him . . . *badly*. Fletcher's grip on me gets tighter, holding my body close to his. In this moment, I'm lost to him.

My body wants more than the kiss, but my mind is telling me to slow this down. A part of me knows this is so wrong, but it feels right.

Fletcher releases his hold and I allow my grip to loosen. We both need a minute to catch our breath.

"Jessica," he grumbles.

"Don't say anything. Go back out to the table. I'll be out in a minute," I say, turning away from him.

"Jess, don't." His hands grip my arms, pulling me slowly

back to face him. "Don't shy away from me."

"I'm not. I need a minute or Lee is going to see straight through me."

"Okay." He kisses the bridge of my nose before turning and leaving the ladies' bathroom at the same time as an older lady comes in. She smiles at me.

I leave the bathroom and take a deep breath before returning to our table. The waiter is serving our main courses, which I suddenly don't want to eat. I've lost my appetite. I sit down and Lee eyes me suspiciously; of course, she *can* see right through me.

"What's wrong?" she whispers as the guys sit talking.

"We'll talk later. When we leave here do you mind if I go home and not come back to yours?"

"I mind if you're going home to mope around and feel sorry for yourself. Now, if you were to tell me you were going home with Fletch, I would send you on your merry way."

"Lee . . ."

"What? Only saying it how I see it."

I order some water when the waiter comes back over and refills our wine glasses. I don't want to be staggering out of here at the end of the night.

Conversation flows with ease, considering the bathroom kiss. I'm certain Lee and Logan know something happened whilst I was gone, but neither have mentioned it.

The waiter comes over to clear our plates at the same time a group of guys come into the restaurant and shout over at Fletcher and Logan.

"Excuse us," Fletcher says as they walk toward the noise. They greet the group that has just arrived. Maybe it's players from the team, or just a group of their friends.

"Jess, I'm not blind or foolish. I know something happened with you two in the bathroom and I also know you're tearing yourself up over it. It might not be obvious to Fletch, but to me, someone who has known you a long time, it is. Go home if that's what you want to do, but talk to him, and please, I know how hard it is for you, don't shut everyone out. To me it looks as though you're about to do that. He might only be after some fun, but if he can bring my best friend back to life then, in my opinion, the fun is worth the risk."

"Lee, I can't. I don't deserve to be happy, or have fun, as you put it." I'm scared to say anything else because I can already feel myself getting teary-eyed.

"You do deserve to be happy. I don't want to hear you say that again. You deserve so much more, but you have to take small steps and I'm sure they will lead you to a great destination. I know this week has been hard. Coming back to work, then Scott, but you've powered through, and yes, at times you've put a fake smile on your pretty face. But I've seen small glimpses of the old you and I've seen a real smile or two with the mere mention of a certain someone."

"It's too soon."

"Says who? There's no right or wrong under the circumstances. The only person judging you is you. No one else gives a shit. Now, I'm going to make excuses when the guys come back over and I'm going to insist Fletcher take you home."

"You're a pushy bitch, do you know that? But I love you."

"Yeah, I know, and I love you. That's why I'm doing this."

Chapter TWENTY-ONE

Fletcher

"I WOULD'VE DROPPED LEE HOME. She didn't have to get a taxi."

"Yeah, I know that, but she . . ." She stops speaking and looks away from me, unsure. I did manage to talk to Lee, albeit briefly. She's worried about Jess. She can see her pulling away again. I know this is my fault. I can see it now that Lee has brought it to my attention. She's pulling away because of her feelings; feelings she doesn't think she should have.

Lee didn't have to tell me that. I kinda worked that much out for myself. I've promised Lee that if me staying away from Jess is best for her, then I will turn my back and walk away. I'll leave her alone to deal with her grief and her past, even though it's the last thing I want to do. I'm still unsure what's drawing me to her. She's completely different from other girls I've spent any time with. Actually, she's the only girl I've spent time with outside the bedroom.

Of course, I would love that more than anything, but part of me is happy to be her friend. I don't think I've ever had a girl that's been a friend. Although, having kissed her twice now, I think it's safe to say I want something more than friendship with Jess. What, though, I don't know.

Pulling into the driveway, I notice Jim's car isn't in the drive.

That could be a good thing. I turn to face Jess, and she fidgets in the seat. I'm going to make it easier on her. She's not getting the option of going into her parents', she's coming into my house whether she likes it or not.

"Come on. Let's go inside. We need to talk." I get out of the car and move quickly round to her side and open the door. She takes the hand I offer without hesitation. She glances at her parents' house. "Are they out tonight?"

"Yes. A charity event."

"Okay, so we have time to talk," I say, opening the front door.

"I have plenty of time to talk. As far as my parents are concerned, I'm meant to be staying with Lee tonight." She closes the front door behind her. Suddenly my thoughts are of having Jess wrapped snugly in my arms all night long, holding her close, keeping her safe.

"I'm not sure what to say now," I tell her. "I want to kiss you, but I don't want you to feel bad about enjoying it."

"I'm trying hard not to, so if you want to kiss me, do it now before I change my mind."

I shouldn't be doing this. I may even live to regret doing this, but right now, it's what I want.

But, I remind myself, *she has just told me to kiss her.*

I inch closer to her and she holds her breath. Slowly, I extend my hands toward her, still looking for a sign that this isn't what she wants. I don't see it. I take her hands in mine. Such an innocent touch with so much meaning.

To me, it means she trusts me. Trusts me not to hurt her, which is something I don't think I ever want to do.

"Well?"

I don't wait for her to ask again.

Pressing my body to hers, I pin her against the door. Our lips lock and everything I should keep in the forefront of my mind about Jessica Taylor disappears. I remove my hands from hers, lift them to her face, and hold it in my hands. Her skin is soft under my touch.

A need and hunger is building between us with each second that passes. She consumes me. Everything about her has me wanting her. I should be questioning the feelings that are sweeping through my body, but I can't. My body yearns to feel her, all of her. I long to have her. Does her whole body feel soft? How loud will she scream my name when she finally becomes mine?

Holy shit!

I push my tongue into her mouth, searching and exploring, and she accepts me willingly. She tastes heavenly. My body responds and I'm sure she feels it as she moans in my mouth. I don't want to, but I'm going to have to pull back before I can't stop myself from taking this further. And, boy, do I wish I could take this moment into the bedroom where I could worship her all night long.

I pull my lips away from hers, but keep her face in my hands, not ready to stop touching her. Tears pool in her eyes and I do the one thing that feels so natural to me. I move my arms, wrapping them around her petite frame, and hold her close. There's no hesitation on her part as she places her hands on my chest.

We stand together in my hallway for who knows how long. Her tears fall and I'm not sure if she's angry with herself for kissing me. God, I hope she doesn't regret it, because I don't. I always have regrets about spending time with girls, but this is the one girl I want to spend more time with and get to know properly.

"I should go home," she finally says, although she doesn't lift her head.

"Jess, please stay. I want you to stay. We have to talk."

She lifts her head, eyes glazed from her tears, and studies me. I don't know what she's looking for, but she must find it. Sighing heavily, Jess nods. I take her hand and lead her into the living room. "Can I get you a drink?"

"No, not yet," she says, sitting down. I sit beside her and silence fills the air. She gets comfortable and I wrap an arm around her. She rests her head on my shoulder and I close my eyes, enjoying the feel of her in my arms. This feels natural. "Fletcher, I'm sorry. You could've been out with Logan and your friends, and yet here you are again with an over-emotional woman in your house."

I move position because I need to face her. "I wanted to spend time with the over-emotional woman in my arms." I see her tears, but I also see a slight smile playing on her lips. "You need to smile more often. So are we going to talk? We've kissed three times."

"Stop."

"Jess, don't tell me you don't feel whatever this is between us. And please don't say you regret it, because I don't, and I don't want you to either."

"I could do with that drink after all and then we can talk properly."

I lean to the side and kiss her. "Yes. A drink." I'm reluctant to leave her, even for a short time. What happens if she leaves whilst I'm in the kitchen? She wouldn't do that, would she? I hope not.

Christ, I hope I have something more than beer to offer her. I make my way toward the kitchen. There's beer in the fridge, and a bottle of champagne that I got from the club. Not sure if Jess will see tonight as a cause for celebration. In my mind it is. I take the champagne and two glasses and go back to Jess.

She lifts her head and smiles. "What are we celebrating?"

"Whatever you want to celebrate," I reply, sitting down. I put the glasses down on the table, open the bottle, and pour. She smiles as I hand her a glass.

"To surviving the storm," she says, raising her glass.

"For being brave and strong enough to survive the storm."

"Thank you," she says softly. "Yes, I admit I feel something between us. I'm not sure what it is, but yes, there is something. I feel . . . I feel . . ."

I stop her because I don't want her upset, "Jess, I get it. I do."

"Fletcher, please hear me out." I nod. "The thing is, guilt floods my mind when I allow myself to be happy. When I remember everything that's happened, I find myself withdrawing again, from everyone. I thought this week would make things easier, clearer even."

"Jess, I can't imagine what you've been through. I'm sure this has been a tough week, back at work and trying your hardest to get back to normal, but here's the thing; nothing is as it was before. Your life has been turned upside down because of that piece of scum." My blood boils just mentioning him. "So, you have to create your new normal." I watch as she mulls over my words as she sips away at the champagne. "You are allowed to start living your life again. You're always going to have your memories, but they don't always have to be painful ones."

She places the glass on the table. "Thank you," she says, before kissing me softly and sweetly.

"What was that for?"

"Because I kinda like how your lips feel against mine." Her cheeks flush with embarrassment at her own words.

"So, do you want to watch a movie or something?" I ask.

"I should go next door and go to my bed. All this alcohol is going straight to my head." She looks too comfy to be thinking about going home.

"Jess, stay." She looks at me, almost puzzled. "I'm sure I can manage to keep my hands to myself. It will be hard, right enough."

"I'm not in the habit of staying over in a strange man's house and I try not to make a habit of falling asleep with my clothes on. But I'm more than happy to sit and watch a movie with you, then I'll go home," she says, trying to hide a yawn.

I leave her alone in the living room and grab a football shirt from my wardrobe and a blanket from the bed.

"Here, go and change." I throw my shirt at her. "You may as well get comfortable to watch a movie, and when you fall asleep you don't have to worry about creasing your dress." She watches me closely. "There are no ulterior motives." As I say the last words, I realise it's true. I don't have an ulterior motive with her, and for me, that's a first.

"Okay." She walks away from me to go and change, and I silently curse myself for this. What the hell is going on in my head? I'm not thinking straight. Fletcher Adams doesn't spend the night with a beautiful woman in his arms and do nothing. Well, nothing sexually. But now here I am, about to spend a second night with Jess because I can't stay away from her.

I'm away in another world when I sense her watching me. Lifting my head, I'm caught totally off guard. She's not supposed to look that good. *Bloody hell*. It was one thing to comfort her the other night in her parents' house, but something altogether different when she looks that fucking good.

My eyes travel down her body, and I can't hide the smile as I appreciate the vision in front of me. I'm done for. I'm never going to look at that football shirt the same way again.

"You can wipe that look from your face," she says, sashaying toward me. "Don't say a word. You handed me the shirt." I've given her a Scotland jersey, and bloody hell, she looks hot.

I don't have any words that would do her justice. She sits down beside me and curls up, resting her head against me as she pulls the cover around her. This is going to be torturous, lying here beside her, knowing how little she has on and how fucking amazing she looks.

In all honesty, I don't think I've ever seen a more beautiful and natural woman. And she is *definitely* all woman.

Chapter TWENTY-TWO

Jessica

SCARED, I DON'T WANT TO open my eyes and realise this is just a dream, but it can't be because I can feel his arms wrapped around me as my body snuggles against his. I can't help myself, I breathe him in. Even after lying here with me wrapped securely against him, I can still smell his aftershave from last night.

"I know you're awake."

I smile, opening my eyes, blinking several times to allow myself to adjust to the brightness. Daylight fills the room; neither of us bothered to close the curtains last night. "Morning. How'd you know?"

"Because your breathing changed. How are you feeling?"

"Really good. I managed to get a decent sleep with no nightmares." The only two nights I've not had any nightmares were the two nights I've spent with Fletcher. I'm not going to try and read too much into this, but it's hard not to when I'm lying in his arms. "Hmmm." I sigh as I remember falling asleep with his warm arms around me. There's a flutter in my stomach as I think about our kisses last night.

Warm and fuzzy. This isn't a good sign. It's too soon for me to become emotionally involved with anyone.

"Perfect. Now, I'm not sure what your plans are for today, but I'd like to spend the day with you."

Fletcher wants to spend time with me! My pulse races at the thought of spending time with him. There's a lightness in my chest that I've not noticed before; it's not heavy or aching.

"Don't you have football today?" Even I know most players have games on a Saturday.

"No. Our first pre-season game is next Saturday, which I hope you'll come along to. So, tell me you'll spend the day with me, please?" He pleads with me with sad eyes.

How can I say no to him when he looks at me like that?

"Yes, but let's go out."

"Deal. How about we start the day with me taking you for breakfast?"

"Okay, but let me go next door for a quick shower before we go."

"Done." He bends down and kisses me on the forehead. That's not where I want him to kiss me, but I'm very well aware I need to brush my teeth. I stand and stretch, and I notice my parents getting into their car.

"Well, that's one problem sorted," I say.

"What?" He looks out the window.

"My parents won't question why I'm here."

How would I explain that instead of staying at Lee's, I ended up here? Dad would buy it that I slept on the couch all night, but not my mum. She would want to know exactly what's going on between Fletcher and me, and how can I explain to her when I don't know myself? Is he my friend? Or something else? I have no idea, but I do enjoy being around him.

"In that case, hurry up. Go and shower because I can be ready to leave in ten minutes."

"I better go and change then. Just so you know, it's going to take me longer than ten minutes before I'm ready to go anywhere." I look at the shirt I'm wearing.

"Jess, who the hell is going to see you? You're only going

next door, and anyway, I get to watch you running next door like that. That might just keep a smile on my face for the day."

I don't say anything to him, I just pick up a cushion, throw it at him, and run out of the door, hoping and praying none of the neighbours see me. I hear him laughing behind me.

Rushing into the house, I go straight to my bedroom and look for something to wear. It already feels warm outside, but I know not to expect it to stay that way all day. After all, this is Scotland, and even during the summer months, we can have four seasons in one day. I pull clothes out, have a quick glance, and hang them back up until I reach a perfect blue maxi halter-neck dress. It has a low back but I have a cream cardigan I can take just in case it gets cold.

I'm happy with my choice as I go and grab a quick shower.

Forty minutes later, I'm finally ready. I've only put on a little make-up, and I've piled my hair up in a loose style with some of it hanging down around the back, and secured it in place with pins. The cut on my face doesn't look so bad, but this is the first day I haven't left all my hair down. When my hair is down, it hides it. No one would know it was there.

Today I don't feel like hiding.

"Jess, are you ready?" Fletcher calls out as I leave the security of my bedroom. I draw in a deep breath. He's standing in the middle of the living room wearing shorts and a t-shirt. I can totally appreciate the view in front of me. Fletcher Adams is hot—like, sexy hot. "I hope you don't mind, I let myself in?" His eyes roam my body and I feel a tad self-conscious. He smiles.

"No, of course not. I'm ready,"

"Yes, so I see. It's about bloody time." He laughs and grabs my hand. And here I thought I'd done well to be ready to go out in such a short time. I lock the front door behind us and we make our way to his car. He opens the car door, always the gentleman, or so he likes to think. Am I fooled by his charm? I could be. Easily.

Glancing at the time, I say, "Bloody hell! Is it only nine a.m.?" I hope it's later.

"Yes."

I sag against the chair. He laughs and turns on the radio. I know it's early, but I'm surprised when I realise he's heading into Glasgow's west end. I'm not sure if I'm up to people stopping him all day when they recognise him.

I smile when I see where we are; Lee and I have been to this café on more than one occasion. The food is to die for.

He exits the car and I don't bother moving because I already know he'll be around to my door quickly. Of course, I'm right. He opens the door and I take his hand as I get out of the car. I'm standing in front of this sexy man and trying not to think of all the reasons I shouldn't be doing this. These thoughts have to go to the back of my mind. Each day this week I've said it's going to get easier, but today feels different.

Maybe this is finally a turning point.

He stands gazing at me, my hand still in his. I can't stop myself. I want to kiss him. Reaching out, I wrap my free hand around his neck and pull him toward me. He doesn't waste time when my lips meet his. God, this feels so good.

Fletcher reluctantly pulls back but keeps his hands on me. My heart pounds heavily as we stare into each other's eyes. "Sorry, I . . ."

He silences me with an all-too-brief kiss on my lips. "Don't say it. Don't you dare say you shouldn't have done that."

"I wasn't. I was going to say maybe I shouldn't have done it in public."

"Come on. Let's go and get some breakfast then we can decide what to do for the rest of the day," he says as we walk away from his prize possession.

There's a slight breeze in the air which is refreshing in this heat. I smile as we walk inside the bistro.

"You're smiling."

"Yes. I'm surprisingly happy."

"Glad to hear it." He turns and places a kiss on my head. I can't remember the last time I felt happy in a man's company. This, whatever it is with Fletcher, feels good.

"A table for two?" a waitress asks, approaching us and eyeing up the man beside me.

"Yes." She shows us to our table, and as we sit down, she can't take her eyes off him. It's no surprise, really. He is very pleasant on the eyes.

"Can we order some juice?" Fletcher asks.

"Of course."

"Jess?"

"Can I have apple juice, please?"

"Make that two."

"Okay. I'll come back in a few minutes and take your order," she says.

We look at the menu, but I already know what I want. I put the menu down and look around. There are a few people in having breakfast. There's a family with a baby girl in a high chair. I turn away. I don't want to be sad, not today.

"Jess . . ." He quickly pulls in and then slowly releases a deep breath, readying himself to start apologising. I lift my eyes. His brows are pulled in as he watches me.

"I'm fine, honestly," I say, reassuring him and myself that I'm not going to turn into an emotional wreck. This is something I have to learn to deal with.

"Are you ready to order?" the waitress asks as she puts our juices down on the table.

"Yes. Can I have a poached egg?"

"And for yourself?" She turns to Fletcher.

"A full breakfast with extra toast and bacon." The waitress

leaves and he turns his attention to me. "Jess, you need to eat more."

"I know."

"The extra I've ordered is for you, and you will eat it." He reaches across the table and takes hold of my hands. "Is there anything in particular you want to do today?"

"No, but I'm sure there must be a lot of sights you haven't seen. Dad says you left Glasgow when you were young, so I'm more than happy to be your tour guide for the day."

"That sounds like a good idea."

I ask Fletcher a few questions about football and Logan. It's clear to see how much he loves playing the game as he answers my questions, which probably sound silly to him. He tells me all about the friendship between him and Logan. He talks about some of the other players on the team, and how he's looking forward to getting to know the others properly.

This is the most natural thing I've done in weeks. Conversation between Fletcher and I flows with ease.

The waitress brings out our food, and Fletcher asks for a pot of tea. The food is as good as I remember, and from the way Fletcher is tucking into it, he agrees. He also puts the extra bacon he ordered on my plate.

I frown.

"What? I'm making it my mission to ensure you eat. Your dad said you're still not eating enough at home."

He's worse than my parents.

I shake my head. "I'm getting there. Slowly I'm getting my appetite back. I ate dinner last night, didn't I?"

"Yes, you did and now breakfast, then lunch, and hopefully you'll spend dinner with me as well."

"Let's see how our day goes first. By dinner time we will have spent twenty-four hours together. You might be sick of the sight of me," I say with a smirk.

"Oh, I don't think so."

"Well, it might be me then, who is sick of you." I can't hide my amusement when he looks at me with a straight face. He studies me for a moment before laughing with me. The waitress brings over the tea and two cups but doesn't linger at the table, only because Fletcher doesn't engage in conversation with her.

As we talk, I can see Fletcher is happy I'm eating. Every time I look at him he's smiling at me. I'm sure he's going to report back to my dad the next time they speak. Placing my cutlery on my empty plate, I look at Fletcher. "What?"

He smiles again. "Nothing, but seeing as we've finished eating, why don't we get out of here?"

"I think that is a very good idea."

We settle the bill, or rather Fletcher does. He won't let me pay. He takes hold of my hand and we leave the bistro.

Chapter TWENTY-THREE

Fletcher

AS WE APPROACH MY CAR, I don't want to let go of her hand. It feels so right in mine. I glance at her as we walk. Her soft hair shines and a few loose strands fly behind her in the light morning breeze. Her skin glows, and I'd like to think she looks that way because of me. She is perfect; there are no other words I can use to describe her.

She has it all.

Jessica Taylor looks as though she would fit right in on a Hollywood movie set. Yes, she would be a perfect leading lady, and I'm sure actors would fall over themselves to play her leading man. But if I get my way, I'm the only one who will have that job, and right now it seems like the best job in the world.

We stop at the passenger's door. I click open the car doors but refuse to let go of her hand. Instead, I spin her around in my arms until she's facing me. I take a step closer and push her lightly until she's pressed against the car.

I've fought an inner battle all week long, trying to control myself around her and not have my feelings on display, and *boy,* has it been hard. But no more. I can't help my feelings for Jess. I don't want to hide them away, not today.

Proceed with caution. I don't want to scare her away.

I run my hands down the side of her cheeks, her face only

inches from mine. Her eyes sparkle in the sunlight and she gives a small smile. But I can see she's scared. After our talk last night, I know she's not scared of me; she's scared of her feelings. Feelings she doesn't think she should have. She feels guilty about enjoying herself.

God, how the hell do I get her to understand, and get her to see life from a different perspective?

I hate that she's still being over-cautious with me. Yes, I can understand it, *totally*, but I don't have to like it. I saw the look when I mentioned having dinner tonight with me too. If I'm honest, I want more than dinner, but I won't rush her into something she isn't comfortable doing.

Her eyes lock with mine and she seems unsure of what I'm about to do next. My thoughts are running in all directions through my head. Passing from one net to another without scoring a goal.

My goal is standing in front of me, and she is all I want.

All I can think about as I stand, my body pressed against hers, is how her naked body will feel underneath me when we finally make love. Because, she can fight it all she likes, but it will happen. Sooner rather than later, I hope.

Her eyes glance downwards and widen. Ah, she feels my growing problem too. My erection presses against her. I wish I could control it, but I can't; that's the effect she has on me. She turns me on and there's not a fucking switch to turn me back off.

I lower my head to hers, our lips almost touching. She bites on her bottom lip nervously. God knows why she's nervous. We've kissed before and she has been the one to instigate it on more than one occasion. Is that because she feels more in control? If it is, she can have control over me any time she wants. My hands still hold her cheeks.

"Fletch." My name rolls from her mouth in a whisper. I stare at her and wonder just how I got to be so damn lucky in spending the day with Jess. I can't stand here a moment longer without kissing her, feeling her lips against mine. Tasting her.

I want to taste so much more than her fucking lips.

My fingers glide through the flowing strands of hair before fisting some in my hands, holding her in place so she can't look away.

My body presses further against her. I feel her nipples tighten under her clothes. This girl before me is addictive. I want more from her than just the physical contact, but in this moment, I'm glad to see her body is craving that side too. I want, and I will, take anything Jess offers me.

My lips brush against hers tenderly. But it's not enough. I want more than soft and tender. She parts her lips, and my tongue slips slowly inside, tasting and teasing. Nothing is rushed. Her tongue strokes lightly against mine and sets off a spark. A spark that nothing on this earth can put out.

Warm sensations sweep through my body as our kiss deepens. She consumes me. Her light moan increases my desire and longing for her. There is now a soothing ache in my chest that spreads through my body like a wild fire on a hot summer's day. Out of control.

I feel alive and desired by this amazing girl.

Her hands slide under the hem of my t-shirt and rest against my lower back. Her touch is warm. The connection between us is electrifying. I know I need to stop kissing her, because if I don't, I'm going to want to take this further. Much further. I untangle my hands from her hair and bring them back to her face, slowing our kiss down until I finally stop with a light brush of my lips against hers.

I sigh heavily as I pull her body back to me. She rests her head against my chest. My heart is beating strong and fast, and

I'm sure she can hear it. I rest my chin on top of her head and close my eyes.

I don't want this moment between us to end.

Chapter TWENTY-FOUR

Jessica

OUR FIRST STOP IS THE art gallery and museum. I used to love coming here when I was young, always so much to do and see, and there's also the bonus of the park being so nearby. I wanted Fletcher to park his car and we could've done a city bus tour, but he wasn't having it. I get the feeling this car is his pride and joy. He parks in the farthest space in the car park. I don't mind the longer walk to the entrance because it's such a lovely warm morning, and also, because Fletcher is holding my hand.

As we walk, I notice a few stares in our direction, but it's not until we almost reach the entrance when a young boy approaches us with a football in his arms.

"Fletcher, please could you sign this?" he asks with a huge smile. Fletcher turns to me, and I smile. I might not know much when it comes to football, but I do know this little boy is so excited to just be near Fletcher. At the moment, I know how he feels.

"Of course I can. What's your name?" He takes the ball and pen from the boy and bends down to talk with him.

"Joe. My friends are never going to believe I really met you," he says with excitement.

"Well, how about we get your dad to take a picture so you can show them?"

I smile at his words. The boy calls his dad over, who has been standing a short distance away. I stand beside him as he takes a few pictures. The boy beams with pride. It seems Fletcher is already a hero and he's not even played for his new team yet. I stand and admire my man and grin.

Oh, no! What the hell am I thinking? He's not my man.

"Joe, it was my pleasure to meet you. Hopefully I'll get to see you at a game." The boy nods. "Now, I should get back to my friend."

"Your friend is very pretty."

I blush at his words.

"Yes, she is," he says, looking directly at me as he walks toward me. The boy's dad shakes Fletcher's hand, thanking him for taking time out for his son. He must get this a lot—kids idolising their hero. And not just kids. I can only presume he gets a lot of attention from the ladies. I try not to dwell on that thought.

We walk inside the art gallery and museum hand in hand.

"The kid was right." He stops just inside the entrance and steps in front to face me.

"About?"

"You are gorgeous, and when he said you're very pretty, I realised I haven't told you just how beautiful you look today. There's something different about you today."

"Different?"

"Yes. I can't put my finger on it. You look relaxed and confident, and dare I say it? Happier."

"Maybe it's to do with the company I keep." I throw my hand over my mouth as soon as the words leave me. His blue eyes brighten as his smile grows wider.

"Come on. Let's go and have a look around. Although, I will say this. At least I know you like me." He winks.

"Oh, I thought you would've worked that out when I kissed you."

I can't believe I said that.

He laughs as we walk. What the hell has got into me today? I'm not usually this forward.

Our morning passes by far too quickly. We've not seen half of the exhibits, but what we have seen has been interesting. You would need to spend days here if you wanted to see everything in the gallery and museum. As we walk around, there are students sitting, sketching various paintings. I remember coming here with my class in high school and doing the same thing, although my drawing skills were and still are non-existent. We've talked and laughed, strolling through this impressive building, and his hand has rarely left mine. It's the summer holidays, and it's really busy with families. From some of the conversations we've overheard, there's a treasure hunt going on.

"How about we grab a drink and go outside for a walk?" Fletcher asks.

"Yes, why not?"

We get a couple of bottles of water before going outside into the sweltering heat. This has to be the hottest day of the year so far. We walk through the park grounds, passing one of the playgrounds. There are kids running around, playing. There's a group of boys playing football. I don't say anything, but I'm silently hoping none of them recognise Fletcher. I'm enjoying this time together, just the two of us. We pass the bandstand and I think I would love to come along here one night when there's entertainment. I'm sure it would be an amazing atmosphere.

"Let's go and sit down," says Fletcher, pointing toward a large oak tree where there's an empty bench.

My phone starts ringing as we sit down. "Hi, Lee."

"Hi! Don't *hi* me. I want details of what happened last night with you and Fletcher," she screeches at me. I'm sure he can hear her. Fletcher is pretending he's not listening; his eyes are on the group of boys playing football but I can tell he can hear her.

"If you must know, I'm with him now."

"Oh . . . I never expected that. Where are you?"

"At Kelvingrove Park." There's a long pause.

"Okay, I'll get all the details tonight, and that brings me to why I'm calling. I have VIP tickets for a new club in town tonight. So, you and me, honey, we're having a night out on the town."

"Lee, no. I don't want a night out." My body sags back and Fletcher puts his arm around me.

"Jess, now you listen to me, we are going out tonight. I want you at mine for eight-thirty. Not a minute late."

"Lee . . ." She hangs up on me, not letting me say I might have other plans. "That bloody bitch has just hung up on me." I throw my phone into my bag. Who the hell does she think she is, hanging up on me? I know what she's up to. She's not giving me the opportunity to say no, that's what she's doing.

"I'm sure she's done it for good reason." Fletcher laughs at me.

"You heard our conversation then?"

"Yes, and I agree with Lee. You should go out tonight and let your hair down."

"Even though it would mean cancelling dinner?"

"We could have an early dinner." He looks at his phone. "Seeing as it appears we've missed lunch."

"What time is it?"

"Nearly three." God, I never expected it to be so late. The time has gone so fast. Why is it when you're enjoying yourself, time seems to speed up? Why did Lee have to call about tonight? I'm not sure I want my day with Fletcher to end. Fletcher's phone beeps, indicating a text. "Well, it looks as though I have plans."

"Oh." I'm sure he can hear the disappointment in my voice; I know I can.

"Yeah. Logan wants to go to the pub for a few beers." He puts his phone into his pocket and I relax back into his arms, closing my eyes. Warm fingers delicately touch the skin on my shoulder. He runs them down my arm and back up again slowly, over and over. I can't help but enjoy the sensation sweeping through me.

Opening my eyes, I turn on the bench. Angling myself so I can see him, I reach up and run my fingers along his unshaven jawline. This man in front of me has no idea of what he's done for me. He's given me belief again in mankind. Yes, I feel something between us, a connection of some sort, but I also know I should be wary of him. Especially after everything Lee has told me about his bad boy image.

The thing is, why *should* I stay away from him? I had a good, decent man, or so I thought, but look where that got me.

I lean forward and gently brush my lips against his. His eyes lock on me. So much passes between us. He presses his lips hard against mine, and his tongue glides along my lips before sliding inside my mouth. Strong hands move effortlessly around me. He holds me tight against his body. I'm totally captivated by him. My heart pounds as our kiss intensifies with so much passion it takes my breath away.

I've never felt this way with a man before, not even in the beginning of my relationship with Scott. I've been missing out on so much, it seems.

"I could sit here and kiss you all day," he says, pulling his lips away from mine. "But, as it is, I can't, so we should think about where to go and have an early dinner."

"I could change my plans," I say breathlessly.

"As much as I love the idea of that, Lee wants to spend time with her friend. Who, I might add, was supposed to stay with her last night."

"Okay, I hear you."

"Come on. Let's get going. I know the perfect place." He takes my hand and slowly pulls me to my feet.

The walk back to his car is long in the warm afternoon sunshine. He gets stopped on more than one occasion by groups of boys wanting to speak with him. He answers their questions before telling them he has somewhere to be.

"Is this what it's like whenever you go out?" I ask him curiously.

"Yes. Kids I don't mind. I'll always try and make time for them. They're the supporters of now and the future. But when it's adults, it can get tiring because they can ask some really stupid questions."

We drive back into the city centre and I feel myself closing off from Fletcher. Not because I want to. I'm trying to rationalise my feelings for him. It usually takes me time to get to know people before I accept them. But for some strange reason, it seems I've already allowed Fletcher into my life. The question I should be asking myself is, *why?* From the minute my dad introduced us, I felt something between us. Is that because of everything I've been through with Scott and losing my baby? I don't know. I wish I did. It would make my life just a little easier to understand at the moment.

The car comes to a stop and I hear Fletcher's seatbelt unfasten. Looking out of the window, I see we're parked outside a beautiful Italian restaurant.

"Jess, what's wrong?" I shake my head. "Jess?"

Slowly I turn. His face is cocked to the side and his eyes are narrowed as if confused. "There's nothing wrong," I say, trying not only to convince him, but myself too.

"Jess."

"It's just . . . I've had such a lovely day and really have enjoyed your company. I'm not ready for it to end."

"We can do it again soon. Anyway, we're not finished yet. Come on. You're going to love this place." We get out of the car at the same time. I don't want him to think I expect to be waited on. It's nice, of course. But I've never been one to sit patiently and be waited on hand and foot. I'm too used to doing things for myself.

"So, how did you find this place?" I ask him. For someone who's only been in Glasgow for a short time, he certainly knows his way around.

"My grandparents brought me here a few times when I was younger. Logan and I came here not long ago and I discovered it's still the same family who owns it, just a different generation." I catch the smile on his face as he mentions his grandparents. He grabs my hand and we go inside.

"Ah, Fletcher, benvenuto. Hai scelto la squadra giusta per giocare a calcio per. E chi è questa bella donna ? Lei è troppo buono per voi." A waiter, or maybe the owner, greets Fletcher as we enter. The restaurant is traditional, full of warmth, and not very busy.

"Sono d'accordo con te. Si tratta di Jessica." I'm surprised when Fletcher answers him in fluent Italian. "Jess, sorry. This is Antonio. This is his restaurant." Fletcher introduces me to the handsome man standing before me.

"Hi, Antonio," I say.

"Bello, bello, Jessica," Antonio says, taking my hand in his and placing a kiss on it. I can feel myself blush, even though I have no idea what he just said to me.

"Antonio, posso avere un tavolo in un angolo, si prega di?"

"Naturalmente, un tavolo romantico per due," Antonio replies as he shows us to a small table in the corner—very secluded and romantic. He hands us the menu and disappears.

"Right, I don't have a clue what either of you said."

Fletcher smiles, looking up from the menu, and says, "Antonio said you're beautiful and I agreed with him."

I can't look at him as I feel myself blush, so I sit and read the menu, which is thankfully in both Italian *and* English. Antonio brings over some bottled water and we order. We decide to share antipasti. I order a veal dish and Fletcher chooses steak. Antonio doesn't linger at our table; I'm beginning to think Fletcher has deliberately asked for privacy.

"So, when are you back at training?" I ask.

"Monday. All players will be back at the club then. Our pre-season games are a bit early, but I suppose that will give the manager time to have a look at his team. Then we also have a few big games before the first games on the domestic front."

"Things will be busy for you?"

"Yes. But I enjoy it. It's what I live for." Something about the way he says it makes me think that's all he's ever had in his life; his football. Dad mentioned that he didn't have his family around him because of his mum, and I'm not sure what the story is with her. It's not my business to pry into.

We spend the whole time in the restaurant talking and eating. He asks lots about the business and my friendship with Lee. I'm glad we stay clear of Scott in our conversation; he's not someone I want to give the time of day to. Fletcher tells me the team has two home games, starting with the game next week, and then they're travelling for almost two weeks. He seems excited about the travelling. Well, who wouldn't be?

Like the rest of the day, time is passing by too quickly. We've been so engrossed in conversation that when I next look at the time, it's after six-thirty. Leaving the restaurant, we say goodbye to Antonio, who says he's very much looking forward to seeing me back soon. I assure him I will be.

Fletcher stops at the car and wraps his arms around my

waist. "I'm doing this now because I don't think you'll be happy about this in front of your parents' house." His lips meet mine with a softness I can't describe. This kiss isn't rushed. A mixture of feelings flood through my veins, my stomach tightens, and I press my legs together, looking for relief.

I know what I want and it's *not* a night out with Lee.

"Thank you for an amazing day," he says, standing back and gazing at me.

"No, thank you. Today has been exactly what I've needed." I want to add I want more, but I don't. He opens the car door and I slide in.

Lee has a lot to answer for. Or maybe she's just saved me from making a huge mistake, because I'm certain if we weren't going out tonight, I know how my evening with Fletcher would end.

With me in his bed.

Chapter TWENTY-FIVE

Fletcher

"YOU'VE BEEN NURSING THE SAME bottle now for nearly an hour. Are you going to tell me what's eating you up?" Logan asks as we stand by the bar.

He's right, of course. This is my first drink and I'm in no hurry to finish it. I have no idea why I agreed to come out. Or maybe I do. I needed a distraction. Knowing Jess is going out with Lee tonight has left me feeling jealous. From what Jess said, they're going to some club, and I'm well aware what happens in clubs. The thought of her dancing and some sleazy man trying to put his hands on her makes me feel sick. I swear to God, if anyone lays a finger on her, I will make them pay.

"What? I'm not in the mood tonight."

"No, you don't seem to be, but I'm sure I know what you are in the mood for. Jessica."

"Leave her out of this," I snap.

"Well, at least I know the cause. You may as well tell me what's wrong."

"She's off out tonight to some club with Lee."

"And why is this bothering you so much?"

"Because I was having a fucking great day with her and I wasn't ready for it to end!" I shout at him, causing a few customers to look in our direction.

Logan waves the barman over. "Can we get another two beers and a couple of shots? Anything at all. My friend here needs to loosen up."

The barman smiles and gets our drinks.

"I do not need to loosen up."

"You do, and you also need to get laid." He might be my friend but that won't stop me from hitting him if he doesn't quit it. I don't want to get laid.

"Fuck off," I tell him. The barman puts our drinks down in front of us.

"Some of the lads are heading to a new nightclub. I think we should join them. You need to put some distance between you and Jessica."

I'm not sure if he's right or not, but I nod as I lift the shot from the bar and down it. What harm can it do going to a club with the lads? Fuck, I know what he's trying to do. He's trying to distract me. Pull me from this God-awful mood I'm in. But a club with the lads? That's the last thing I should be doing. He has me questioning myself. Would putting some distance between me and Jess help? No, it won't, because I want to spend as much time with her as I can.

Logan and I make our way to the entrance of the club, much to the annoyance of the clubbers waiting in line. It would seem our names are on the guest list. How that happened, I have no idea. As clubs go, this place looks pretty trendy and up-market, not like some of the dives I've been in over the years. By all accounts, whoever owns this place has gone all out, including a red carpet for tonight. Someone calls my name and I turn, and the flashing of cameras momentarily blinds me. I should've expected it. Logan and I stand for a few moments, letting the photographers get some shots. Let's hope I don't leave here tonight completely wasted. The last thing I need is bad publicity.

The club is crowded as we make our way through the bar area and up the stairs to the VIP section where most of the noise is coming from. From the looks of things, most of the football team is here tonight. Fuck, I'm going to need more than a drink. We join the lads who all look as though they're in the mood to party. A waitress approaches and asks Logan and me what we're drinking. Logan tells her shots and beer, and to keep them coming.

So much for a quiet drink! This is about to get messy.

The VIP section is filled with most of my teammates, and Logan introduces me to a few players from other teams. I stand over at the rails and look out across the club; the place is packed. There are two bars on the lower level and one up here. I hope they have enough staff here because the guys all look and sound as if they're up for a good night, making the most of tonight and tomorrow's hangover before training.

A hand slaps me on the shoulder. I turn to see Logan. "Tonight is all about getting pissed and having fun."

"Okay," I say, sighing heavily.

"At least pretend you'll enjoy yourself," he replies. I turn back to the sea of people on the dance floor. "Fucking hell, Fletch. Get your act together. Forget about Jessica. Look at all the women here, and you, my friend, can have the pick of any here tonight."

I flash him a smile. He's right. I know most of the women in the club would be happy to get up close and personal, or just scream with excitement if we invited them up here with us. But there's no one I would want up here with me. Christ, I wouldn't even want Jess here with all the lads.

"Fletcher? I thought it was you." I cringe, hearing her familiar voice. Blondie from a few weeks ago. Slowly, I turn to face her. I take a large drink from my beer as my eyes roam the body in front of me. Nothing. Not a single twitch. Logan wanders away. This is a part of me he doesn't like, when I'm about to tell a girl I'm not interested. "I thought you would've at least called."

"I think we both know how it is. It was always just going to be one night," I say dryly, trying to brush her off. "Now, I'm sure you can have your pick of any of the *players* here tonight." I stress the players part because I know that's all she's interested in. I turn back to the dance floor, hoping Blondie will take the hint and leave me in peace to enjoy my beer. I've been there once; I don't usually go back for a second course.

"Fine," she huffs before moving on to her next willing victim.

My gaze moves slowly around the room, taking everything in. The DJ booth is to the far side of the dance floor. I notice there's a photographer inside, taking various shots. Well, I suppose it is opening night; the owner will want to get lots of press coverage. I'm just finishing off my beer when Logan appears back at my side.

"You're a pussy," I say as he hands me another beer.

"No, but I could sure do with some." I can't help but laugh. One thing about Logan is that he always says what he thinks, even when he should maybe stop and think first. "Fletch, I'm sorry for dragging you out tonight. I should've left you feeling sorry for yourself."

"Leave it out. I'm here and you never know, I might find someone to go home with." I try to sound confident but I'm not even fooling myself.

"Oh, shit! Fletch . . ."

"What is it?"

"You're not going to like it, but you should turn back to the dance floor." I raise my eyebrows, questioning him, but he stands glued to the spot, his eyes fixed on the dance floor. Following his gaze, my eyes stop when I see her. Fuck, I'm done for now. There is only one woman I would consider going home with tonight, but she's the one person I'm meant to be staying clear of, according to Logan, anyway.

Jess.

And boy, does she look hot. She's wearing a red strapless dress that clings to her curves, and her hair . . . loose curls flow down her back and frame her face. The way she moves to the music, hips swaying. I stand paralyzed, watching her as she dances with Lee, wishing it was me with her on the dance floor. I silently pray to God that she's not with some guy.

"What are you going to do?" Logan asks.

"I know what I want to do."

"Is that wise?"

"Fuck knows, but I know no matter how hard I try, I can't get Jess out of my head, and until this happens between us . . ." I let my voice trail off. As if she senses someone watching, she turns away from Lee and her eyes scan the room. Her eyes lock with mine. Even from up here, I see her shocked reaction as it registers with her. Then she smiles.

I finish the beer in my hand, hand Logan the empty bottle, and walk away from him. "Fletch, be careful," he shouts after me. Being careful doesn't suit me, and after spending the day with Jess, I have no plans to careful.

Reckless, most definitely.

Striding with purpose toward Jess, I can see Lee is questioning her. Lee lifts her head, looks at me then back to her friend before smiling. Jess's eyes stay on mine the whole time, burning with desire, never losing our connection.

The music changes as I reach the dance floor. I smile. *Wild Ones*. Now the question is, will Jess allow herself to live a little on the wild side tonight? The music might be loud but I still hear the hushed voices of a few women, wondering who I've set my sight on tonight. I'm sure they will work it out in a matter of seconds as I close the distance between Jess and me.

"Fletch . . ."

"Jess . . ."

Neither of us says anything else. I grab her hips, pulling her against me. I hold her tight, feeling her body pressed against me, and breathe her in. She pulls out of my hold, turning her back to me and lacing her fingers with mine. We both start to move. I mean *really* move. She grinds against me, and I let out a low groan. I catch sight of Lee; she's now dancing with Logan. I'd put money on it; he's keeping an eye on me.

The song changes and I spin her around in my arms because I need to see her. Our eyes lock. Her eyes darken, filled with desire and lust. I place my hands on her backside and pull her against me, letting my erection rub against her through our clothes. Clothes I hope we lose at some point tonight. We continue dancing as the song leads into another, and the sexual tension between us rises.

I lean down towards her face. Her lips part, and her breathing . . . well, it sounds just the same as mine—we're both panting. I smirk when I feel her press her thighs together. I'm glad to see we're both thinking about the same thing.

I'm mesmerised, watching her. We're both barely breathing. It would be so easy to kiss her . . .

Fuck it.

My lips meet hers with such passion and force, and I'm losing myself to her. She throws her arms around my neck. I want to lift her from the dance floor and find somewhere we can relieve the sexual tension that has been building between us all day. Jess deserves more than a quick fuck in a club. She is the type of woman a man should worship, and I intend to do just that.

We both pull from the kiss at the same time. She slowly

threads her hands through my hair before running them across my jawline. *I need her in my bed. I need to bury myself deep inside her.* She shakes her head, and then I see her smile. Does she know what I'm thinking? She shrugs her shoulders and raises her eyebrows, silently questioning me.

So much can be said without actually speaking.

She nods.

I take her hand and walk toward Logan; he's still dancing with Lee. "We're leaving," I tell him. "Lee came with Jess. Please make sure she gets home safely."

He nods, although if I know Logan, after all the flirting between the two of them last night, he'll end up going home with her. Right now, I couldn't care less who he goes home with.

As we leave the dance floor, Blondie approaches us, and from the look on her face, she's not happy. *Fuck.* I watch as she casts her eyes over Jess and looks at our joined hands. I protectively pull Jess closer to my side and wrap my arm around her waist.

"Fletcher," she says, and I can already tell her claws are out, looking to stir up some trouble. "Where are you going? I thought you and I would . . ."

"What part of no did you not get earlier?" I spit out impatiently, because she is keeping me from my girl. *My girl.* I can feel Jess's body tense at my side.

"She can't give you what you need," she says, her eyes on Jess. Jess glances between the two of us, wanting to find out what's going on. I rub my thumb across her knuckles.

"I think I made myself clear earlier tonight. Now if you don't mind, me and my girl are leaving." I don't believe I've just said that out loud. My girl. Blondie steps aside, drawing me a dirty look, and we walk away. I feel Jess relax again. I hope and pray Blondie hasn't fucked up my plans for the night.

Chapter TWENTY-SIX

Jessica

ALCOHOL FLOWS THROUGH MY VEINS. I'm not drunk, but close to it. Lee and her bloody cocktails. She dragged me out tonight, and brought my day with Fletcher to an end. But now here I am. His arm is wrapped around my waist as he flags down a taxi. Fletcher hasn't let go of me since the blonde spoke to him inside. I have so many questions I want to ask him about her; like who the hell she is? But it can wait. I heard him say he told her earlier tonight he wasn't interested. Maybe I should just put it to the back of my mind. After all, it was a brief conversation. Although she didn't look amused as she ran her eyes over me. Was I too natural-looking for her, with her fake eyelashes and hair? And I'm sure it didn't stop there.

Jealous! I was jealous when she approached Fletcher. It's obvious something has happened between them. I saw it in the panic on his face.

"Come on, this is us," he says, leading me into the waiting black cab. He gives the driver his address.

He reaches out and turns me to face him. "You are who I want, not her. It could never be her." The muscles in his jaw clench, frustration in his eyes as he watches me. He's thinking our little encounter with the blonde has changed our plans. Even if I wanted to use the blonde as an excuse, my body craves him.

I couldn't walk away from him tonight. I need this as much, if not more, than he does.

He angles his head to the side, his eyes burning with desire through to the depths of my soul. It's almost unnerving. *Almost.*

Without hesitation, I wrap my arms around his neck and his lips are on me. I'm lost to the sensations sweeping through my body. Every single inch of my body is suddenly on high alert. Pent up frustration from not just tonight, but today and last night, explodes between us. Fireworks and stars rain upon me. Until tonight, I never really believed in that. I read about it in books, saw it in movies, but never before experienced it for myself.

There is nothing gentle about our kiss. Need burns through me as he pulls me closer, his lips still on mine. His tongue slides inside, teasing and tormenting, and I love the feel of it against mine. He pulls back, breaking our kiss, leaving me wanting more. Cupping my face with his hands, his eyes stay on mine. They're dark and almost demanding.

"We're here," the taxi driver tells us. I glance at my parents' house as Fletcher pays him. All the lights are out. Well, they should be considering the time; it's almost two a.m.

We exit the taxi and it drives away. Fletcher takes my hand, walks quickly to the front door, and stops. He turns, facing me, and rests his forehead against mine. "Jess, I'll give you exactly one minute to change your mind because once we're on the other side of the door, there's no going back. You will be mine." There's no quiver as he speaks. His tone is even, he's giving me a back-out clause, but I won't use it.

I watch as he closes his eyes and waits for my answer. My heart is beating so fast I'm sure he can hear it. He's wrong if he thinks I'm going to run. I'm done with running away from everything. From now on, I intend to face every challenge and obstacle in my life head on. Tonight I want to be carefree. Forget about the grief I've been drowning in these last few weeks. I must be feeling brave, or maybe it's just the alcohol. I reach out, running my hands up the front of his shirt. His eyes fly open when I start unbuttoning it.

"Holy fuck, we need to get inside." I watch in amusement as he reaches into his back trouser pocket for the front door key. It takes him a moment to open the door, but when he does, he drags me inside quickly and pins me against the door as soon as it's closed. "Jess, I want you."

"You have me."

Three simple words are all it takes as his mouth crashes on mine, hunger building between us. Without breaking our contact, he picks me up. I wrap my legs around his waist and he carries me effortlessly through the house. I lose myself in our kiss. A door opens and closes behind us. He removes his lips from mine.

"You are so beautiful, Jess," he whispers, trailing small kisses from my face and down my neck.

Closing my eyes, I throw my head back and moan as his lips caress my skin.

"Jess." His voice is a whisper, yet it still manages to send shivers down my spine.

He pulls my head back. I open my eyes and I'm met with those mesmerising blue eyes of his. Need fills me and I know there's no point in fighting against us.

Us? I like the sound of *us*.

I press my lips to his lightly and tighten my legs around his waist, urging him to make the next move. His grip tightens, pulling my body closer to his. My breasts rub against his firm chest, nipples standing to attention. I can feel his erection through his jeans and the flimsy material of my knickers. I want to press my legs together to alleviate the growing need, but I can't in this position. Instead, I grind against him. He groans in response.

When it's clear he's waiting on me to make the next move, I unwrap my legs from him and slide down his body until my feet touch the floor. I turn in his arms with my back to him and lift my hair away from my neck. He takes my not-so-subtle hint and pulls the zipper down on my dress.

Turning back to face him, I let my dress fall to the floor and step out. I smirk when I hear his shocked gasp. I lift my eyes to meet his, and if there were ever any doubts in his mind about me staying, I don't see them. All I see is that he wants me as badly as I want him. His clouded eyes roam my body, not lingering on any one part for too long, and he smiles.

I step closer to him and continue with the job I started on the front doorstep. Sliding my hands back up his chest, I pause for a second before loosening all the buttons on his crisp white shirt. Slowly, I peel the shirt from him and let it fall to the floor.

The bed catches my eye. I place my hands on his chest, and with one step at a time, I move toward it. His eyes stay locked on mine as we move. Brave and bold is what I am. I've never been this forward with a man before, never taken the lead, especially in the bedroom. Fletcher makes me feel different. He makes me feel bold and slightly naughty.

When we reach the bed, he stops and reaches out, quickly pulling my body to his. One hand grabs my hair, the other is pressed against my back, holding me in place, leaving no room to run. My thoughts are lost and jumbled as his lips crash onto mine in a frenzy of lust and passion.

Desire unfurls deep within as I feel the heat of his chest against my bare skin. The pleasure of our kiss far outweighs the pain in the back of my neck as he pulls harder on my hair. His lips leave mine, and instantly I miss our connection. He releases my hair and I almost sigh in relief. He grabs my arms, turns me around, and pushes me down on the bed. I giggle as this is not where I thought I was going to be. No, in my mind, I was going to do this to him.

He hovers above me. Deep blue eyes burn through me. I try to move my hands but they're held firmly in place. All I want to do is touch him. Feel the warmth of his skin. Run my fingers gently across his jawline. I just want him. All of him.

"Trying to go somewhere?" His breath tickles my skin and I giggle again.

"Me? No. Never. I just want to touch you."

"I promise you will. Do you trust me?"

"Yes." There is no hesitation in my voice as I answer him.

"Close your eyes."

"No. I want to see you."

"Jess . . ." His voice is low but demanding.

As I close my eyes, he releases my arms and I have to fight the urge to touch him. He delicately runs his fingers across each breast, sending a charge of electricity through my body, taking my desire and excitement to another level. A level I have no control over. I want his hands all over me. I want his mouth on every part of my body. To touch. To taste.

I moan as my desire intensifies.

He shifts on the bed and I open my eyes. "No turning back, Jess," he says.

"No. No, turning back." My eyes burn into his. "I want this. I want you."

His hands glide down my exposed body until they reach my knickers. He tucks his thumbs in the waistband and slowly pulls them off. My hand instantly reaches down in an attempt to hide my scar, and tears pool in my eyes. I turn my head to the side because I don't want him to see me cry.

Suddenly, I'm not feeling brave anymore.

"Jess . . ." I hear the pain in his voice as he says my name. His hands reach for my face, and gently, he turns me to face him. I close my eyes in an attempt to hide. How can he possibly want me after seeing that scar? "Jess. This doesn't change anything. It doesn't change how I feel about you. Open your eyes, please." I do. "That's better. Don't hide from me, ever. You are beautiful. Don't ever doubt that."

I nod as my tears fall.

With his words, I try and pull myself back together. I'm trying hard not to brush off his compliment. There's an uncontrollable rush of heat throughout my body. I take several deep breaths and wish my tears to stop.

He places feather kisses around my neck, and I moan. The bed shifts underneath me and he moves slowly, licking and kissing until he reaches my breasts. Swirling his tongue across my nipple, he pulls it into his mouth, sucking and nipping, while his other hand massages and teases my other breast.

"Oh God," I moan as he changes direction.

My senses have heightened and I'm on the verge of losing control. Fletcher moves his attention, kissing and licking as he moves down my body.

Don't panic. Don't panic. I repeat the words over and over in my head as he gets closer to the one part of my body I'm no longer sure I want him to touch.

I hold my breath as he places the softest of kisses at the edge of my scar. "Jess, breathe."

I let go and breathe as he carries on kissing me.

As his mouth lowers, I start to tremble. I fist the sheets, feeling the first touch of his tongue as it swipes through my folds. It feels fucking incredible. All thoughts of moments ago drift into the background of my mind. He continues to lick and suck, and then pauses, then starts again, continuing with my torment, pushing me closer and closer before suddenly stopping again. My need for a release is painful as he starts teasing me again. I try to hold back because I'm scared he's going to stop if he thinks I'm close.

Fletcher licks and sucks, pushing me higher, and I'm close. So fucking close. He pushes a finger slowly inside me and I'm done. That sends me over the edge, repeatedly calling his name. But that doesn't stop him. His tongue travels back and forth, and he continues pushing deep inside me, drawing out my orgasm until I can't take it anymore.

Holy fuck! That has to be the most intense orgasm I've ever had. I'm aware that my heartbeat is racing. Warmth filters through my body. There's no way I can come down from the high I'm on to do anything else.

The bed shifts, and I open my eyes to see him standing by the bed, unfastening his jeans with a look of smug satisfaction on his face. Well, in my opinion, he has every right to look that way. I watch with interest as he removes his jeans and boxers in one go.

Oh, God! My eyes drift lower; there's no way that is going to fit inside me. My eyes travel to his and he lets out a low chuckle.

I sit up and make my way to the edge of the bed. He watches me curiously. I take him in my hand, stroking him. Glancing up, I see him close his eyes as I lick him from root to tip.

"Fuuucking hell, Jess."

That *was* the plan, but for now, it will have to wait.

I circle the tip as I continue to stroke him in my hand. Sheathing my teeth, I take him into my mouth. His fingers run through my hair before grabbing hold of my shoulders. He groans. Licking and sucking, I take him deeper. His body reacts and he pushes against me. I work him up and down with my hand, at the same time applying pressure with my tongue. I feel him growing inside me. He's close, close to losing control. His grip on my shoulders tightens as he continues to thrust against me. Reaching down lower, I roll his balls in my hand then turn my attention to the skin underneath.

"Jess, enough. You need to stop before I can't." He pulls out and we both crawl up the bed at the same time.

When his face is in line with mine, he brushes my hair away from my face. "Are you ready?" I nod, because in my present state, I don't think I'm capable of forming the words. He reaches over to the bedside cabinet, opens the drawer and then sits up. I watch as he rolls a condom on. Part of me wants to tell him he doesn't have to wear it because of my pill, but the sensible part of me says, this is a conversation for another day.

He gazes at me and I take a deep breath. "You have no idea how much I want to do this. You bring out feelings unknown to me. This makes you mine, Jess."

My eyes widen as he slowly enters me and stills. This feels so good. He moves slowly, pushing deeper inside me. Every part of my body aches for his touch. A shiver of pleasure runs down my spine. My body trembles beneath his and I feel weak.

He pushes deeper and pulls slowly back, and this time slams back into me. Again and again. He said moments ago this makes me his. I am, in every sense of the word, with every breath I take, and with every beat of my heart. In this moment, he owns me completely.

He reaches down between us and applies pressure to my clit. He's going to send me spiralling again and I'm not sure my body is ready. He pounds into me harder, reaching new depths each time. I'm not going to last; my breathing is becoming erratic and my need is building. I find myself clawing at his back as he continues pounding, over and over. Looking for my release, I thrust against him desperately. Our eyes lock and I cry out his name as I shatter around him. I ride out my orgasm as Fletcher follows, calling out my name. He falls to the side, pulling me with him so we're still facing each other.

He kisses me sweetly on the lips before lying on his back and pulling me until my head rests against his chest. The beating of his heart is soothing and I feel my eyes getting heavy. Everything about tonight has been gentle and caring.

"Sleep," he says. I close my eyes and allow myself to drift off, happy and content.

Chapter TWENTY-SEVEN

Fletcher

IF ONLY I COULD FALL asleep as easily as Jess. But I can't. I can't take my eyes off her, this vision of beauty, and she's sleeping with her arms wrapped around me, her head resting on my chest, her gorgeous just-fucked hair splayed across my body. And the best bit of all, she's gloriously naked.

Every time she moves, I have to pinch myself that this is real. And it is. So bloody real. Something inside me has changed. I'm still me, but my feelings have changed. Jess is an amazing person, and I hope and pray when she wakes up in the morning, she has no regrets. Because I sure as hell won't.

When we parted company after the restaurant, I never imagined this is how my night would end. With Jessica Taylor in my bed.

Her body was made for me.

I'm desperate to hear that sweet sound she made right before her orgasm. I loved the sound of her calling my name. For me, this isn't some one-night stand. I want more with Jess.

For the first time in my life, what we shared wasn't just sex. No, for me it was a whole lot more and I'm trying not to think about that. What it means.

This is going to be a long night. I already have the urge to wake her so I can have her again. This feeling is unknown to me. I've never wanted anyone as badly as I want Jess. And now I've finally had her, I need her to stay in my life.

Chapter TWENTY-EIGHT

Jessica

MY EYELIDS ARE CLOSED, AND I'm sure it wouldn't take much for me to snuggle back in and fall over again into a deep sleep. His arms are still draped around me and my head is still resting on his chest. We're in the same position we fell asleep in. As I stretch, I can feel we're still naked as we lie in each other's arms. Opening my eyes, I blink against the light that floods the room and focus on Fletch. I watch as his chest rises and falls as he breathes. He looks so peaceful as he sleeps. I want to run my hands up and down his body one last time before leaving.

My parents might still be in bed. If I'm lucky, I'll be able to quietly slip through the house without disturbing them. I glance at my watch; it's nearly six a.m. It's starting to become a habit, falling asleep in his arms. A habit I could take great pleasure from.

Leave. I should do that, but at this moment, I'm selfish. I lie next to him, admiring the view as memories of our day and night come flooding back to me. Memories of a perfect day together, followed by what turned out to be an exceptionally good night.

I glance down our bodies. We're lying in a tangled mess of covers which are barely covering either of us.

I can't help but smile.

I remember every touch of his against my skin; soft, gentle, and caring. Tears. I remember my tears as he removed my underwear and the embarrassment I felt as he saw my scar. The delicate kisses along it eased my fears. He made me feel wanted. I've not felt wanted or desired in such a long time. My body was burning with lust for him the moment our eyes locked in the club.

Our night together started on the dance floor but ended with me in his bed. Was it bound to happen? I'm not sure. I can't say the thought hasn't crossed my mind. But now what? I've never found myself in this situation before. Do I leave now? Or . . .

Tears fill my eyes. *You, silly, silly girl.* I shouldn't be in this position. Shouldn't have let this happen between us, no matter how much I wanted it. What the hell was I thinking?

But I wasn't thinking. I try to rationalise this situation in my head, but I can't. I could put it down to my own grief, but even that doesn't justify me sleeping with him.

What will people think of me, sleeping with someone so soon after everything that's happened? My parents . . . they're going to be so disappointed in me. I've let them down.

Guilt eats away at me as I look at Fletch. In my own selfish way, have I used him? Or has he been the one to use me?

Lifting my head, I meet his blue eyes. "Morning." A slow smile curls at the corners of his mouth and my heart skips a beat.

"Morning," I murmur back. His fingers draw circles on my skin, sending warmth through my body. He looks happy and content. I want to feel that too, but with doubts and grief lingering, I'm not sure I can. I have no right to be happy and content.

My imagination has gone into overdrive; it's as though someone has pressed the accelerator and cut the wires to the brakes, sending me out of control.

I can't do this. I can't lie in his arms and pretend this is okay. Far from it.

I turn away from him as panic and fear grip me, cutting me in two and sending me in different directions.

"Jess?" The concern in his voice pulls at my strings and I know I need to leave before it's too late.

It's already too late. I wanted him and now I'm going to punish myself because I have to walk out that door and leave him.

"Jess, stop thinking."

"Fletch," I finally say as I turn to him. "I need to go. I shouldn't be here." I try to pull from his hold but he's too strong.

"No way. You're not going anywhere. Jess, we need to talk. I can see you're struggling with this, but I don't get it. You and I both know there's something pulling us together. Why fight it?"

"Why? There's a million fucking reasons for me to fight it. Please let me go."

"No! Go on then. Tell me your reasons. I'm waiting." He sits up in the bed, pulling me with him. I pull the covers up, covering my body, needing the security they provide.

"My parents, my dead baby, Scott. Need I go on?" I sigh as tears leak from my eyes. "And this." I lift my hand to my face. "I'm an emotional mess. Why would you want me when you can have someone like the Barbie doll from last night, who comes with no complicated baggage?"

"Let's get one thing straight; I don't want her. I want you. I can help you. Help you overcome the insecurities caused by your fucking ex. Not all guys are like him. I could never treat you the way he has." He laughs before stopping himself.

"What's funny?"

"I might not be like Scott, but I am an arsehole. I've never wanted to treat someone with respect. Never have I woken up in the same bed as a woman the morning after the night before until now, with you."

"This is your place. The thought had crossed my mind of leaving . . ."

"If I'd woken up and you weren't in bed beside me, I would be hammering on your parents' door wanting to know what the fuck happened." Now it's my turn to smirk. "Jess, I've never had a proper relationship in my whole life. Fuck, I never even had a relationship with my mum. Logan is the closest to me, and at times I shut him out. I want to spend time with you, enjoy your company. But most of all I want to get to know the real you. The one hiding behind layers of grief. Let's take this a day at a time. I'm asking you to give me a chance and let me in. Don't put the barriers back in place. Leave them down a little."

I've already allowed him into my life. Could I just shut him out again? No, I don't think I could. But I'm scared of the feelings I have around him. I don't think clearly.

"You're thinking again. Don't. Just let whatever this is between us happen."

Do I really have any say in this?

"Okay," I whisper.

His face lights up. "Do you mean that?"

"I think so. Fletcher, this won't be easy. I'm still dealing with everything life has thrown my way lately."

"Stop! Just stop talking because now I have an overwhelming urge to kiss you."

"Hold that thought because I need to pee." He laughs as I get out of bed. I look for something to put on, but what the hell. Why bother? He's only going to remove it as soon as I leave the bathroom. I feel his eyes on me as I walk toward the bathroom. Before, I would never have walked away from a man in just my birthday suit, but there's something about the way he makes me feel. Confident, yet weak. Confident to be myself and not be scared about anything or anyone when I'm around him, and weak because I'm scared of my growing feelings.

What a fucking combination!

After a few minutes, and brushing my teeth with his toothbrush, I leave the bathroom. He's still exactly where I left him, sitting up in bed with his eyes on me as I walk toward him. I had considered wrapping a towel around me to walk back here, but as his smile grows, I'm glad I didn't.

Warm hands reach out and playfully pull me back on the bed. I fall on top of him and both of us start laughing. "What do you want to do today?" he asks, smirking, eyebrows raised. I already know what he wants to do. To be fair, he's not the only one.

He pulls me closer to him and kisses my neck, then nibbles on my earlobe. My imagination is now impatiently anticipating his next move. A tingling sensation sweeps across my body and heat flares deep within. "You haven't answered my question, yet."

"Oh, I don't know. I'll happily spend all day in bed with you."

"You will?"

"Yeah, why not? Although you will have to feed me at some point."

"I'm sure that can be arranged. Now, how about that kiss?"

Lowering my mouth to his, our lips meet. His tongue slides across the seam of my lips, seeking entry. His tongue brushes lightly against mine as I let him in. This kiss is soft and slow, and in this moment, it's perfect. His warm hands travel up and down my back as I try to steer us in the right direction. We both want it, so I don't know why we're holding back.

"I want you," I say, pulling myself out of his hold, moving position so I'm straddling him.

"This could be very interesting," he says, eyes assessing our current situation. "You have a whole load of sexy going on. A man could get used to this view."

"Don't get too used to it," I say, lowering my head and crushing his mouth with mine, putting an end to our conversation. Already, I like the way my morning is going, despite how early it is. Now would be the perfect time for what I hope is a quick conversation, and I do hope it's a *really* quick conversation because I want to feel all of him. Nothing between us.

Stretching out, I'm alone in the bed. Not how I wanted to wake up. I open my eyes and notice the curtains are now closed. Fletcher must've closed them. I hear voices in the distance; one belongs to Fletcher, the other is my dad. *Shit.* Why is he here? Does he know I'm here in Fletcher's bed? Fuck! Fuck! Fuck! I look at the time; it's just after one p.m. I snuggle under the covers. There's no way I'm going out to face my dad. The front door closes and I hear footsteps coming up the hall. He stands in the bedroom doorway, hands leaning on the woodwork, face unreadable. That's a first. I can usually tell how he's feeling.

"Please, just put me out of my misery," I say. He sits down on the bed and I sit up and relax into the warmth and comfort he provides.

"Let's just say I'm glad it was Jim who came to see me and not your mum. I'm sorry. Your phone had been ringing non-stop. I thought you would answer it. But when I saw there were missed calls from Lee and your dad, I finally answered and told him you're here. Then he paid me a visit."

"Oh no. I was having a good day and now I'm going to have to face my parents." I sink deeper into his arms.

"It's not as bad as it seems."

"How can you say that?"

"Jess, your dad only came over, I think, to pacify your mum, who by all accounts, is more than happy to hang me on her washing line by my balls." I frown. "Hey, your mum's words, not mine. But seriously, your dad is fine with you being here. Well, he accepts it better than your mum. Having said that, I was given a fair old warning from him, which of course, I expected."

"Really?"

"Really. Stop worrying. You're not some silly young girl. You're twenty-five years old."

"Yes, but I don't want to be a disappointment to anyone."

"Jess, you could never be a disappointment to anyone." He lifts my chin so he can see me clearly. "Never. Your parents just want you to be happy, but in your mum's eyes, I'm not the right person to do that." He sighs heavily as he finishes saying it, as though he's now got doubts. After all my doubts and insecurities earlier, he's now having them.

"And what do you think about that?"

"I think she makes a good point. The image I've had over the years isn't a good one, I can't deny it. But I do want to be the one who makes you happy, brings a smile to your face."

"That's good enough for me," I say, pressing my lips softly to his.

"Also good enough for your dad too, it would seem. Now, why don't you grab a shower and then we can eat."

"I have a better idea. Why don't you join me in the shower, then we can eat."

"You are going to wear me out. I need to be fit for training tomorrow."

"I'm sure you can keep up," I say, getting out of bed, taking his hand, and leading him to his own bathroom.

Chapter TWENTY-NINE

Fletcher

"DO YOU REALLY HAVE TO leave me?" Jess asks me from the comfort of my bed. Oh boy, I wish I was still in there beside her after spending an amazing day with her yesterday. "It's only six a.m."

"Yes. I'm sorry. First morning, full training and all that. What time are you heading into work?"

"I'll grab a shower if that's okay with you, then I'll get dressed and maybe head in early."

"Of course it's fine with me. Help yourself to some breakfast. I'm not sure what the manager has planned this week. I should know better after today. I'm hoping I get to spend time with you," I say, watching her as she wriggles under the covers.

"Give me a call later and let me know. I should probably face my parents tonight." She sighs heavily. She's not looking forward to this, even after I tried to reassure her yesterday after her dad was here. "I'm also thinking about looking for a new house for me."

"Don't rush in," I say, surprised. I know she originally thought she would only be staying with her parents for a few days. But days turned in weeks. "What about the apartments?"

"No. I love them but I see me in a house with a garden if I buy, but I might rent something for a while. It would give me my own space. Might also give me some independence that I've lost. It would give me time to find my ideal house."

"And what is your ideal house?"

"Somewhere in a good estate, houses not too close together. Plenty of space inside and out. Nothing too old. Something new, ready to move into."

"As I said, don't rush in, and your parents . . . well, your dad at least, won't give you a hard time about spending time here with me."

"It's my mum I'm dreading facing," she says, looking away. I sit on the bed beside her, taking her chin in my hands, and capture her mouth with a slow, meaningful kiss. The meaning behind it . . . I'm not sure what it is yet.

"Don't worry. I'm sure everything will be fine." I try to sound confident, but even I'm worried about seeing her mum. Jim made it clear Elaine isn't happy with me. Or rather, how I've led my life over the years. She doesn't want her daughter mixed up with the likes of me. She doesn't think I'm good enough, and she might have a point.

Fuck. I don't think I'm good enough for Jess. I just hope I don't fuck this up between us, whatever this is.

"I'm sure it will be. Hopefully when I go next door to get ready for work I can avoid Mum," she says. "Now, you should go before . . ."

"I'm going because you are a temptation I'm afraid I have to resist this morning." I kiss her softly. "I'll drop you a message later." She smiles as I walk away, leaving her in my bed.

"Fletch, I swear to fuck, you are going to fucking kill me," says Logan as we walk back out onto the training pitch. We've done an early morning weight session in the club gym. I'd thought a few other players would have been there as well, but it was only the two of us.

"I'm not going to kill you. Make you fitter, now that's a possibility."

"Right, lads," the manager calls out to all the players, rounding everyone up. "I know some of you will feel as though you haven't been away from the training ground for long, but I do hope you enjoyed the break. Now, we have a long season in front of us. I'm sure you all know Fletcher. There may still be one or two new faces joining us before the domestic season kicks off. But for now, this is my squad. If you want to make it into my starting eleven, you have to earn that right by working hard during training. I expect no less than one hundred percent. Less than that, you won't even make the bench."

There are a few grumbles from some of the boys, although I'm not sure why. The manager is only telling us what he expects.

"Now," he continues. "We have a few pre-season games and you will all feature in these games, before our first European game. So the hard work starts today."

The morning is spent playing small sided games, as the manager and coaching team watch over every single player. The manager is new and I'm sure he's watched replays of the original squad, but he'll want to see for himself where everyone is at. A few of the lads are really good, and I'm sure I could name my starting eleven from this first training session with them.

Logan has some good competition from the goalkeepers, but I'm sure he'll remain the first choice keeper. There's also a couple of really young lads who have impressed me; I hope the manager feels the same.

"Right, lads. Take a break. Go and have lunch then we'll meet in the conference room in an hour," the manager calls out. Everyone stops and heads inside to the canteen. Logan walks with me and Jackson, who has been told he will remain club captain. Jackson is a central midfielder and has great presence; the younger lads in the team look up to him. He was a bit worried the new manager would want to revamp everything in the team, but he had nothing to be concerned about.

"Spill!" Logan says as we sit down in the canteen with our lunch.

"What's going on?" asks Jackson, looking between Logan and me.

"Fletch has spent most of the weekend with a certain lady."

I'm going to fucking kill Logan.

"As in the same lady? What's wrong with her?"

"Jackson! I would watch your mouth," I warn him. "And as for you." I turn to Logan. "If I wanted everyone knowing my business I'd take out an ad in the fucking paper."

"Oh, come on. Neither of us meant anything. Can you not take a joke? You used to have a sense of humor," says Jackson. "Are we talking about the girl from Saturday night? She was fucking hot. I wouldn't kick her out of my bed."

I slam my cutlery down. One, two, three, four, five, six, seven, eight, nine, ten. That hasn't helped. I'm trying to rein in my temper because I know the gaffer would have me on the bench for the foreseeable future if I caused any sort of trouble on the first day.

"Fletch. Fletch." It's Logan's voice. "Sorry. I shouldn't have brought it up."

"No, you shouldn't have, but seeing as you have . . . yes, I've spent the weekend with Jess, and yes, that was who I left with on Saturday night."

"So, you have a special someone in your life." Jackson smirks.

"Let's wait and see."

"When do we get to meet her?"

Do I really want Jess meeting the lads? No, but I have said I'd like her at Saturday's game.

I may as well tell him. "She'll be at the game on Saturday."

"So, you won't be coming out Saturday night to celebrate with the boys?"

"Oh, shit. I never thought of that when we mentioned it to Jess and Lee. Fuck!" Logan says. He never thinks when it comes to the opposite sex.

"What the hell? One leopard changing his spots I could believe, but not two." Jackson looks between us, laughing.

"There's no way I'm changing for anyone. No matter how good they are in the sack," Logan says, putting us both straight.

"So Lee got home okay then?" I ask him.

"You know she did, because I know Jess spoke with her yesterday. So are you going to spill what's going on with you and Jess?"

"I don't know."

"She's nice and all, but she comes with too much baggage."

"Fuck, this gets better. My mum would love your gossip. It beats her soap operas on TV. Does she have a kid?"

"Jackson, you are fucking pushing it. No, she doesn't." Jess isn't up for discussion.

I push my plate away and stand up. I've hardly touched my lunch, but I've lost my appetite. As I walk away, I can hear Jackson ask Logan questions. If he knows what's good for him, he won't answer.

I make my way to the conference room; there's no point going anywhere else. I'm bloody missing Jess now they've mentioned her. I drop her her a text.

Me: Hope you're not working too hard.

My phone beeps.

Jess: I'm always working hard.

Me: What are you doing?

Jess: Just leaving the office to go to the apartments. I need to get my car. Getting taxis everywhere is driving me nuts.

Me: Are you fit to drive?

Jess: Are you serious? After some of the things we've done, you ask if I'm fit to drive. What are you doing?

Her reply makes me smile. Maybe I should have thought about that before.

Me: Manager wants to have a meeting with everyone. Heading there now.

Jess: Ok. Behave and I'll speak to you later.

If only she knew.

I enter the conference room and the gaffer is already there. He looks surprised to see me as he sets up the projector.

"Fletcher, you still have a good twenty minutes left of lunch."

"Yeah, I know. Can I help with anything?"

"Not being funny, but, are you alright?"

"Of course. Just making sure I start off on the right foot."

"Well, in that case, put out bottles of water for everyone." He points at the cases on the floor. "After this meeting have you got time for a chat?"

"Of course," I reply wondering what, if anything, I've done wrong. It's not long before the rest of the players start filing into the room. Jackson comes straight over to me and apologises for his comments about Jess, and says he's looking forward to meeting her after Saturday's game. Logan smiles as I accept his apology.

The three of us sit together as the gaffer starts talking. He tells us that on Friday afternoon we're all going to visit the children's hospital. The club is making a large donation for new equipment, but we're also donating toys. Next, he goes through the timetable for the week ahead, telling us where we should be and when. He then mentions we should each think about a charity we would like to be associated with. Lastly, he talks about Saturday's game and ticket allocation for players. This part never interested me before with any of my other teams, but today it does. I know a few of the players are married with kids, so there will be some wives and girlfriends at the game.

And Jess, too.

The gaffer lets everyone head home for the day, and I stay behind for our chat.

"How's the first day with all the lads been?" he asks.

Shit. I wonder if anyone has said anything about me and Jackson. But no one knew.

"Yeah, they seem a good bunch. It helps having Logan and Jackson here."

"Yes, it must. Look, what I really wanted you to know is that I know it must be hard for you being back here in Scotland, not having family around you . . ."

I don't let him finish. "It's not been too bad. Having to sort out my gran's things is probably the hardest thing about being back here. But I meant what I said. This is a fresh start for me. You've given me a chance. I don't want to fuck up."

"You and I are going to get along just fine, but if you need anything, anything at all, just say."

"Thanks. There are a couple of things. Who do I see about tickets for the game?"

"How many do you need?"

"Four, but two with family, and can you arrange the other two for hospitality? Those two I can pay for." I want to give the other two to Jim as a thank you for all he's done the last few weeks.

"Of course, and there's no need to pay for those, just don't tell the others. Now, the two within the players' family section . . . I will need names to go on the list for security."

"Jess Taylor and her friend, Lee. I will give you her surname later."

"Someone special?" he asks.

"I think so. This also brings me to what you were talking about earlier. Can someone check out a charity against domestic violence? I'd like to do something with that."

"I never expected you to say that. Yes, I will get the player liaison officer to look into that for you, if you're sure."

"Yes."

"Right. Get off home, and I'll see you in the morning."

"Thanks, boss." I leave him feeing happier than I did at lunchtime. Now I have a phone call to make to Jim. I want to go and collect Jess's car for her so it's sitting there for her after work, and also speak to Jim about the charity.

Chapter THIRTY

Jess

"BLOODY HELL!" I SAY, ENTERING the office. "I'm exhausted."

Lee looks up from her desk, smirking. "Well, if you hadn't spent all day yesterday in bed, doing God only knows what, you wouldn't be exhausted." I can't help smiling. She has a valid point. I am tired and there are only two people to blame: me and Fletch. "Glad to see you smiling. Fletch brings out all that's good in you. Now, how did it go over at the apartments?"

"Really good." I sit down at my desk, taking the weight off my feet. "Everyone that bought off plan is happy and I have another two reservations."

"That's brilliant. I knew these apartments would sell themselves. If only I wasn't heading off to the other side of the city, we could've been out celebrating."

"There will be no celebrating for me on a Monday night, and anyway, I need to go and face my mum. Although, after talking to Dale today, I might not be staying at my parents' for much longer."

Lee is moving folders and tidying up her desk when she stops and stares at me with a puzzled expression. "Hold on, what did you say about Dale? And why do you need to face your mum?"

"Mum isn't happy with me because of Fletch. Dad came around to his yesterday for a friendly chat," I pause. "And as for

Dale, I asked if he would be interested in renting any of the apartments out."

"Right, let's take this one thing at a time. I presume your mum reads the newspapers, so she would know all about your Fletcher Adams?"

"I suppose so, but is there anything in particular I should know?" I ask, now slightly worried about how little I know about him. Yes, Lee has mentioned the fact that he's been a bit of a player, but I had already guessed that much for myself.

"You should do your own research on Fletch and then come to your own conclusion. Now, are you moving into one of the apartments? And why are you not buying?"

"Because when I buy it's going to be a permanent move and a house. I've always pictured myself in a house with a garden or a fair bit of land. From my point of view, it makes sense to rent for a bit until I find the perfect house for me."

"Oh. My. God. This is going to be so good. So do you know which one?" She walks over to my desk and she's almost bouncing with excitement. God, what's she going to do when I tell her what he's offering to rent me. "Oh, tell me . . ."

"The penthouse."

She screams. "NO way."

"Yes way. I was as shocked as you are but he's not ready to sell it. So I can have it anytime."

"Just like that? What's the catch?"

"There's not one. His wife agreed today. We all agreed on a price, and after this week I can move in anytime."

"Maybe he's after a younger model to replace his wife."

"Lee . . ."

"What? You never know, or maybe it's the wife who's taken a shine to you. They might want to share you."

"You have some imagination!"

"Hey, things like this go on all the time." She laughs. "Now, seriously. I know you wanted to look at what we have on our books. Are you sure this is what you want?"

"Yes. It feels right, and most importantly, I feel safe there with the security. I need my own independence back. The other good thing is I don't need to rush out and buy furniture." She wraps her arms around my neck, and I relax back in my chair.

"Well, in that case, I'm pleased for you." She kisses my head. "Now, are you going to be okay locking up?"

"Of course. Go. I have a few things to do then I'll be leaving."

"Okay. See you in the morning. Try and rest tonight." I can hear her laughing as she leaves the office. I don't plan on spending the night with Fletch, but I never planned on staying with him yesterday, either.

I've just finished replying to some emails and I'm about to shut down my computer when the front door opens, and in comes a delivery man with a bunch of red roses in his arms.

"Miss Taylor?" he asks. I nod. "These are for you." He hands me the flowers. They look and smell amazing. "If you could just sign for them."

I put them on my desk. "Of course." I scribble my signature on the paper. "Thank you." He leaves and I take the card from the envelope;

To a beautiful lady who looked amazing in red. x

Fletch. He must've sent these. If his car is in the drive, I'll go in and thank him for these before facing my mum. I grab my bag and the roses, and lock up before flagging down a taxi.

The ride back to my parents' doesn't take long. I'm sure I've sat in the back of this taxi with a silly grin on my face for most of the way as I've stared at the roses. Fletcher's car *is* in the driveway. I pay the driver and exit the cab.

The first thing I notice is my car parked alongside my dad's, and my dad and Fletch are talking beside it. I walk toward them and I can't help but smile.

"Jessica," my dad greets me. "Those are lovely. Are they from a client?"

"Hi. No, I don't think they are," I say, staring at Fletch, who considering he's sent me flowers, doesn't look all that happy to see me with them. "These are gorgeous. Thank you."

He screws his face up and his brows knit together. "Jess, I didn't send you flowers. I wish I had, but I can't take credit for these."

"Oh! I just thought when I read the card they were from you." Fletch and Dad exchange glances, both of them frowning.

"Why? What's on the card?"

"To a beautiful lady who looked amazing in red."

"Can I see the card?" Fletch asks.

I hand it to him. How the hell did I not notice there's writing on the back? I drop the roses to the ground.

"Jess, what's wrong?" Dad asks.

"Fucking hell. *But then again, you always looked good in red.* Is this from who I think it is?" Fletch asks, his voice raised. I can only nod. "I'll fucking kill him."

"That won't help," Dad says. "Let's get inside and not discuss this in the street."

Fletch takes my hand as Dad picks up the flowers. I don't want them now, so why is he bringing them into the house?

"What the hell is he doing in here? I don't want him here!" Mum shouts as we enter.

"Bloody hell, woman. Can you give it up?"

"Jim, I don't want him in my home. He's no good for Jess."

"Elaine, leave it. Now is not the time."

Mum looks at me as I go and sit down.

Fletch kneels down in front of me. "Jess, we have to report this."

"I know. Dad, do what you need to do."

"Can someone please tell me what is going on?" Mum shouts.

Fletch speaks up. "Jess received some flowers and thought they were from me, but they're not."

"Scott?" My mum's question hangs in the air.

"Yes," I finally say. "With what is on the card, that means he was watching me on Saturday night," I say, looking at Fletch.

"It would appear so. But you were always safe."

I nod, knowing he means what he says, and deep down, I believe I'm safe with Fletch.

"The safest place for you, Jess, is at home, not out all night with him."

"Elaine, come and help me get something to drink," Dad says, trying to keep my mum under wraps. They both leave the room.

Bloody hell, I know she means well and she wants to look out for me and take care of me, but she has to realise I'm not a child. Even though at times I might come across like that. I think she forgets that I'm twenty-five-years-old and run a successful business.

"Jess, are you okay?"

"Yeah. I suppose it was just wishful thinking on my part that I wouldn't see or hear from him again. I don't know what to make of this, though. I was coming home to face my mum and then I wanted to come and share my news with you."

"What news?"

"Well, bad news is the penthouse is no longer up for sale because Dale has taken it off the market and is going to rent it. I'm moving into it."

"Is that wise, considering this?"

"I don't know now, but as I said before, I can't stay here forever. I need to get my life on track and I'm not going to allow this to set me back. I don't . . . no, I *won't* allow myself to become Scott's victim again. I don't want to be constantly looking over my shoulder, wondering when he's going to pop up in my life."

"Jess . . ."

"Fletch, honest, I'm fine. Why don't you go next door and let me deal with Mum? Let's face it, she's not happy, and I suppose I need to know the reason why. The question is, are you going to be the one to tell me or do I have to go looking myself?"

"I'll tell you anything you want to know. But I can understand her reaction to me," he says.

"Maybe, but she was fine with you until the weekend. So I need to ask her if it's just because of you or does she think me moving on is too soon. I think it's both, and if it is, I can't stay here because I've made a promise to myself not to live in the past. I have to try and move on from what has been the worst thing I've ever faced. No one should have to face what I've been through, yet thousands of woman do so on a daily basis, and some never have the courage to do anything about it."

"You should consider going into politics with that speech."

"Don't tease, because it is true."

"I know it is. I'll go and give you time with your parents. I wanted to cook dinner for us, though."

"Why didn't you say? How about I come around in an hour? That gives me time to talk to my mum, and if the police want to come and see me at some point, they only have to come next door."

"If you're sure, but just to warn you, it won't be anything fancy."

"That's fine with me." I lean forward and kiss him. "I'll be over soon." He reluctantly leaves me to deal with my mum.

Mum comes back into the room carrying two cups of tea.

She sits down on the couch beside me and I wait as she hands a cup to me.

"Jessica, about you and Fletcher. Don't you think you're rushing in?"

"Mum, I'm spending some time with someone whose company I enjoy. What's wrong with that?"

"It's just, well, you've just come from one bad relationship and jumped into a disaster," she says, her voice calmer than how I feel.

"Mum, that's not fair. You're not even giving Fletch a chance. He's done nothing wrong. In actual fact, all he's done is go out of his way for all of us."

"That may be so, but his past isn't clean cut."

"We can't all have perfect lives."

"That's not what I'm saying." She raises her voice. "Yes, he helped us all, but I can't help how I feel about you being in a relationship with someone who is known to use women only for one thing."

"Mum . . ."

"Sweetheart, it's true. He doesn't have a good track record. There has always been some bimbo selling her story of their night together. You are too good for the likes of him."

"Elaine." My dad's voice is a warning to her. "Enough. Can't you see Jess is happy?" He smiles at me. Yes, it has to be said, I'm a daddy's girl. Always have been, and I suppose always will be. I don't like it when he takes my side against my mum, but this time I'm grateful he doesn't share her opinion.

"Yes, but . . ."

"Look, I've already warned him what will happen if he hurts her in any way. Why don't we just leave the two of them to get to know each other?"

"Look what happened the last time we left her." Mum's eyes fill with tears. This isn't just about Fletch, this is about Scott. I put my tea down, move closer to her, and wrap my arms around her.

"I'm sorry, Mum."

"You don't have to be sorry. It's my job to look after you and protect you."

"You've done your job. I love you, but I do want to spend time with Fletch and I would rather do it with your blessing."

She sniffs and her tears fall. "Of course you can have my blessing, but God help him if he steps out of line."

I tell them about the apartment and that I can move in next week. My news makes mum cry even more, but she tells me I'm not allowed to move into the apartment on a Saturday.

'Saturday flitting, short sitting,' she says. It basically means bad luck and that I won't stay in the apartment for long.

Dad tells me the police might call around to collect the card that came with the flowers. I don't really listen as he tells me the details. I don't want to think about Scott anymore.

Mum isn't too happy when I tell her I'm going to have dinner with Fletch. Dad winks as I leave. I know Mum will be fine; he'll make sure she is.

Chapter THIRTY-ONE

Fletcher

FUCK. I NOW KNOW WHAT Elaine thinks of me. It's no less than I deserve, but I admit it fucking stung hearing that she doesn't think I'm good enough for Jess. Even though deep down I know it; she's right. Jess deserves so much better than a footballer who doesn't treat women with the respect they deserve. It's not all my fault when I have women like Blondie and her friend offering everything on a silver platter. But I don't do myself any favours.

I stand chopping a salad with more force than I should. There's chicken in the oven and rice cooking in the pot. The doorbell rings, startling me.

"Ouch!" I shout as the knife slices down and I cut my finger. I grab a towel and go and answer the door. With the towel wrapped around my hand, I open the door to Jess, who's standing with her back to me. She's changed out of her work clothes into leggings and a T-shirt. Her hair is piled up in a messy style. I run my eyes up and down her, letting them linger for a moment on her arse. She still looks fucking amazing.

"Hey," she says, turning to face me. "Shit. What have you done?"

"I should blame you."

"Why?" she asks, wide-eyed.

"For ringing the doorbell instead of just coming on through. I cut my finger."

"Let me look at it." She unwraps the towel. "It looks worse than it is."

She holds my hand as we walk back through the house into the kitchen. We go straight over to the sink, where she turns on the tap and puts my hand under the running water.

"Bloody hell!" I shout as the water hits it.

"Be quiet," she scolds me. "I'm sure you've had worse on the pitch than this tiny cut."

"Maybe, but this fucking stings." As I say it, I realise I'm being a bit of a pussy, especially when I look at the stitches on her face. "Sorry. I'm being a prat."

"It's fine."

"When do you get those removed?" I ask, watching the concentration on her face.

"Tomorrow, first thing. I can be honest and say I'm not looking forward to it. I'm hoping it looks okay. Now, let's see." She pulls my hand away from the water to have a closer look without all the blood. "See, it's not bad. Do you have any plasters?"

"Yeah." One thing I do have is a fully equipped first aid box. I leave her to go and get it from my kit bag. I grab a plaster and put it on. "See? Good as new," I say, joining her again in the kitchen. "Dinner won't be long."

"Sounds good." She walks toward me, eyes wide. A woman on a mission. I lean back against the counter as she stops in front of me, stands on her tiptoes, and kisses me. Her lips crash desperately against mine. Suddenly all thoughts of having a nice dinner are gone. I was calm and relaxed until she walked toward me, hips swaying, and now . . . Jess holds all the power over me. I'm weak when it comes to her.

I need to slow this down. Placing my hands lightly on her jaw, I try to control this kiss. She smells of coconut, fresh from a shower. God, I wish she had showered here and I could've joined her. Right now, I want nothing more than to remove her leggings and take her here on the kitchen counter.

But I'm trying really fucking hard to be a better man.

I push her face away. Her stare is intense and oh-so-intimate. Why is she making it so damn difficult? It would be so easy to fall into my old habits, but I want more. What? I'm not sure yet but I suppose I'll find out in time.

"I want you," she murmurs. Three words that sound so fucking sexy coming from her sweet, innocent mouth.

"I'm all yours after dinner."

"What. If. I. Say. I. Don't. Want. Dinner?"

I melt. She punctuates every word and kisses my neck in between each.

"Then I will have to force feed you."

"Spoilsport."

"I've been called a lot of things over the years, but never that. Now, make yourself useful. There's wine in the fridge if you want some," I tell her as I take the chicken out of the oven.

"Are you having some?"

"Nope. Need a clear head to deal with you," I tell her with a smirk. She doesn't look amused. "I tend not to drink during the week when I'm training."

"What will you be drinking?"

"Water."

"In that case, it's water for two." She grabs two bottles of water from the fridge and puts them on the table. "Who the hell were you cooking for?" she asks, looking at the chicken.

"What?" I put two chicken breasts on each plate that I've laid out.

"Only one for me. There's no way I can eat all that."

This isn't a lot of food, just some chicken, brown rice and salad, but then it's what I'm used to.

We sit and eat in what I can only describe as a comfortable, relaxing silence. I catch her watching me. I bet she's thinking, 'where the hell does he put it?' But that's easy—I work it all back off. And I'm looking forward to working this off later, with Jess.

I've not mentioned Scott and the flowers because she's so relaxed and I don't want to put a damper on our night. But I also don't want her to think I don't care. When I think of him, how I wished I had fucking dealt with him the other night. Because now I get the impression this fucker is out to make her life a nightmare. Hasn't he done enough to her already?

As soon as she's finished, she takes our empty plates over to the sink and starts running the hot water.

"There's no way either of us are doing those," I say, wrapping my arms around her waist. She leans back against me and I kiss her neck. Her whole body relaxes. The mess I've made in the kitchen from making dinner can wait. Some things are more important, and right now, Jess is far more important than a pile of dishes.

"Stay. I want you in my arms all night, after I've finished with you."

She turns and lifts her arms, wrapping them around my neck at the same time as thrusting her breasts against me. I pick her up and put her legs around my waist. She smiles coyly. It's too late for her to be acting all shy; she's anything but shy, especially in the bedroom department.

I carry her to my room.

I stop right beside my bed and put her down so she's facing me. She is the most beautiful woman I've ever seen. Everything about her is natural. I reach for her top and pull it over her head. She's perfect. She studies me curiously, her eyes never leaving me, anticipating my next move.

Her hair looks great, but it will look better when I remove the hair tie. It's not as easy to take out as I thought it would be.

She shakes her head and lets her hair tumble down her back.

"You have no idea how beautiful you are, do you?"

Her mouth twitches at the corners as she shakes her head. It's up to me to make sure she knows it. I pull my own T-shirt off. As she stands in front of me, I need to be inside her. I watch in approval as her eyes leisurely travel from my face, taking in the scenery in front of her. I'm almost drooling as I watch her checking me out.

Bloody hell! Her smile is full of confidence as her eyes travel back upward and meet mine. Her eyes darken, smoking hot and sizzling. I'm done for.

I can't wait another fucking minute. I have to have her. Now.

I fix my eyes on her and unbutton my jeans. She bites the corner of her lip as she watches. She draws in a long steady breath as she waits. Her eyes are greedy and filled with desire as I slide my jeans and boxers off in unison.

For what I have in mind, she's wearing too much clothing. There's nothing romantic in the way I make quick work of removing the rest of her clothes.

She is the only woman who has ever looked at me the way she does, with so much need and passion. I smile softly.

Jess wraps her arms around me, pulling me closer to her, and we fall to the bed, our lips crashing desperately against the other's. Skin-on-skin contact, there's nothing like this. Or is it because it's Jess? Her tongue sweeps softly along my lips before entering and exploring. In and out. There is something so fucking erotic as she takes the lead. But not for long.

My tongue sweeps along her bottom lip and I growl. My cock pushes against her and she's fucking wet; soaking wet just for me.

This is not going to be sweet. This is going to be hard and fast because it's what we both need. Pulling my lips away from hers, I look into her smouldering eyes. "Jess, I need you."

She raises her hips to meet me and I enter her slowly and still for a moment. She grabs my arse, squeezing it tight, and I rock slightly, allowing her to adjust before entering her with force. She lets out a soft whimper, her muscles contracting around me. She feels like home.

Totally turned on by the unknown feelings sweeping through my body, I thrust against her. Slowly in and out. Over and over, building up pace. Each stroke brings new pleasure and desires for me. Her nails scrape against me and she arches her back, allowing me to go deeper and deeper. The connection I feel between us consumes me.

She pushes against me harder. Her muscles tighten around me—she's close. I thrust harder and deeper. She cries out and grinds against me as she shatters around me, and with one more forceful thrust, I explode.

She pulls my body down on top of hers and I kiss her. Conscious of my weight on her body, I pull us both to our sides and gaze at the beautiful woman in my arms. Reaching out, I smooth her hair away from her face.

I can't get over how fucking lucky I feel, having her in my bed, but more importantly in my life.

She yawns.

She wriggles closer, resting her head on my chest. I hold her in my arms and it's not long before she's sleeping. With an early start in the morning, I should close my eyes and sleep too, but I can't take my eyes off the beautiful woman in my arms. I know I don't deserve her, but for as long as I have her, I'm going to worship her.

Chapter THIRTY-TWO

Jessica

AS I SIT IN FRONT of the mirror, putting my make-up on, I can't believe how quickly this week has gone. It's Saturday already, and I get to watch Fletcher run about a football pitch. Yes, I'm excited, but also nervous. I've never been to a football game before. What if I do or say something stupid? I don't want to embarrass myself or Fletcher.

I've not seen him since I left his house on Tuesday morning. He's been away early every morning and I've been late most nights what with working over at the apartments. We've texted lots and spoken on the phone most days, but it's just not been the same. I've fought the urge to sneak out of my parents' at night and go to him. When I told him about this only this morning, he couldn't stop laughing, but he did ask why I hadn't done it.

My reply was that I didn't want any of the neighbours calling the police and reporting me as an intruder. It was great hearing his voice this morning. He sounded excited and upbeat about his first game for his new club. He wants us to go for dinner after the game, but I told him to wait and see what happens.

Fletch got Dad tickets for the game as well; he's taking one of his golfing buddies. He did ask my mum if she wanted to go but her reply was, 'not in a million years.' She's not happy about me and Fletcher, and I can understand why, although I do wish she would give him more of a chance. She was okay with him until I started spending alone time with him. I know I shouldn't have, but I did dig up some information on him this week. I had to know why Mum was so dead set against him, and part of me wishes I hadn't looked. From his many wild nights out in his early playing days to well documented nights with women who have sold their stories over the years to the national press—there was also an incident on the pitch with another player, which resulted in him being fined several weeks' wages and serving a six game ban. The article I found this information in says the two players, on opposing teams, came to blows over Fletcher's treatment of the sister of the other player. It told me the names and the teams involved, but this is me, it didn't matter, and I have no clue who they are. I'm more interested in the story, but there was nothing else about it. No other mention, which I found strange considering all the other articles about him.

So, I now find myself feeling uneasy at what I know about him.

He's had a string of women over the years. Never, from what I can find out, had a serious girlfriend. And there has been more than one bar room brawl. My guess is that there was always a woman involved in those.

I need to push these thoughts to the back of my mind. The Fletcher I've gotten to know recently is nothing like the articles describe, so I shouldn't allow these to cloud my opinion of the man I'm spending so much time with. Everyone has a past. But I do believe maybe the past is better off staying where it belongs.

Fletch also made the news this week, along with the team. They visited the local children's hospital. It was strange seeing his picture in the paper this morning. I did leave the paper open on my parents' table, hoping my mum would see the picture of

Fletcher with the kids. Her seeing him in a different light may help.

He's not the only one who has been busy. Work has been hectic because I've had a few personal appointments this week. First up was Tuesday morning and my hospital appointment to get my stitches out, which I drove myself to, and then regretted it because my face was a bit sore after. I'm left with a tiny scar which I know will fade over time. If I'm honest, it's barely noticeable, but I know it's there.

I also had my meeting with Doctor Harry Fieldman, who is happy with how I'm doing, considering the flowers Scott sent me at the start of the week. He said I'm strong and very independent. He doesn't breach patient confidentiality, but does tell me it takes a strong person to walk away at the first signs of domestic abuse. I can't understand why someone would stay in an abusive relationship, but I know many do. He also asked me to consider going to speak to a small group of women. This, I'm not sure of. I don't think I'm at that stage yet where I'm ready to talk about it. Everything is still too raw. He says my story would help encourage those who want to take the first step but are still unsure.

We talk about how I'm feeling about the baby. He knew he hit a sensitive nerve, but I told him I'm coping and that some days are harder than others. I told him I feel bad when I'm happy, when I suddenly remember what I've lost. I got emotional at the mention of James and cried. We talked through the many stages of grief and he made me finally realise that I am allowed to be happy, and that all my thoughts and feelings are completely normal.

Although, he is concerned about what's making me happy, or rather who. Fletcher. He's worried I might be latching onto the first person who has shown an interest in me. I've been urged to take it slow. Harry, as he has told me to call him, is worried because of Fletcher's high profile. That concerns me too. I don't want what happened to me to become public knowledge. I don't want to walk down the street and have people stare at me and feel sorry for me. I'm good at doing that on my own.

Before I left our meeting, Harry made me promise to think about doing a talk or something that might help and encourage others.

"Jessica, Lee's here," my mum calls through to me from the living room. I forgot she was still in the house. She's been so quiet. Usually she would be in and out of the room, checking on me. With a quick glance in the mirror, I'm happy with how I look, although for a football game, I'm overdressed, in my opinion. I did ask Fletch what I should wear. His reply was something smart but comfortable that I would feel okay wearing if we go to dinner afterwards. So, here I am wearing another halter-neck maxi dress because it's warm and sunny outside.

I find Lee in the living room with my mum. Dad left a few hours ago, something about hospitality. He's going for a meal before the game; I'm sure he will love that.

"Wow, check you out," Lee says. Mum turns around and smiles. "Fletch, won't be able to concentrate on the game if he sees you."

Mum frowns and walks out of the room, shaking her head.

"Thanks a bunch, Lee."

"What?" She raises her hands and shrugs.

"Mum isn't a fan of Fletch."

"Since when? I thought she liked him."

"Oh, until he and I hooked up. Now, you don't look so bad yourself." She gives me a twirl, showing off her dress. Yes, my best friend looks amazing. She's wearing a navy blue knee-length dress that nips in at her waist, with a white cropped sleeve cardigan. Her make-up is minimal and her hair is braided in a very loose style. One of those hairstyles that look as though someone has done it for you, but I know Lee. She's great at doing all the latest styles. Maybe I should've gotten her to do mine.

A horn beeping outside has my attention.

"That's our taxi," Lee says. I draw in a deep breath and try to prepare myself for the afternoon, but it's not working. I'm just so nervous about being there amongst other players' closest family and friends. "Time to go."

"Bye, Mum," I call out as we get to the front door. She doesn't answer, which doesn't surprise me.

We chat the entire journey to the stadium. Lee is really excited. She's been to a few games, but she says today is different. I still don't understand it. The taxi comes to a stop and I pay the driver. Stepping out, I gasp.

"Bloody hell." I don't know where to look first. I'm standing in front of an amazing entrance. There are people everywhere, heading in all directions.

"Oh, honey, if you think this is impressive, wait until you see the rest. Come on, it's only fifteen minutes to kick off." We go inside and I give my name to security.

"Ah, Mr Adams' guest," he says with a quirky smile. "I'll have someone take you upstairs."

It's not long before we're shown upstairs, outside, and into the stand. WOW! And I thought the entrance looked great. Bloody hell. I stop and look around the stadium; it's huge. I have no idea how many people are here. All these people here to watch a football game. As Lee and I are shown to our seats, I no longer feel overdressed as we pass lots of men in suits.

Lee points out that this is the directors' box, and our seats are just below that. This area feels more spacious than it looks around the stadium.

"Enjoy the game, ladies," our escort says as we take our seats. The view from here is amazing, everything so clear. I had imagined it would be hard to see the pitch, but it's not.

"I'm sure we will," Lee says, her voice full of excitement. A few women in front of us turn and offer us a small smile.

A lady beside me introduces herself. "I'm Fran, the manager's wife."

"Jess, and this is my friend, Lee," I reply.

"Good to meet you both. I'm guessing you're with Fletcher?" At her words, the ladies in the row in front turn around and stare.

"Yes." I hear a few mumbles from the women in front.

"Thought so. Only because all the other wives and girlfriends seem to know each other. You and I can be the newbies together." She lowers her voice before adding, "I was dreading today."

"Why?"

"Because you never know how the wives and girlfriends are going to be. If they're going to accept you into their group or leave you on the sidelines for the entire season. The good thing for me is I always have our sons at all games with me."

"Where are they today?"

"They're in the dressing room. They couldn't wait to meet our new star player. A bit like everyone else connected with the club. So, you and Fletcher?" I can hear the question in her voice, but I don't know what to say.

"He's a friend." She smiles, raising her eyebrows as if not satisfied with my answer. Just when I think she's going to say something else, the stadium erupts with noise and Lee nudges me to stand as the players take to the field.

"Well, your friend is in the starting eleven today, how exciting," Fran says as I look out. There he is, standing beside Jackson, I think, although I haven't been introduced to him yet, but I do know he's the captain of the team. Fletcher has spoken about him once or twice and I can admit to doing a search for him on the internet.

Fletcher's eyes meet mine and I'm lost, so fucking lost in the current wave of electricity that is flowing between us. A slow smile plays on his lips that I can't help but return. He looks hot. So fucking hot in his football shorts and shirt. Now I have the image of what's underneath his football kit running through my mind, and that's an image that turns me on. He turns and makes his way to the halfway line; it's then I notice his shirt number. Number nine, one of my favourite numbers, and also part of my date of birth.

"Friends?" Fran says. "There's no way you two are just friends. That was so intense. I'm sure everyone here felt the heat and desire between you." Lee agrees with her and both of them smile. Lee turns her attention back to the game.

"Can I let you in on a secret?" Fran nods. "This is my very first football game and I was anxious about coming here today."

"Hmmp." Fran and I look at the row in front. One of the ladies is not impressed with my comment as she shakes her head and turns back toward the pitch.

"Jess, don't worry about it. We all had to start somewhere. And as I've said, I'm at all the home games so you always have me here. And as for her." I know she means the woman in the front row. "Ignore the likes of her. She's the type that wants a player and will do anything to get into bed with any of them."

"Thanks." I turn my attention back to the pitch as the whistle blows and the game starts. Totally mesmerised by the scene in front of me, I can't take my eyes off Fletch. Well, I do when he doesn't have the ball at his feet. As I watch the game, I wonder why I've never shown any interest in this before. I may not know much about football, but Logan, the keeper, looks to be having a great game. He's saved each shot that has been fired toward him.

"This is great! They're all over the opposition," Lee says excitedly beside me. She's almost bouncing on the seat.

I smirk and turn back to watch the game. The ball is passed

from player to player, the opposition not getting in between. I hear Fletcher's voice, it's so clear above everything else, and my eyes turn toward him. He's making a run. The ball is passed to him; he looks at the goal and takes a shot.

Scores.

The crowd rise to their feet, and Lee pulls me up with her, and screams and claps her hands. Fletcher runs to the half way line, stops, looks at me, and I can't help but smile as he blows me a kiss. The manager approaches him and gives him a great big hug and kiss on the side of his face; not what I expected.

"Friends," says Fran with a wink. "After that performance, no-one will ever believe you're just friends." Fran wraps her arm around me and smiles. As her husband looks into the stand, she waves. "He's off to a great start."

"He sure is," Lee says. "Celebrations all around." Lee and Fran give me a knowing look; what for, I have no idea.

The game restarts and Lee and Fran sit beside me, each of them fidgeting in their seats. Lee can't seem to keep her hands still and Fran, well, she can't sit bloody still. I wonder if my dad is enjoying the game. Who am I kidding? He will be loving this. I turn my attention away from the pitch and look around the stadium; it's packed, I have no idea how many fans are in here. The atmosphere is electric. I don't think I've ever experienced anything like this. Not even at some of the bigger live gigs I've been to.

Lee tells me it's almost half time; only a few minutes to go. Jackson has the ball and he's just over the halfway line when he lifts his head and passes the ball to Fletch. The crowd all stand, including me. I watch wide-eyed as he takes the ball around the keeper and scores his second goal. Fran and Lee both hug me and jump up and down.

"Someone's waiting," Lee says as they both let go of me. I look down to the pitch and Fletcher is again smiling, blowing me a kiss and, of course, lapping up the attention of the crowd and his teammates.

The halftime whistle blows and the team are two-nil up. Fran takes Lee and me inside for a drink. I hear some of the wives and girlfriends talking as we enter, but I don't hear what is said, although I have an idea. Fran tells me to ignore them. She tells Lee and me that we have made it easier for her today, having people she could stand with and talk to. She seems like such a lovely person.

The second half starts just the way the first half ended, with a goal, but not from Fletcher. No, this one comes from Jackson. But as Fran says, the only thing that matters is the team is winning. The three of us talk in between watching the game, and I have to admit, I'm a little disappointed that it's almost over.

Fletcher has the ball at his feet, lifts his head, shoots, and scores his third goal of the game, or as Fran and Lee tell me, a hat-trick. Again, he heads toward the halfway line to celebrate. I can feel his excitement and happiness as he beams with pride. I'm so pleased for him; a perfect game for not just him, but the whole team.

Chapter THIRTY-THREE

Fletcher

I'M DESPERATE TO SEE JESS. Between the atmosphere in the dressing room and then the manager wanting me to talk to the press with him about how today went, I can't believe it's taken so long to get upstairs. I'm thrilled for him. What better start is there for the new manager than a win? A four-nil win. And for me, what better start to my career at my new club? It means the fans are already on my side. I don't have to try and win them over. No, there's nothing better.

The boss and I are the last of the team and management to enter the room, and we do so to loud applause and cheering. Everyone stops us to talk and offer us congratulations, and we talk with each one, but my eyes are fixed on Jess, who is standing with the boss' wife, Fran, and Lee, at the other end of the room. I notice Fran and Peter's boys talking with some of the other players. They seemed like great kids when I met them earlier in the dressing room. Jess smiles, watching me, and I just want to go to her, scoop her into my arms, and kiss her.

We're talking to the chairman when I make my excuse. "Do you mind?" I ask the boss.

"On you go," Peter says, looking to where my eyes are focused. "Tell Fran I'll be there in a minute."

I walk towards her. Lee is talking, but I can clearly see Jess isn't listening to a word. No, her eyes are still on me and I can't help the fucking grin on my face. Jess Taylor holds me captive with the look on her face. That one look has me wishing we were anywhere but in this crowded room.

A few more people try to stop me from reaching my destination. I swear it's being done on purpose; I try not to be rude, when all I want to say is 'fuck off and let me get to my girl.' I catch her smirking as I try to leave an older gentleman who wants to talk to me.

Bloody hell!

"Finally." I sigh as I wrap my arm around her and kiss the top of her head. She smiles.

"Fletcher," Fran says.

"Boss will be over in a minute," I tell her.

"I have to say, I'm a tad disappointed in you, Fletcher," Fran says with a straight face.

Shit! What the hell have I done?

"What?"

She looks between Lee and Jess before addressing me. "All that sexual tension between you two before the game started, and blowing kisses after each goal. And all you can do now is kiss the top of her head. I, no, *we* expected more than that."

I stare at Fran and look at my girl. She shrugs her shoulders as though saying, 'nothing to do with me.'

I wanted to take her in my arms as I watched her from the other side of the room, and I still want to do that.

"Well, I would hate to be the one to leave you all disappointed," I say, stepping in front of Jess. "But I'm afraid the only opinion that matters to me is yours." I reach out and wrap both arms around her frame, pulling her tight to me, and press my lips to hers. She doesn't react straight away, probably because of where we are, but I don't let up until she does.

After a few moments, she returns my kiss. Our kiss is packed full of emotion, of days spent apart because of our schedules. Every nerve in my body is buzzing with desire for her. She lifts her hands and cups my face, holding me as tight as I'm holding her.

Loud clapping and cheering has us tearing our lips from the other. Jess is embarrassed when she realises every set of eyes in the room is on us. I step in front of her, shielding her from the crowd, and hold her tight in my arms.

"Well," Fran says. "That's how you should greet Jess every time you see her."

"Does that mean I have to do that as well?" Peter asks, approaching us. He kisses Fran briefly on the lips before turning to face Jess. "Miss Taylor." He holds out his hand in greeting. Jess lifts her hand to shake his, but instead Peter lifts it to his mouth and kisses her. My poor girl is going to hate being the centre of attention. "You are now our lucky mascot. Fletcher will need you at all the games after today."

"Me? I'm not sure I can be classified as a lucky mascot. I don't know the first thing about football," she says bashfully. Yip, my girl is still embarrassed by the attention.

"It doesn't matter what you do or don't know. What *I* know is that's the best game I've ever seen Fletcher play. And I've been watching him for a number of years." Peter smiles at Fran as she hands him a drink. We continue talking as Logan joins our group, standing beside Lee. I'm not sure how Jess is dealing with today. She seems fine, but I have a feeling this might all be a bit much for her. Especially as I can feel every unattached woman's eyes in the room on us. Fran and Jess seem to have hit it off; I say as much to Peter. He says it's probably because today they have been thrust into the same situation. Newcomers in amongst all the wives and partners.

Shit! I never gave that a thought. Some of these wags can be complete bitches, so I'm glad she had Lee and Fran.

"Fletcher, Fletcher." I turn to see Peter and Fran's boys, Connor and Nathan, racing toward us. "What are you going to do with the match ball?" they ask.

Jess looks a little puzzled.

"If a player scores a hat-trick, he gets to keep the match ball," I tell her. "I don't know yet, boys. Maybe put it up for auction for charity."

"That's a great idea," Fran says enthusiastically. "Which charity?"

"Scottish Women's Aid." The words are out of my mouth before I've thought about it. Jess tenses beside me. Shit! I knew there was something I wanted to discuss with her. She doesn't look at me, but I can see Lee's raised eyebrows. The boys take off again, this time in the direction of Jackson.

"Oh," Fran says. "Not a charity I would have thought of. But a very good one."

"Yes, it is," Peter agrees. "Now, what's everyone's plans for the rest of the evening?"

"We were going out for dinner, but it's up to Jess," I say, thinking about how my bombshell might be affecting her.

Lee offers me a slight smile, obviously thinking along the same lines. She cuts in, "I'm heading home after here. I've got an early start tomorrow over at the development." I can see the disappointment in Logan's face, although he does try to hide it.

"We need to get the boys home," Fran says. "Although I have no idea how you, dear husband, are going to get them to leave. Look at them! They are loving this today."

"I'll think of something." Peter smiles lovingly at his wife.

Peter is still a young manager, at only forty-one, and if the truth be told, he doesn't look his age. Now, as for Fran, she is a stunning woman a few years younger than Peter. It's obvious how much they love each other. I've met them a few times over the last few years at various events and charity functions.

"So, dinner?" I ask Jess, who has now relaxed beside me.

"How about a takeaway instead?"

"And some wine?" Fran adds with a knowing look. "Oh, to be young again."

"Less of that," Peter says.

We all say our goodbyes. Fran and Jess swap mobile numbers before we leave. I offer to drop Lee home, but Logan insists on doing it.

The car park is quieter now, with very few people around as we walk toward my car, although a few kids are hanging around and ask for my autograph. Jess stands quietly to the side as I chat with the boys.

I leave the boys and we continue to my car in silence. A silence I hate. I've hurt her, something I never wanted to do. Why do I have the feeling when I stop the car in the driveway she's going to take off into her parents'? Because I'm a fucking idiot. I should've remembered to tell her about the charity.

She waits at the passenger door with her back to me, waiting on me opening the door. I suppose I should be grateful she didn't rush out and get a taxi home.

"Jess." My voice is soft as I call her name. I watch as her posture straightens. "I meant to tell you."

"I wish you had." She turns to face me. "I'm not pissed off about it. About the charity. I happen to think it's a charity people often forget about. They help women and children who find themselves in extreme circumstances and have run out of options to consider." I can hear the sadness in her voice as she speaks.

"Jess, I'm sorry."

"Don't be sorry, especially about helping others. I just don't want my situation to become public knowledge and I'm hoping my reaction hasn't aroused suspicion."

"Oh, God. I don't want you to be uncomfortable." I lean

forward and press my lips to her forehead. "Mine or your parents'?" I ask her, hoping it's not the latter.

Lifting her head, she looks me in the eye. "Yours."

Thank fuck.

Chapter THIRTY-FOUR

Jess

MY HEART SANK AT THE stadium, and I'm sure Lee saw the look of surprise on my face, even though I tried to hide it. I just hope no one else picked up on my expression; I don't want anyone to feel sorry for me, or to think about what they say to me before they speak. I never expected him to utter the words 'Scottish Women's Aid.' Would he have picked this charity on his own? Had it not been for my circumstances, I'm sure I know the answer to that question.

As we drive back, my mind wanders. I think of myself as one of the lucky ones. Some women aren't so lucky. Yes, I lost my baby, but some lose a lot more. Especially if the abuse has been going on for a period of time. One time was more than enough for me.

My therapist's words play over and over in my head. Maybe I should give it some thought, go and speak to some women. If Fletcher can help raise awareness for this charity that hopefully leads to extra funds being available to them, more women might get the help and support they need. Maybe I can help too.

"We're here." I turn to him. His eyes are on me, creases at the corners of his eyes as he frowns at me.

"So we are," I say softly, teasing, trying to divert the atmosphere surrounding us. I lean across and kiss him, taking him by surprise. "Surely we're not going to sit out here?"

"No. Come on. Let's go because I'm sure I can sense your mum's anger and hostility toward me."

I shake my head and open the car door. Mum is standing at the window, watching us. I wish she would give him a chance. A proper chance. Yes, she grudgingly gave me her blessing, but it would be nice if she could try with him, if only for me.

His phone buzzes, indicating a text message, and he smiles as he looks at me.

"What?" I ask.

"That was your dad, thanking me for today." We walk toward the house.

"He would've loved today."

"What about you?" He stands at the door, waiting on my answer.

"Me? Different to what I expected, but yeah, I have to admit, I enjoyed what I saw."

He laughs, entering the house. He dumps his bag in the hallway and we make our way into the living room. I pause and look around. It's different. Spacious.

"What's wrong?" he asks.

"You've been busy," I say, noticing the room is clear of all the boxes that were here the last time I was.

"Yeah, well I had to do something this week to keep me occupied." He steps in front of me and takes off his suit jacket, throwing it down on the couch. "To keep my mind off a certain someone."

"Does this certain someone have a name?" I tease.

"A name? She has so much more than a name. She has this really sexy smile, beautiful long hair, and a sexy body that most women would die for." He leans forward and I can't wait. I take his face in my hands and kiss him deeply. He responds with fire and passion. Tongues dance and tease, and I lose myself to him easily.

He pulls away, as breathless as I am. "I've bloody missed you this past week," he says. "What are your plans for tomorrow?"

"Nothing yet."

"In that case, you're spending tonight and tomorrow with me. We can go out tomorrow. But for now, I'm starving, so what do you want to eat?"

"Chinese."

"Glad you said that. Me too." He kisses me before asking what I want to eat and then phones in our order to be delivered. I go into the kitchen and open the fridge, hoping he has something to drink. Bottled water, beers, and a couple of bottles of wine. Opening a bottle of water, I take a long drink.

"Someone's thirsty."

"I am," I answer with a smile. "Hope you don't mind."

"Why would I mind? I'm glad you're comfortable and relaxed here. Do you not want to open the wine?"

"Maybe after dinner. What are our plans for the night?"

"Well. . . ." His eyes roam my body and I can see the glint in his eyes.

"We've got all night for that. Why don't you tell me about the charity?"

"If I have to talk about the charity then you have to talk to me."

I sigh heavily, knowing he wants to know how I got on with the therapist. He's asked more than once, but I've been reluctant to tell him. I've skirted around the whole conversation. A part of me is scared to tell him how I was in those early weeks after Scott. I'm frightened of what he'll think of me.

"Okay, you win. I'll talk, but after dinner."

"Deal. Make yourself comfy. I'm going to change."

"I can help you with that." I stalk toward him.

"Christ, don't distract me. We start this now and we won't be doing anything else for the rest of the night."

"That works for me."

"It would work for me too, but I've already said I'm hungry." He turns and walks away. It would be so easy to follow him to the bedroom, but I don't. Instead, I grab another bottle of water and return to the living room. Taking my shoes off, I get comfy on the couch and flick through the TV channels.

My phone beeps. A text message.

Lee: Hope you are ok after Fletcher's revelation.

Me: Yeah I'm good. I just hope no one else picked up on my shock.

Lee: Only Logan.

Me: Oh.

Lee: JESS, it's fine. Don't worry about it. Enjoy your night with that handsome man because I'm going to enjoy mine. X

I smile at her message. I can only presume Logan is with her. There's a surprise. I don't reply to her because what is there to say?

Why is it there's never anything decent on TV on a Saturday night? It's always a load of crap. Surely there must be a half decent movie to watch. I continue flicking through the channels until Fletch comes back into the room. Gone is the suit he was wearing, replaced by jogging bottoms that hang low on his hips. He has a T-shirt in his hand. I run my eyes over him and smile.

"See something you like?"

"Me? No, I'm just hoping you're going to put that on to eat dinner."

"Of course."

The doorbell rings and he grabs some money before going to answer it. I can hear him talking to the delivery driver. They're talking about today's game. I go into the kitchen and grab some plates and cutlery, and take them into the living room.

Fletch comes in carrying the food, looking pleased with himself, and I'm sure that's to do with the conversation at the front door.

He puts the food down on the coffee table and puts the T-shirt on. Not much is said between us as we plate up the food and start eating. He sits back. Everything about him looks relaxed and comfortable. There is a smug grin on his face. I, on the other hand, don't feel it. I'm slightly nervous as to how our conversation will go after we've eaten. I'm going to need some wine.

"Jess, have you finished?" Fletch asks as he starts to clear away the containers.

"Yeah, sorry. I guess I wasn't as hungry as you." I move to help him, but he takes my plate from me.

"Stay where you are and try to relax. If you don't want to talk, we can leave it 'til another time. I'm sure we can come up with something else to occupy our time together," he says with a smile and a low glow in his eyes.

"Do you mind if I go and change out of this dress?"

"Go on. Grab one of my shirts."

I quickly change into a white shirt and make my way back to him. Stopping, I watch him from the doorway. He's sitting on the couch. A bottle of wine with a glass and two bottles of beer are on the coffee table. He must sense me because he turns. His eyes leisurely travel down my body and stop at the hem of his shirt, which is midway down my thighs. A slow smile plays on his lips as he pats the couch beside him.

He picks up the wine and pours it into the glass. "Thought you might need this."

I take the glass and slowly take a sip. Fletch wraps his arm around me and pulls me close to him. The hem of the shirt rides further up my thighs, and he laughs as I try to pull it down.

"Jess, are you okay?"

"Yeah. Let's get this over with because I'm bloody nervous."

"You shouldn't be nervous with me, ever."

I take a deep breath. "As you know, I saw my therapist this week. I'll be going to see him weekly until he thinks I'm in a better frame of mind." I turn slightly so I can face him because I need to see his reaction to what I'm about to tell him. "I suppose I should start at the beginning."

"Best place to start."

"I won't go into all the details about the night Scott attacked me, because it will only result in me shedding more tears, and I've sworn to myself he gets no more of my time. You already know my injuries were so severe that I lost my son."

"I never realised," he says with sadness. "A son . . ."

"Yes. With being so far along in my pregnancy they had to do a C-section because I was unconscious when I arrived at the hospital. You've seen my scar. When I came around, I got to hold him. He was so tiny." I pause and close my eyes for a second. "He looked perfect. After speaking with the nurse who was looking after me, I named him James, after my dad. The week in hospital was horrible. I was really struggling to come to terms with what had happened."

"Jess, I can understand, but I have a question. Was this the first time he lifted his hand to you?"

"Yes, it was the first. Scott changed over the last year from the man I first met. When we met he had a great job as a bank manager, but last year he was laid off due to cutbacks and he started drinking heavily. That's when I first noticed he'd changed, but he got another job; night shift in a factory. Not what he had been used to. He stopped drinking and we carried on with our lives, but something was off between us. Then I found out I was pregnant, and my work picked up. We had more clients and I was working longer hours, which resulted in us arguing about trivial things when we were around each other.

"After I came home from hospital, the midwife paid me several visits to check on me. She had her job to do, to see how I was coping. The thing was, I wasn't coping. Only Lee knows how bad things got for me."

"What are you saying?"

"I'm saying I was so depressed I couldn't pull myself out of the darkness that was consuming me. Lee stayed with me after I told her I didn't want to carry on."

"Jess, no . . ." His arm tightens around me and he pulls me closer and kisses my head. "Please tell me that's not how you feel."

"You should know it's not," I say, meeting his gaze. "Lee made me promise to speak with someone, which I have done, and I will continue to do so. Scott took away so much from me that night. The therapist thinks I've come a long way in such a short space of time. But I still have my moments when it all gets too much for me. This last week I've been happier than I have been in such a long time, even before that night with Scott, and I've felt guilty for it. For trying to move my life forward instead of looking back."

I watch him as he takes in my words.

"Jess, I'm truly sorry for what you've been through. And I'm sorry you feel bad for being happy, but if it's me that's made you happy, I won't apologise for that. When you smile, it makes everyone around you smile. I love your smile. I can understand having dark days, but I want you to know you can always talk to me. I don't want you thinking you can't talk to me about this."

"Thank you."

"How did you feel last week when he showed up at your house?"

"Scared. Anxious. Lee told me to stay in my room and she

would deal with him, but when I heard him shouting at her, I couldn't stay there and do nothing. When I got out into the hall, he had his hands around her throat, shouting at her. Well, you know the rest."

"Jess, you're strong. So much stronger than you give yourself credit for. You need to give yourself time to heal. You'll never forget about James but it will get easier."

His kind words could be my undoing as one lonely tear rolls down my face. "Can I ask a question?"

"Of course."

"Does Logan know?"

"Yes, he does, because he's my friend and I trust him with my life. I told him just after you came home from hospital because I needed someone to talk to after all my conversations with your dad."

"I understand. Now, the charity?"

"Jess, I'm sorry about today. It completely slipped my mind."

"It's fine. Honestly. Don't worry about it."

"I could have picked any charity, I know. But you are the reason behind it. I spent some time this week going through information about the Scottish Women's Aid, finding out everything they do for women who have suffered domestic abuse. Jess, what you've been through is terrible, but what some women go through for years just doesn't bear thinking about."

He's right. I will always say I'm lucky because I didn't go back to Scott. Some women go back time and time again.

"This isn't a charity that I can go and get some PR pictures with the victims to make me look good. This is a charity that needs all the help and funding they can get, to highlight the problems that are going on. I promise you there is no hidden agenda for me other than raising funds and awareness."

Chapter THIRTY-FIVE

Fletcher

AS I FINISH SAYING THE words, I realise, for the first time in my life, I mean it. There is no hidden agenda. I really and truly want to help. And some of the stories I read were harrowing. No two situations are the same. I know Jess told me she left Scott the first time, but what I don't understand is how some women can put themselves through the same ordeal time and time again. And they just learn to live with it and accept it as part of every day life.

Jess has said she counts herself as being lucky, but I don't see it. For fuck's sake, he killed their baby. How does he live with himself knowing what he's done? Does Jess see herself as lucky because she's alive? After reading some stories, I know of some cases where the women haven't survived. Yes, these are extreme cases, but no woman should have to suffer abuse at the hands of a man, ever. Why does a man feel the need to have his partner suffer at his hands? Is it a power trip, or is he just fucked up?

I hate what Scott has done to her, but at the same time, if it weren't for her situation, our paths would never have crossed, and I wouldn't have the chance to get to know the amazing, strong woman she is. Because she can deny it all she likes, she is an amazing person.

There's always a price to pay in life. I just wish Jess wasn't paying for what that bastard has done.

"I believe you. My therapist also wants me to do a talk to a small group of women, but I'm not sure I'm ready for that yet," she says quietly. That might help her, but if she thinks she's not ready, I won't force the issue.

"Well, until you are ready, I will do enough raising awareness for both of us."

She has a sad smile on her face. I lean forward and kiss her because I long to see her proper smile.

"I should also tell you," she says, pulling back from me. Her body is tense now. "The therapist seems concerned about me and you."

Shit. I never expected that.

"Why? Because . . ." I have no idea what to say to her.

"He's worried about my fragile state of mind. And given your profile . . ."

"Jess, all I wanted coming home to Glasgow, because this is my home, was a quiet life. I'm hoping that in a few weeks things will settle down for me. The media has been speculating for weeks which club I was going to sign with. I've never had much of a private life as far as the media is concerned, but that's what I want."

"Fletch, you don't need to say anything else. I just wanted to be truthful with you."

I nod in understanding, frightened to say anything in case I say the wrong thing. This between us, I'm not even sure what it is, but I do know I've probably fucked up big time today with regards to keeping a low profile.

I should've thought about Jess before I decided to celebrate each goal with her on the pitch today. I'm sure the media will have a field day trying to find out who she is and what she means to me. I should share my fears with her, but I can't. Not tonight.

We both take a drink and she settles back into my side. We

decide to watch a movie, but my thoughts are running wild in my head at everything she's been through. I can't get it out of my head that she felt so bad that she didn't want to carry on. She has great parents. Even if her mum isn't happy with me, they both support her. She has Lee, and I know she has other friends. Then there's her business, which, from what Jim tells me, is very successful.

The movie we're watching is meant to be a comedy, but neither of us seem to be in the mood for it. At a guess, our conversation is playing over and over in both our minds. She's resting against me, her fingers running lightly up and down my arm. I smile because I don't think she realises she's doing it. I brush her hair behind her ear, tucking it out of the way, and gently stroke the side of her face. Her body still feels tense.

It's crazy. I want to take her and kiss her until she forgets all the pain and hurt. If I could take it all away from her, I would. I now realise I'm in way over my head with Jess. These feelings I have for her run deep. Deeper than I thought possible. I'm unsure what they mean, but I know I won't be taking the chance in telling her because I don't want to scare her away.

She sits up facing me. "I'm not really in the mood for this movie," she says, then takes a sip from her wine glass.

"What are you in the mood for?"

"You."

Not what I was expecting after our conversation. I hesitate before pulling her until she sits straddling me, my shirt now around her waist. Fuck! How the hell did I not know before now she has no underwear on? Instantly, I'm hard. The only thing between us is my jogging bottoms. She blushes and tries not to look at me.

Jess Taylor is a fucking tease; all in a good way, of course.

I lower my lips and gently kiss the corner of her mouth. A low moan escapes her, making her sound and look so damn cute. I pull back to look at her and her smile is as seductive as her lips. She wraps her arms around my neck and pulls me back until our lips are touching, but I don't let her control the kiss. I slide my tongue between her lips, tasting and searching. My hands roam down her back until I reach her arse. I groan as I pull her closer to me. Tension is building between us and everything else that has happened or been said between us fades into the distance.

I can't help myself, I allow my fingers to wander. One hand is firmly on her arse, holding her tight against me. She tries to squeeze her legs together but my other hand is in the way. My fingers slide with ease through her soft folds. God, she's wet. Soaking wet and only for me. It would be so easy for me to slip my bottoms down and push deep inside her. I slide my fingers back and forth over and over as our lips stay joined and our kiss intensifies.

I want her. And badly.

I remove my fingers and she moans in my mouth. Her hands tighten around me but I pull out of her hold. Slowly I pull my shirt over her head, leaving her straddling me, completely naked. Reaching down, I shower her neck with adoring kisses, because that's one thing I know for sure; I totally adore her.

In a rush, she pushes my bottoms out of the way, freeing me. My erection nudges against her. She lines herself up and slowly lowers. My eyes close momentarily as I take stock of the feeling of her tightly around me. The muscles of her walls contract around me, pulling me in deeper. I groan as she stills. She pushes her mouth back onto mine. I moan loudly as I give in and let her have control.

Jess is the one in control tonight, and right now, I'm happy to let her.

She moves slowly up and down, over and over. Her lips

are still on mine, demanding more from our kiss. We're both hungry for the other, devouring each other. My tongue grazes against hers and she moans. Her arms are still around my neck, holding me in place. Moving my arms, I grip her hips. Her need is burning through our joined bodies. Scorching heat sizzles between us and there is only one way the flames are going to go down.

At this moment in time, Jess needs this more than me. She's using me to forget about her pain and suffering, and I'm more than happy to be used, just so long as she doesn't regret it.

Our lips part at the same time and our eyes lock.

She's panting and close.

She's stretched to the full as I'm buried deep inside her. I hold her steady, not allowing her to control our movements.

"Eyes on me. Can you feel that?"

She nods, feeling me pulsing deep inside her. Her eyes roll and she bites the corner of her lip and lets out a low moan. I thrust against her wildly, holding her, not breaking eye contact, watching her as pleasure consumes and takes over. We come together, each crying out the other's name.

I wrap my arms tightly around her back and her head rests against my shoulder. Moving her hair, I kiss her neck softly, not wanting to break our moment together, or the connection.

She stays resting against me, her breathing evening out. Finally, she lifts her head and I can see an array of emotions. Lust and desire, but I also see worry. The last emotion is not one I want to see on her beautiful face.

"What's wrong?" I ask her.

"Nothing."

"Jess?"

"I'm just emotional. All our talking and sex has taken a lot out of me."

"Well, in that case, how about we go for a bath and go to bed, and I can hold you in my arms all night long."

"I love the sound of that."

God, me too. Me too.

Chapter THIRTY-SIX

Jess

I STRETCH, OPENING MY EYES, not expecting to feel so rested. But I do. Fletcher's arms are still wrapped around me snuggly, my head on his solid chest. There's no better way to start the day. It's so quiet and peaceful. This is what I've missed most this week; having him beside me. That's what happens after being spoiled last weekend and sharing his bed.

I remove myself carefully from his arms so I can go and pee, and brush my teeth. As I leave the bathroom, he's sitting up in bed. His warm eyes roam over every inch of my exposed body and I can almost feel the heat radiating from them.

I know he mentioned going out today but I'm more than happy to stay here and share a physical connection with my man. *My man*. I like the sound of that.

He folds his arms behind his head, and leans back, eyes wide as he watches me walk back toward the bed. The covers are barely covering his naked body. I have an inkling as to how our day is about to start, because the evidence of his arousal is standing hard against his body.

"Good morning," I say, climbing back into the bed beside him.

"And what an amazing sight to wake up to. Good morning. Now, how about I show you just how good a morning it is?" He moves quickly, pinning me in place with his body, and kisses my neck.

I don't answer; I don't need to. He always seems to know what I want and how I want it. In this moment, all I want is Fletcher Adams.

Gliding my hands over his firm chest and abs, I scrape my nails lightly against his skin as they travel. His kisses nip lightly on my neck and I moan. My hands travel lower, tracing and teasing the deep V just above where his body meets mine. I want to move them lower but he stops me and pins my arms to the bed. I'm trapped beneath him and completely at his mercy. He lowers his face to mine and his lips crash against me. His tongue invades my mouth, tasting and teasing, and I know I'm lost to him. My hips rock against him and I feel his erection harden further against me. I moan loudly at the large and much welcomed intrusion in my body. Fire soars through me, starting from my core.

His lips leave mine and my head falls back, into the soft pillow beneath me. My eyes close as Fletcher starts to move. He rocks gently against me; not hard and fast as I had expected with the force of his kiss. No, this is something totally different.

I open my eyes, bringing them back to his. I gasp, seeing the emotion in not only his mesmerising blue eyes, but also his face. He's watching me with intent.

His eyes are glazed. Neither of us are in a hurry to change the pace or direction. His grip on my arms loosens, but I don't move them. His gaze moves and my eyes follow, locking to where our bodies are joined. We move together slowly as one, no rush.

He brings his hands toward my face, and his fingers dance delicately on my skin. Soft and sincere. Slowly, he moves his hands lower, and cups my heavy and ever-so-sensitive breasts. He takes my nipples between his fingers, pinching them. My eyes are heavy but I want to watch him, watch us, so I fight against closing them.

He's still caressing my breasts, but my eyes travel beyond, to where we're joined. The speed has picked up slightly. Instead of rocking gently, he's now moving in and out of me. My mouth goes dry, watching as his hard erection peeks out with the movement. The red, wet swollen flesh has caught my attention and I can't look away.

My body trembles as I watch the connection between us.

Sensations are building within me and I'm not ready for this to be over yet. Needing to slow the pace down, I draw light circles on his back with my fingers. His eyes still don't leave mine, but his hands release the teasing hold of my breasts. Instantly, I feel relief from the building pressure.

He sits back on his heels and continues with the slow in and out movement. His eyes leave mine, travelling down my body, and stop. He lifts his hand and softly runs his finger along the scar. He's always so delicate when he touches me there. My reminder. I remember only last week I had tears in my eyes when he first saw it, but with his actions, he made me feel better with myself.

A tear runs down my face.

Moving his hands to my hips, he grips me lightly and our pace changes again. This time I know the end will be in sight. The in out rocking is now hard thrusting as he slams into me. I no longer have the ability to move; the pleasure is way too intense.

He pulls my hips closer with each movement. The pressure is building to heights I've never reached before. The feelings sweeping through my body are alien to me. Part of me is scared, but the other part of me is excited about all the possibilities that lie ahead. New experiences to look forward to.

I know I shouldn't allow my thoughts to drift in the direction they're going, but I can't help it. Fletcher brings out all these emotions in me.

Fletcher is exciting, and alive, and fills me with so much confidence in myself and my own abilities again.

His eyes are wide as he holds my gaze. The pleasure is becoming too much, and he knows it. He feels it.

My breathing quickens as his thrusts continue. I never knew my body could climb so high. My body tightens and the explosion starts to spread through me. Unable to think, unable to breathe, I close my eyes and cry out his name.

His own groans come thick and fast, and with one final, powerful thrust, I feel the warmth of him inside me.

We lie, heavily panting from our morning activities. This is the best start to my day. Nothing can beat this. Nothing will ever beat this.

Finally, I open my eyes. "Well, Miss Taylor, this I could get used to. You in the morning for breakfast." I blush at his words. I feel the heat rising in my cheeks.

He hovers above me, his smile full of contentment. "Now, I think we should have a shower before I make you something to eat," he says, leaning down and pressing a chaste soft kiss on my lips. "I have plans today."

"What plans?" I ask with interest.

"I want to go to Edinburgh Zoo. The last time I was there I went with my gran. Do you fancy it?"

"Why not?" It does sound like a fun day out.

"Well, in that case, up and showered."

Our shower took a little longer than expected, because as soon as he stepped into the shower with me, I wanted him all over again. I seem to have a very healthy sexual appetite when it comes to Fletcher Adams. I exit the bathroom a good twenty minutes after he left me alone, and find fresh clothes laid out on the bed. A pair of my cropped jeans, a T-shirt, and my Converse. Do I even want to know how he got them? No, I don't, but I smirk at the thought of the look on my mother's face when he appeared at the door, fresh from a shower. I dress quickly and give my hair a blast with the hairdryer that he's left out for me, and then pin it up loosely.

Fletcher is in the kitchen, cooking, and there's a pot of tea on the table.

"What are we having?" I ask him.

"Just some toast and bacon. Is that okay?"

"Of course. I would eat anything. I seem to have worked up an appetite."

"Yes, I've noticed," he says with a smirk before turning back to his cooking. I can't help but smile at his comment. He finishes making breakfast and we sit down and eat. When he's finished, I ask how he got my clothes.

"Well, your dear mum looked at me in disgust when I went over. I'm not sure I'll ever win her round."

"You will. I'm sure of it."

"When I asked for some clothes, she did go and get them, but left me standing on the doorstep. Your dad came out and spoke to me and I told him we're going to the zoo. When your mum came back, scowl on her face, clothes in hand, Jim was just telling me that he hopes we enjoy our day at the zoo. Your mum tried to hide it, but I saw the slight smirk on her face. I can tell she approves of our outing. So, maybe there is hope for me after all."

"There's definitely hope for you, Fletcher Adams."

"Right, we should get out of here if you're finished eating, because if we don't go now, I'm only going to get side-tracked with your sexy mouth. As much as that appeals to me, I want to take you out and have a fun day without caring about anything else. Let's face it, you're moving into your new apartment tomorrow night."

"I know. Can you still give me a hand?"

"Of course I can. I could have all your stuff there by the time you finish work, then all you have to do is unpack."

"I'm more than capable of helping."

"Whatever you say."

Our day has been amazing. We've laughed all day long. Fletcher kept my hand in his, caressing it most of the time. Today has been exactly the sort of fun day I needed. I feel as though we've walked for miles. I'm so glad I had my Converse; I'd forgotten how steep it is at the zoo.

We visited all the major attractions, including the pandas, penguin rock, Budongo trail, home to the chimpanzees. Those three were the highlights for me, but if I'm truthful, the whole day has been special. I'm not ready for our day to end, but I know it has to.

We talked a lot. I've learned more about the man in my life—because he does have a place in my life. His love of football was evident when we talked, as was his love for his grandparents. I feel sorry about the fact he only had them in his life for a short time.

We're now in Fletcher's car and heading back home after stopping off at a lovely restaurant for dinner. Sadness is overwhelming me the closer we get to home. I feel his eyes on me every now and then as he drives, but he doesn't ask any questions.

"Thank you, for today," he says, his voice low. Slowly I turn to face him. "Jess, what's wrong?"

"I've had an amazing day. Why does tomorrow have to be Monday?"

He takes my hand in his, lifts it to his mouth, and lightly brushes his lips against my knuckles. This small gesture spikes my senses.

"Can I . . ."

He doesn't let me finish speaking. "Stay."

"Yes." No other words are said between us as we exit his car and walk toward the house, hand in hand.

Chapter THIRTY-SEVEN

Fletcher

"WHAT THE HELL IS WRONG with you all this morning?" Peter's voice echoes in the changing rooms. If he could've dragged each one of us off the pitch by the scruff of our necks, I'm sure he would have. Some of the lads look as though they had too much alcohol over the weekend. They've not even managed to give the boss fifty-percent effort this morning.

"Lads, I get you might still be excited after our win on Saturday, but we have an abundance of games coming up. You all need to be committed to not just the games, but training. Yes, we have some great experience in this squad, but those players won't be prepared to carry the lads that aren't pulling their weight." His eyes shift around the room and focus on the younger lads in the team.

"Jackson, Fletcher, and Logan, go and take a thirty-minute break, then I want you three back on the pitch. Each of you will be working with a group." The three of us look at one another, confused by what he wants us to do. "Go have a break and come back with something for your group to work on. Either a training session or a fitness test." We nod and leave the room. As we close the door behind us, we hear Peter's voice roar. I feel sorry for the rest of the lads.

"Well, I think I'll work on some goal practice," Logan says as we enter the canteen. We each get ourselves some coffee. "May as well see if any of the lads can catch a ball."

"What about you?" I turn and ask Jackson.

"I don't know, maybe some training drills," he says with a shrug of his shoulders. "What about you?"

"I'm thinking something like a HIIT workout. Short, sharp, and intense exercises."

"Fuck. The lads will hate you. The boss, on the other hand, will love it." Logan laughs as he speaks, and I have to agree. My old boss used to do things like this all the time. Sometimes it was a fun exercise, other times it wasn't.

"Logan, are you still okay to give me a hand this afternoon?" I ask.

"Yeah. Who else is helping?"

"Just Jim."

"What are you doing?" Jackson asks.

"Jess is moving out of her parents' today and I offered to move her stuff this afternoon while she's working."

"Someone's got you wrapped around her finger," Jackson says smugly.

"What?"

"Nothing. Nothing at all."

We all head outside onto the pitch. Peter and some of his staff are standing at the side of the pitch and the lads are doing laps. "Come on, faster!" Peter shouts, urging them to move their legs quicker. I feel bad for what I've planned.

Peter calls the lads back in and splits them into three groups. I give them my instructions. They all moan and frown. I already sensed Logan and Jackson were more than happy to stand back and give their groups orders. As I look at them, my suspicion is confirmed. I might be giving the lads in my group instructions, but I will be doing these exercises as well.

We start, and the lads curse me before we even reach the end of the first exercise. I can hear Peter laughing but I don't take any notice.

At the halfway stage, the lads are puffing and panting. I try to keep encouraging them as I do my own workout, but some of the younger lads drop out. A few continue to push themselves to the max. When our thirty minutes is finished, there are only two lads still on their feet.

"I'm impressed," Peter says as he stands beside me, looking at the players. "I can't believe you joined them."

"I wouldn't give them something I wasn't prepared to do myself."

Peter calls everyone around, and instead of a telling off, he praises us on how hard we've worked over the last thirty minutes then tells us to go home for the day.

I'm glad we've finished early. It means, hopefully, by the time Jess finishes work, all her things will be moved into the apartment.

"Does he have to help?" Elaine makes no attempt to hide her question to Jim. I already know she's not happy about me seeing Jess. She looks at me as though she wants to throttle me as she stands watching and giving out orders to poor Jim.

"Yes, he does. Now, if you won't help or say anything nice, please just stay out of the way. Or better still, go and make the boys a cuppa," Jim says, not mincing his words. Elaine sighs heavily, but walks away in the direction of the kitchen. "Thank Christ, for that. I was beginning to think she wouldn't stop. Sorry, Fletcher."

"It's fine. I'm not taking it personally. She's only looking out for Jess."

"Bloody hell! What does she have in these boxes?" Logan

asks, taking in the room filled with boxes. "To think we're not even moving furniture. Women. They must keep some amount of crap."

Jim and I laugh at what seems like an accurate assessment. There are a lot of boxes and a few suitcases filled with Jess's clothes.

As we load the three cars, I'm certain we'll only need to do one run to the apartment. Well, I hope so, because we only have an hour and a half until Jess finishes work.

Elaine enters the room and hands me a cup of tea. I thank her and she smiles. Jim notices and raises his eyebrows with a smug grin. She even manages to make small talk with me, much to my surprise.

We finally have all three cars loaded and I'm glad Logan was able to help out, otherwise it would have been two trips for us. He's also talked non-stop, which helped when the atmosphere earlier in the afternoon was a little on the frosty side between Elaine and me. Now, as we all get ready to go to the apartment, she seems much more relaxed, which can only be a good thing.

Jim and Elaine leave, with Elaine saying they're going to the shops first to get a few things for Jess before they meet us at the apartment.

I send Jess a text: *See you soon at your new home x*

Jess: I told you I would help move my things!

Me: Too late. It's all done x

This is an exciting time for Jess. A new chapter of her life.

Chapter THIRTY-EIGHT

Jessica

"PLEASE SOMEONE TELL ME THE kettle is on?" I shout, entering the apartment with Lee. It's moving day for me. Lee and I were hoping to finish early, but no, Mr and Mrs Richardson had other ideas. That couple infuriate me with their attitude toward the sale of their house. But, for tonight, I'm going to push it to the back of my mind. I can deal with them tomorrow afternoon when they come into the office for our meeting.

I can hear my dad's and Fletcher's voices coming from the kitchen. There are boxes piled up in the hallway—Dad and Fletcher have been busy. I did tell Fletcher last night to wait until I'd finished work, but he was having none of it, saying it could all be here before I finished. And from the look of it, all my belongings *are* here.

"Well, I can see Jess has kept you all busy," Lee says as we enter the kitchen.

"Yes." Dad smiles. "And the kettle is on."

"Perfect, because I need a drink." I walk to Fletch who is making tea. I slip my arms around his waist and kiss his neck. "A girl could get used to this," I whisper, hoping my words only make it to his ears. He angles his head slightly and flashes me a warm, knowing smile.

"You girls look tired. Tough day?" Dad asks with concern.

"Just an awkward client," Lee says. "One that, after tomorrow, I hope *won't* be our client."

"We'll see." My voice is blunt because I want to try and forget about work for tonight. Lee knows I don't like discussing work with my parents, especially because most of my clients like their business kept confidential. "Where's Mum?" I ask, even though I know she's probably at home, keeping out of Fletcher's way.

"Would you believe me if I say she's just left?"

I laugh but stop when I see the smile on Dad's face. "Really?"

"Yes. Logan is dropping her off. She has a meeting tonight. Logan was going in the same direction and was happy to take your mother and leave me here to see you."

"That has surprised me."

"Why?"

"Because Fletcher is here."

"Now, Jess. That's harsh. Let's just say your mum is a bit more, how shall I put it . . . understanding. She had hoped to see you before she had to leave. She's kept us right today, hasn't she?" Dad turns to Fletcher.

"She did." I frown and search his face, looking for answers. "Jess, your mum and I will be fine. Don't worry about it."

Lee and I exchange glances. She knows what my mum's like and I can't believe she would be happy about being in the same room as Fletcher, especially if I'm not around.

Fletcher picks up two mugs of tea and hands them to Lee and me. I leave the three of them talking, wander out to the living room windows, and stare along the river.

"Jess, are you okay?" I turn to Fletcher as he walks toward me.

"Yes, everything's fine. It's just been a long day."

"Don't worry about your mum. She was actually very pleasant to me. I think your dad has said something to her about us."

"Us?"

"Yes. Us."

I sigh heavily. "What is us? What is this between us?"

"Jess, I don't want to rush you or put pressure on you. Don't overthink this. It's not the time for a conversation with Lee and your dad here. We can talk later."

"Okay." I take a drink of my tea. Fletcher stands behind me, wraps his arms around me, and kisses my head.

I feel totally drained. All I want to do is lie down and sleep, but I can't. I'm going to have to unpack some boxes and open the case that has some of my clothes, otherwise I'll be going to work tomorrow wearing today's clothes.

Footsteps entering the room have me turning. Lee and my dad join us.

"Sweetheart, do you need me to do anything else for you before I go home?" Dad asks.

"No. I'll get to everything later in the week." He comes over to me and kisses my cheek. Fletcher releases his hold and I give my dad a tight squeeze. "Thanks for this today."

"You don't have to thank me. Right, I'm going. There's a game I want to watch on TV."

"I'll walk you out," I say.

"You don't have to. I'm going to head home for a long hot bath," Lee says, her eyes darting between me and Fletcher. I would have to be pretty dumb not to get what she's up to.

"I thought you were going to stay?"

"Two's company, and three . . . well, let's not go there," she whispers softly. I want to laugh. "You and Fletch can have a nice quiet night together, if you know what I mean?" She winks. Oh, I know what she means alright, but given how I feel, maybe that's not the best idea.

"Go then. See you tomorrow. I might be late in," I tell her.

"Planning on a heavy night? Doesn't Fletcher have to be at training early?"

"Yes, he does. Dale is coming over. We have a meeting at nine then I have a meeting with new buyers. But don't worry, I'll be in the office long before Mr and Mrs Richardson get there."

"Good, because I can't deal with them." With that, she and my dad leave, shouting goodbye. I slip my shoes off, walk over to sit down on the couch, and finish drinking my tea. Fletcher joins me, studying me curiously. "Jess, are you sure you're okay?"

"I'm tired. It's been a really long day and I have a mountain of unread emails to check, but other than that, I'm fine."

"Would you like me to run you a bath or order some dinner?"

"Dinner sounds good. I see someone went shopping for me."

"Yes, that was your mum. She thought you wouldn't have time to go shopping tonight. It's only essentials, she said."

"More like I don't have the energy. I'm going to grab a quick shower, see if that wakes me up." I stand up.

"Okay. I'm sure your mum said she put some toiletries in your bathroom. After we have dinner I'll head home and let you get some rest."

"Does that mean you were thinking of staying and keeping me up all night?" I ask, my mood suddenly lifted. He smiles, picking up his phone to place an order for dinner. I leave him and go to shower and change out of these clothes.

"Did your shower help?" Fletcher asks, turning his head away from the TV. His eyes roam over what I'm wearing. He nods in approval of my shorts and vest. His shoes are off and he's sitting with his feet up. There is something so incredibly sexy about seeing him so relaxed.

"It did. Do I have time to check emails before dinner arrives?"

"Of course. You don't mind me watching the sports news?"

"Nope, do what you want." I grab my laptop. I should go and sit at the table, but I want to be close to Fletcher. Making my way to him, I sit at the other end of the couch and start working my way through my emails.

Most of them are enquiries about this apartment block; potential clients looking to arrange viewings. I open my calendar and start replying, sending off appointment times. Early to mid-morning or later in the evening would suit me better, but at the end of the day, it's entirely up to the client.

My inbox pings, alerting me to a new email, and I hesitate on seeing the sender, but I open it.

To: JessTaylor@tcproperties.co.uk

Jess, we need to talk. There are things we need to sort out face to face. Bills and bank accounts. I know I'm meant to keep my distance, but if you could find it in your heart to meet with me somewhere public, I promise I'll be on my best behaviour. My number hasn't changed, so call me. PLEASE.

Scott x

Not what I was expecting to see. Although, I suppose it was to be expected sooner or later that he would get in touch with me through the business. And here was me feeling better after my low mood from earlier. I wasn't sure what was wrong with me.

The intercom buzzes and Fletcher answers it, and then I hear him in the hallway.

I stare at the computer screen in front of me. This needs to be dealt with because if I don't, I know he will continue to pester me. So the question I need to ask myself is, do I meet with him, or just let the police know he contacted me?

I know what the right thing to do is, but a part of me is also hoping if I meet with him, we can put an end to everything that was once between us and move forward with our lives separately.

I'm going to put Scott and Mr and Mrs Richardson to the back of my mind and try and enjoy dinner.

"Mmm, something smells amazing," I say, entering the kitchen. Fletcher has just finished setting the table and transferring the food onto plates. "Where did you order this from?" I ask, looking at the delicious steaks on the plates, along with what I can only describe as a healthy portion of vegetables.

"The Italian I took you to. As I've already told you, I try and be good food wise when I'm training. Is this okay?"

"Okay? This is perfect." I press a kiss to his lips before sitting down.

Dinner is relaxed and I manage to chat with Fletcher, but I don't mention the email because I don't want to worry him. He reminds me he's away on Sunday with the team. They fly out late Sunday night for a week's training in Spain before going on to Italy for a game. So in total, he will be out of the country for ten days. They come home on the Thursday afternoon and then have a home game on the Sunday.

It will be strange not having him around for a while, but he assures me he will still be in constant contact. I should use the time he's away wisely, but I'm sure my time will consist of work.

"Are you finished?" Fletcher asks.

"I can't eat anymore. That steak was to die for."

We clear away the plates and I load the dishwasher.

"Jess?"

"Yeah."

"Do you want me to stay tonight or would you rather be on your own?" he asks, grabbing hold of me. He leans against the kitchen counter and holds me in his arms, facing him, a warm smile on his face.

I draw in a deep breath and hope and pray my words don't offend him. "There is part of me that wants you to stay and hold me in your arms all night long, but the other part of me is telling me to be a big girl and spend tonight here alone." I look into his eyes for a sign that he's not happy, but he's still smiling. "It's been so long since I've lived on my own, I want to know if I can do this."

"Of course you can do this. In that case, I'll go now and you can call or text me later if you need to speak to me." He pulls me closer to him.

"You don't mind?"

"No, Jess. I don't mind. I'm going to miss you, but I understand your reasons. I also know you're completely safe here with twenty-four-hour security."

"Thank you." I kiss him, and he pulls away. "What?"

"If you keep that up I won't be going anywhere," he says with a teasing smirk. He grabs his car keys from the counter and I walk him into the hallway. He gives me the briefest of kisses before saying goodbye and leaving me on my own.

I wander from room to room, and I'm grateful to Dale and his wife for letting me stay here. Now I just hope I manage to get a full night's sleep on my own.

Chapter THIRTY-NINE

Fletcher

"FLETCHER?" THE BOSS CALLS ME over as we wrap up our last training session of the week.

"What's up?"

"Nothing, I just wanted to let you know you have a meeting with an advisor from the women's aid charity when we get back from our trips to Spain and Italy. She wants to meet with you on the Friday morning."

"But won't we have training?"

"Yes. She's prepared to come here and speak to you. See what ideas you have and how you can help raise awareness."

"I'm more than happy to meet her as long as you're fine with that. It also means I can give her a cheque. I still can't believe how the online auction went for the match ball."

"Yes, that was a great amount and I'm sure the charity will be more than happy with the donation." Someone paid five thousand pounds for the match ball that I signed, of course, and I added a signed football shirt with it. It was the least I could do when a fan spent that amount of money.

"I'm going to match the amount we raised," I tell him.

His eyes widen and the smile on his face, well, it looks as though I've surprised him. "Well, it's for a good cause. Is there a special reason for this charity?"

It's not the first time he's asked the question, but I'm not about to reveal Jess is the reason behind it. I wouldn't want this becoming public knowledge. She's had a bad enough week with being named by the media as the significant woman in my life.

"No reason."

"Okay. I'll let you get off. No doubt you're spending some quality time with Jess."

"Yes, that's the plan."

"Don't be late on Sunday."

I leave him and make my way to the car. Speaking with Jess isn't the same as seeing her. I'm heading to the office to pick her up from work. It's Friday, and the weekend starts now. She doesn't know I'm going to get her; I arranged for Lee to keep her afternoon free so we could start our weekend early. Well, I do have to leave her on Sunday afternoon, so I plan to make the most of our time together.

As I drive into the city, my thoughts are of my girl. Of how she's coped with being linked to me. And truthfully, she's coped better than I expected, or at the very least, she's made out that she's coped with it. It's been me who hasn't coped that well. Some of the papers were, shall we say, a bit revealing of my past, which pissed me off. I'm sure Jess was hurt seeing some of the stories about me and various women, but she hid it well. Or maybe that made for an interesting meeting with her therapist.

Jess doesn't think it, but she is one strong and independent woman. Now I just hope she's not angry with me for pulling her away from work. I have a bag in the back of my car, and as soon as I pick her up, we're heading to St. Andrews for two nights. Lee managed to pack a bag for Jess and will have it at the office.

With me leaving on Sunday for ten days, I thought it would be nice to do something different for just the two of us. I also let Jim and Elaine know of my plans because Jess had mentioned during one of our conversations that she might call her mum and arrange to go shopping on Saturday.

I park the car just outside her office and I can see from the windows she's busy at her desk.

Leaving my car, I look back at it and hope I don't get a ticket for parking in a no parking zone.

As I open the door, Lee looks at me and smiles. Jess lifts her head, her eyes narrowing as she sees me. She glances at Lee then back to me. She brings her fingers up and touches her lips which makes her look really cute.

"What are you doing here?" she asks.

"Me? I'm here to collect you."

Lee is grinning from ear to ear. She's moved from her desk and is now standing by Jess.

"Am I forgetting something? Because I still have a few things to do and it's only . . ." She stops talking and looks at the time. "One. I don't finish for another few hours."

"Jess," Lee says, reaching down, and I presume saving whatever Jess was doing on the computer. She spins her chair around. "You are leaving now and . . ." She walks away, opens a door, and lifts out the bag I asked her to pack for Jess. "This is yours." My poor sweet girl now looks more puzzled. "Go on, take it, and enjoy your weekend with your man."

Jess smiles, reluctantly taking the bag from her, and looks at me. "You've both been very sneaky, and as for you . . ." She turns to Lee. "Can you manage?"

"Of course. Now get out of here."

My girl shakes her head as she walks toward me and straight into my open arms. I kiss her because I've missed the feel of her lips against mine.

"Get out of here, you two, and get a room. Oh, that's right, you have one booked." We turn and look at Lee before I take Jess' hand and lead her from the office.

"Fletch," Lee calls after us. "You can thank me later when

you see what's packed." She laughs as we leave.

"Oh, God. What the hell has she packed for me?"

"With a bit of luck, not a lot," I say, opening the car door.

"You are impossible. Where are we going?"

"St. Andrews," I tell her, and close her door.

I put her bag beside mine, walk around the car, and get in. My girl is grinning. She really does have an infectious smile. I can't help but feel warm and happy.

Starting the car, I pull into the traffic. Getting out of the city centre on a Friday afternoon is harder than I thought. We have to stop at every single set of traffic lights. By the time we get out of the city and onto the motorway, we've already wasted twenty minutes, but Jess doesn't seem to care. She's singing away to the radio.

"What?" she asks, catching me watching her. "Shouldn't your eyes be on the road?"

"They should but there's this really beautiful, sexy woman who has me distracted by her singing."

"Shit!" She blushes.

"You have nothing to be embarrassed about. You have an amazing voice. Is there anything you're not good at?"

"I'm sure there must be something." I catch the glint in her eye as she speaks, and I wonder what she's thinking about. "So, what are our plans for the next two days?"

"How about some golf?"

"I suppose I could try. You would have to teach me." I have a vision of me standing behind her, my arms wrapped around her waist, helping her to swing a golf club. There's no way we can play golf. I'm getting hard just thinking about that little scenario.

"No, we're not playing golf. This weekend is all about relaxing and spending time with each other."

"I like the sound of that, but I should probably phone my

mum and cancel our trip tomorrow."

"You don't have to."

"She knows I'm with you." It's more of a statement than a question, and I nod.

We spend the drive talking about our week and my upcoming trip. I wish Jess was going with me; I'm going to miss her like crazy when I'm gone. When we've spoken about it, I've made out I'll be too busy with training to miss her, but that's not true. I know the boss has packed a lot into our time away in a bid to keep us players away from pubs and nightclubs, although, I have no interest in either. I will be more than happy to spend my evenings on the phone to Jess.

Fuck, I've got it bad.

When did I turn into such a sap?

Chapter FORTY

Jessica

WOW. BLOODY HELL, I HAVE no words. This place looks spectacular, and I've only just got out of the car. Fletcher hands his car keys to the doorman and someone else comes and takes our bags. I stop and stare, taking in my lavish surroundings, with views across St. Andrews and out toward the North Sea. It's breathtakingly beautiful and so peaceful.

"Come on, let's go inside," Fletcher says, taking my hand. I lift my eyes to his and shiver, but not from being cold. Far from it. No, this is because I'm excited about what our weekend away holds for us.

It's the end of July. There's still some heat in the air, which, considering this is Scotland, isn't too bad. We aren't known for our hot summers. It's overcast, but I don't think anything could overshadow today, not even if it started pouring with rain.

I slowly turn to the incredible, sexy man by my side; his blue eyes light up as he watches me. Yes, he and Lee have been sneaky in organising this, but it's the best surprise I've had in such a long time.

"You look happy." He places a hand on my chin and leans closer to me, our lips almost touching. I want him to kiss me but I know he's not going to. Not here at the main entrance to the hotel, when there is all this chemistry sizzling away between us. Heat fires through my body, and I take a deep breath to try and compose myself.

No, we don't need an audience.

"I am happy. But I'll be happier when we get checked-in and I can thank you properly," I say, letting him know exactly what I want when we reach our bedroom. "You, my sexy player, are about to be thanked in more ways than one."

His eyes are now smouldering and completely seducing me. "Now, that I love the sound of. So, tell me, woman, why are we standing here?" His voice not only teases me, but caresses me.

I smile as we walk inside, and I pause.

"Jess, we've no time for you to be admiring our surroundings. I want to get us checked-in *now*." His voice is low and strained, and his gaze is distracted. He pulls on my hand, urging me forward to the reception. I try to take everything in as we walk, but it's not as simple as it should be.

My heels click as we walk over the beautiful wooden floor, solid oak, if I'm not mistaken. The seating is luxurious, with a mix of velvet chairs and tartan sofas; not something I would put together, but it works in contrast with the grey/blue tones of the walls. All this amazing space, and it still feels homely and welcoming.

"Ah, Mr Adams. We do hope you both enjoy your stay with us," a lad behind the reception desk says. I turn away from them, leaving Fletcher to check-in, and wander around, looking at various pictures on the wall. There are a few of the view and lots from the golf course.

"Jess?" Fletcher calls out. I walk toward him and a porter who is waiting to show us to our room. We travel in a lift, with the porter chatting away to Fletcher about his European game next week. I've tuned out of the conversation. Fletcher has my hand in his and is stroking mine with the pad of his thumb. I close my eyes and draw in a deep breath. He lets out a subtle low chuckle, almost unrecognisable. But not to me. I seem to have picked up on his little moans and groans. I'm so attuned to him. How can that be? Especially given we've only known each other for such a short time.

My steps falter as we walk along the brightly lit hallway to the farthest room. The porter opens our door, taking our bags in. Fletcher gives him a tip and he wishes us a good day before leaving us.

I walk through our private hallway and look in at the separate lounge and dining area; it's all beautiful shades of cream and grey, with lots of tartan. I then make my way toward the bedroom, and wow! Just wow. My eyes focus on the full-length traditional sash windows with stunning views over the golf course and beyond. I could easily sit by the windows and watch the world go by. Again, the colour scheme is very similar to the lounge, and there's nothing I don't like about it.

"I love it," I say, feeling Fletcher's body against my back as he slips his arms around my waist. "Thank you for bringing me here."

"It's my pleasure," he whispers against my neck. Warm lips kiss me softly. My body melts against him. "You are driving me crazy."

His choice of words surprises me, and I turn in his arms to face him. "Not yet, but I'm going to," I say boldly, finding courage and a hint of excitement to my voice. My body aches for him. Craves him. I've gone too long without him and need him, *now*.

I wrap my arms around his neck and he pulls my body closer to his. There have been so many stories of Fletcher Adams in the news this week, most of them not very supportive of the man before me. But the man before me is nothing like the stories printed. No. My man can be sweet, possessive, controlled, and demanding. And all of those qualities describe all aspects of his life, not just in the bedroom.

I pull his lips to mine and kiss him tenderly. He returns my kiss greedily, devouring me; so much passion, yet his hold remains gentle and tender. He's holding back, and he's not the only one. I want to savour our time together. There's no rush, even though we both need the intimacy we share.

My hands slide down his back and my nails scrape against the fabric of his T-shirt. He starts walking backwards, forcing me to go with him; he doesn't break our connection. A shiver runs through my body as I realise the direction we're going; toward the bed. Moments ago, I was prepared to go slow and savour our time together, but now, as he deepens our kiss, all I want is sex.

My feelings for Fletcher consume me. I love the way he makes me feel precious. The feel of his hands on my body drives me wild with desire. I can't get enough of my very own star player.

He backs up and stops by the enormous bed. Our kiss deepens and our tongues glide against each other. There is something so erotic about hearing him groan into my mouth as we kiss. My breathing quickens.

One hand slides quickly up my back. I can feel him fumble with the zip on the back of my dress, then cool air hits my skin as the zip slides down. Still not breaking our kiss, he slowly works my dress off my shoulders. I stifle a laugh because I'm sure this is nothing like how it looks in the movies when a guy undresses his partner. I wriggle, and the dress drops to the floor.

My back arches against him as I feel his hands on my bare back. His hands dance delicately up and down my skin before he reaches the fastening on my bra, which he unhooks first time then drops it to the floor.

Drawing back from our kiss, I lift my eyes to his, silently questioning why he still has so many clothes on. I stand before him in nothing but my knickers and my heels. He pulls his T-shirt over his head, revealing his muscular torso; a perfect sight. Standing back, he smiles in appreciation as his eyes roam my body.

The physical closeness we share is hard to put into words. Everything we share, from the friendship we have, the laughing and talking, to the familiarity I feel with him. He makes me feel at ease with not just him, but myself. It's about knowing each other so well. Wanting to spend time with the other.

I reach out, taking his hands and threading my fingers with his. He lifts our joined hands and places small, soft kisses across both. Such an innocent gesture brings more than a smile to my face. There's a fluttering in my stomach and a chill running down my spine.

"You see what you do to me?" he says.

My eyes follow his and stop at his erection straining in his jeans. "Well, I might if you remove those," I tease him.

He laughs and shakes his head. He lets go of my hands and I smirk as he removes his shoes and the rest of his clothing.

"Yes, now I see." I can't help it, but I giggle.

He frowns. "I see someone is in a funny mood. We need to change that." I shift restlessly on my feet, step back, and watch as he drops his hand. "See something you want?" he asks, pleasuring himself, and at the same time, teasing me.

Fuck! I've never seen anything so hot as Fletcher is right now. I press my thighs together. Never did I think I could come without someone touching me, but now . . . now I know different.

Surely he's not going to deny me?

My body responds to his actions, heat slowly simmering through me. Drawing my eyes away from what he's doing, I look into his. My heart stops and I have to take a deep breath.

He's getting pleasure from me watching him. He's waiting for my reaction. Something about the way he's looking at me tells me he is about to take me hard and fast.

"Now I think it's you who's wearing too much. Time for you to remove them," he says, stopping what he's doing. I kick my shoes off and slowly step out of my underwear.

Looking back into his eyes, tingles of fear and excitement shoot through me. My desire for Fletcher has only intensified. I knew all those weeks ago as he sat at my parents' kitchen table that there was something about him; it was in his eyes, the way he looked at me. And it was more than the sadness I had first seen.

He's slowly putting the broken pieces of me back together. I'm finally starting to believe in myself again. My memories are there, but I'm starting to feel not so broken anymore.

He lowers me gently to the bed. I pull him close to me, our noses touching, eyes locking.

"I'm taking you the way I think we both need because I know we have two days for slow and sensual, but right now, Jess, it's been too long since I've been buried deep inside you."

My breath catches at his words.

He settles between my legs, his erection hot and hard against me.

"I want you," I breathe against him, rubbing myself along him.

"You have me."

He pushes against me and slides inside me. I gasp, my walls tightening around him, holding him captive. Everything with Fletcher feels so right.

He sits back on his heels and pushes my bent legs back against me and pushes deeper. Deeper than I've ever felt him before. I moan and close my eyes.

"No, Jess. *Open.*"

I open my eyes at his command. Staring, I watch his expression change to that of heavy lust and desire. He starts to move, and I mean really thrust against me, each time pulling all the way out and then thrusting back in, going a little deeper each time.

His blue eyes cloud over, his lips part, and his chest heaves with his laboured breaths as he moves in a wild rhythm. My pulse quickens as the pace increases to something almost unbearable. His body glistens above me. I'm paralysed to move as he's pinning my legs against me. I'm unable to move and I want to.

Over and over. Harder and harder.

I'm so close . . .

"Jess!" He calls my name, thrusting against me and stilling. My own orgasm hits hard and I cry out. He lets go of my legs and they flop to the side, and the weight of his body falls on me. He nuzzles against my neck, his teeth nipping lightly against me. We lie still, allowing our breathing to return to something that resembles normal.

Fletcher lifts his head, rests it on his hand, and stares at me. With his other hand, he runs his fingers up and down my face.

"What are our plans now?" I ask.

"My plans include taking care of my beautiful girl. A bath, dinner, and then I'm going to worship your sexy body all night long. And tomorrow we can spend a relaxing day at the spa."

"That sounds perfect."

Chapter FORTY-ONE

Fletcher

THE LOOK ON HER FACE when we arrived was priceless, but the look on her face right now is something else. Happy. Content. Spent. She's anticipating my next move.

Emotions seep through me. I've never before felt all these feelings, and it scares the holy crap out of me. My feelings for Jess are so intense, and I'm not sure if that's a good or a bad thing. Either way, I'm going to enjoy every single moment we share.

I kiss the top of her head before leaving the comfort of the bed. The luxurious bathroom is my destination, to run us a bath, where I get to lie back with a beautiful woman in my arms and relax.

Switching the taps on, I pour some of the smelly stuff hotels leave in bathrooms and watch as bubbles form in the water. I sit on the bath edge and watch as the water slowly rises.

It's funny, I can't imagine not having Jess in my life. She fills a gap I never knew existed. The more time I spend with her, the more I get to know her. I want to know every last detail of her life; all her favourite and least favourite things. I can easily admit to enjoying the time we spend together.

Soft footsteps pad across the bathroom floor. "I see you're a man of your word," she says, stopping beside me. I turn my gaze away from the running water to find her standing, still naked, before me.

Her hair flows down her back, her cheeks are still glowing, and her eyes . . . her eyes are filled with lust. Fuck, I want her all over again. Her eyes travel downward and she shrugs her shoulders as she takes in my current problem.

"You don't make this easy for me," I say, standing up. I switch off the water before turning back to face her. "Why do you have to look so fuckable?"

"And here was me thinking I must look a state." There's no way she's getting in that bath right now. Not a hope in hell. I want her and I will have her. Slowly and very deliberately, she runs her tongue along her bottom lip, and Christ, I can't fight the urge.

I lose it. My lips crash against hers and my fingers thread through her hair. She reaches up and rests the palm of her hands on my chest. Her mouth moulds to mine. Her tongue sweeps along my bottom lip. I pull her closer roughly by her hair. She moans.

"I want you," she whispers. After God knows how long, I pull back and I'm met with those eyes, and I know she means the words that slipped from her mouth. With a smile and a glint in my eyes, I move her backwards until we're at the sink. I spin her around and pull her hips toward me. She braces herself against the sink.

I will make it up to her many times over this weekend.

I almost cry out as I enter her. She gasps, pushing that sexy-as-fuck arse closer to me. Her arse is perfect, totally flawless. My hands tightly grip her hips and I slowly thrust against her. She turns her head slightly and I bend over and kiss her lips roughly.

A heavy scent of sex fills most of the air; the rest is filled with the strong scent of honey bubble bath. The aromas mixed together smell so sweet, and all I can think about is tasting her after we share a bath.

My hands slide from her hips to her back, and I find myself drawing circles on her now damp skin. Her soft moans turn louder with each calculated thrust. She lifts her head until she's looking in the mirror in front of us, watching. Our eyes connect, and all I see is my other half. We share something special; I see it every single time I look into her eyes.

She trusts me completely. And I know how hard that must be for her, but it means the world to me.

I watch as she struggles to keep her eyes open. Her legs shake, and I move my hands back to her hips, holding her in place. I'll always be here to catch her fall. *Always*. She opens her eyes and focuses on us, watching intently, eyes heavy with lust. Her walls tighten around me, pulsing, and we both lose ourselves to the other.

No words are spoken. None are needed between us.

Slowly, I withdraw, and make sure she's steady on her feet before checking the temperature of the bath. It's perfect. I turn and walk back toward her, scoop her in my arms, and carry her the short distance to the bath then lower her in.

Her lazy smile is infectious.

"Now, what are we doing?" she asks playfully. "You said a bath first."

I climb in the bath behind her and pull her into my arms. "Yes, I did, didn't I? Well, in my book, that doesn't count as worshipping your body all night long. So we will have dinner and then I intend to follow through with my original plan."

"Oh, fuck!" She gasps.

"No. We won't fuck. I'm going to worship you all night long, so call it what you will, but I can assure you, we won't be fucking."

And there, I've just given her a clear indication of how much she means to me. I feel her body relax against me. This I could get used to.

Chapter FORTY-TWO

Jessica

I TRY TO STRETCH BUT I can't; his body is wrapped tightly around me. My body aches in all the right places and I can't help but smile. He was right; he worshipped me all night long. I feel used but certainly not abused. Everything about yesterday, from surprising me at work until we fell asleep in the wee small hours, was perfect. I don't think anyone has ever made me feel the way I do when I'm with Fletcher.

He's attentive, caring, and makes me feel alive. Something I didn't think was possible a few weeks ago. I'm loving the time we spend together, and although I've spoken to him every single night, I've missed seeing him. Missed everything about him.

As I open my eyes, there is a small sliver of light breaking through the small gap in the heavy, velvet grey curtains. It's bright yet still dark in the room. I know it's early.

Slowly turning, I want to face him, to watch him sleep. But as I turn, I see his eyes are wide open. "Good morning."

"Morning, beautiful." He kisses me on the lips. "How are you feeling?"

"I feel a little over-used, if I'm honest with you," I say with a smile.

"In that case, I will leave your aching body alone for the time being." My core clenches at his words and I want him all over again. I pout, hoping it means I get my own way. "No, Jess." He looks at the time. "We have enough time for showers before going for breakfast and then we hit the spa. You can have anything you want at the spa."

"Anything? All I want is you."

He ignores my comment and carries on speaking. "I'm sure we can go for a swim as well. I did ask Lee to pack a swim suit for you."

"What about a workout in the gym?" I ask, knowing how much he enjoys his workouts. After all he does workout most days.

"You want to work out with me?"

"It could be interesting."

"I'm sure I could put you through your paces."

"I'm sure you could, but what you don't know is that before my life got fucked up, I was always in the gym. I miss it."

"I'm sure I could do a cardio session with you, if you want?"

"Cardio? Do I look like a girl who is only going to do a cardio session in the gym? It's been a while since I did weights, and I would rather have you with me the first time."

"I'm more than happy to help with first times, for anything or any situation." He winks at me.

Oh, dear God. What have I let myself in for?

He kisses me in a way that leaves me wanting more. "It's about time we get your sexy arse in that shower."

"Yes, sir," I say moving from his hold and getting out of the bed, naked. I walk away, his eyes watching me.

The shower is quicker than I'd hoped. I thought Fletcher might join me, but he's sticking to his word and leaving my body alone. That's probably a good thing; it will make tonight much more interesting.

I should've checked yesterday what Lee had packed for me, but, well, I never got around to it. Fletcher climbs out of bed as

I lift my bag and put it on the bed. Distracted from the job in hand, my eyes follow his naked body into the bathroom until he closes the door behind him. I sigh and I'm sure I hear him chuckle.

Opening my bag, I take out a black underwear set that's sitting at the top. I frown because I don't recognise it. It's brand new, still has the tags on. What is Lee up to? It's a stunning set; a beautiful satin and lace basque that fastens low and I'm sure leaves a lot of flesh on show at the back.

I shake my head as I think about Lee buying this, and put it to the side before carrying on. She's packed a pair of jeans and a couple of T-shirts and some gym gear, but not packed anything that would be suitable for going for dinner tonight. What the hell was she thinking? All my make-up and even my hair straighteners are here.

Well, Fletcher did say we're going to the spa, and then hopefully we'll go to the gym, so it looks like I'm wearing the gym gear because I'll need the jeans to wear going home tomorrow. I dress and sort my hair because it looks a bloody mess.

"Bloody hell, woman. I hope you have a jumper or something to put on." I turn to him; he's standing with a towel around his waist, eyes running over what I'm wearing.

"What's wrong?" I ask, already knowing the answer. My leggings are fine, it's the top he has an issue with. It's almost like a sports bra. There is a hooded top in my bag, but at the moment, I'm not telling him that. It's actually quite amusing watching him become territorial.

He walks toward me, eyes hooded and breathing laboured. "There's no way you're wandering about like that." I can hear the seriousness in his tone.

"What? Like this? This is what I wear to the gym."

"Jess, I'll give you a T-shirt." He turns away from me and I hear him moan. I watch as he gets ready, pulling on his jogging pants and a T-shirt.

"Are we ready to go?" I ask as he laces up his trainers.

He lifts his head, grabs one of his T-shirts, and throws it at me. "We will be when you put this on."

"Nope. No can do."

"Jess. Fucking hell. Every man in the hotel will be a walking hard on seeing you like that, so please, for me, put the fucking shirt on."

I walk back to the bed, shaking my head, and grab the hooded top from my bag. "No, thank you. I'll wear my own."

"You are a fucking tease."

"Yip. You better believe it."

We leave the room hand in hand and go for breakfast. I have butterflies in my stomach. I can't remember the last time I was this excited. Last Saturday I was excited, but also nervous about going to watch him play football. Fletcher is good for me in more ways than I know.

"Jess?" Fletcher calls over to me. "I think that's enough for one day."

"Okay, spoil sport. I was enjoying that."

"Yeah, I can see that. I just don't want you overdoing it." I slow down on the treadmill before stopping. "Now, stretches."

I jump down off the treadmill and stand so close to him we're almost touching. "I know a very good exercise for stretching out my muscles," I whisper, so no one else in the gym can hear me.

"I'm sure you do," he says with a smirk. "But it's not happening. We have time for a shower before getting ready for dinner." I look at the clock on the wall, and I'm surprised that it's just after six p.m. The day has flown by so quickly.

"Lee hasn't packed anything for me to wear to dinner."

He smiles but stops himself, takes my hand, and we leave the gym. I get the feeling he's up to something.

As we walk back to the room, I reflect on what has been an amazing day. We went swimming together, and that was so much fun, although Fletcher's face was a picture when I stepped out in the bikini Lee had packed. He really didn't know where to look. I have to give credit to Lee for picking the sexiest two-piece I own. The spa was perfect; we got a couples' back massage. I also got a facial and had my nails done. We had a light lunch and we've talked most of the day. I've enjoyed his company.

He opens the room door and we enter. I pause, noticing two suit carriers hanging up.

"What's this?" I ask.

"This is what we need to get dressed for dinner." He hands me one and opens the other. In his are a suit, shirt, and tie. "You need to open that because we don't have a lot of time."

Opening it, I gasp. The black dress inside is exquisite. I take it out and admire it. A beautiful black satin cocktail dress. Turning it around, I know the underwear in my bag is going to go perfectly with it. The dress has a low back, and yes, a lot of flesh will be on show wearing this.

"Who . . . How did you get this and the underwear?"

"Ah, so you found those. I went shopping one day after training. I had to ask Lee about sizes. I arranged for the dress, and there's shoes and a bag as well, to be delivered here today." No-one has ever bought me clothes or done anything so thoughtful for me. "Now, the question is, have I picked well?"

I put the dress down and close the distance between us. "You have done more than well. Thank you." I kiss him. "After I've showered, you'll have to help me with the zip."

"Jess, I look forward to it."

Twenty minutes later, I emerge from the bathroom with a towel wrapped around me. He smiles, passing me to go for his shower. I use my time wisely, putting on make-up and drying my hair. My eyes glance to the dress and back to the mirror I'm sitting in front of. I need to do something more with my hair, I can't just leave it straight. It takes a lot of time, but it's worth it. I sit curling my hair and then pinning it up, leaving a few curls hanging down.

I take my clothes into the lounge area so Fletcher can't see me getting dressed when he comes out of the shower.

"Don't come through here," I call out, hearing him moving around in the bedroom.

The only thing about getting dressed in here is I don't know what I look like. I manage the zip at the side of the dress without Fletcher's help. I slip the black shoes on my feet, take a deep breath, and walk back into the bedroom to see what my man thinks.

I stop, my heart rate picking up pace. He has his back to me, putting on the suit jacket. As if sensing me, he turns around. His jaw drops and he stares, not saying a word. As I wait for him to say something, I nervously run my hands down the sides of my dress. I have butterflies in my stomach as he gapes at me. I can't make up my mind if his reaction is a good thing or not.

He looks every inch the sexy footballer. Powerful and handsome. What a combination!

He walks toward me and stops, taking my hand in his, and turns me around. "Fucking hell. Jess, you look breath-taking." He turns me back to face him, lifting my hand to his mouth, his eyes on me, gaze intense and completely focused.

The feel of his lips against my sensitive skin sends goose bumps racing up my arm, and shivers lace my spine. I close my eyes and try to regain composure that I'm suddenly lacking from his presence.

"You don't look so bad yourself," I say light-heartedly, trying to take the sting out of the air simmering between us.

"Come on. We have time for a drink in the bar before dinner." He keeps my hand in his as we leave the room, but as soon as we enter the lift, his hand is on the small of my back. The feel of our skin-on-skin contact is electric and intense.

Why are we going for dinner? Because all I need now is *him*.

I'm glad the ride down is short because there's no way I could cope with all the sexual tension between us. We make our way to the lobby bar, and Fletcher's hand stays on my back until I sit down at a quiet table.

"What do you want to drink?" he asks.

"Wine."

He leaves me and my gaze follows him to the bar, where he orders our drinks. He turns and smiles. I notice a few people talking as they recognise Fletcher. A waiter carries our drinks as he comes back to the table.

"I thought you said a drink before dinner?" I say, looking at the bottle of champagne.

"I did." The waiter opens the champagne and pours into the two flutes then leaves. "A toast. To us."

"To us," I repeat.

"So what are you going to do whilst I'm gone?"

I've tried not to think about him being away for ten days. "I don't know. Work and work, I guess. Maybe watch some football."

"I'll give you all the kick off times as soon as the boss tells us."

We continue talking and sipping our champagne until a waiter comes and tells us our table is ready for us in the restaurant.

The hotel has several restaurants catering for everyone. The relaxing and warm atmosphere was perfectly blended, and dinner was totally amazing, but my company was even better. I'm certain everyone in the restaurant could feel the sizzling chemistry between us.

"Are you having dessert?" our waiter asks.

Fletcher keeps his eyes on me and answers, "No, thank you. But can you arrange for another bottle of champagne to be sent to our room, and some strawberries, please?" Fletcher pushes his chair back and stands.

"Yes, sir."

"And here was me thinking we would be having a quiet night," I say as I take Fletcher's out-stretched hand.

"Quiet? No. Our night will be anything but quiet. I'm about to tease you and bring you to the brink over and over until you're crying out my name and begging me to stop. I have had to watch you all day, from the bikini in the swimming pool to the top you wore during our workout. You have teased me all day." I smile at his very accurate statement. "I've sat, quietly amused at the longing looks other men have had on their faces as they've watched my girl."

"The only longing look that concerns me is the one on your face," I whisper in his ear, then gently nip my teeth against his earlobe.

"We need to leave now."

Chapter FORTY-THREE

Fletcher

OUR WEEKEND IS OVER, AND I, for one, don't want it to be. We've had an incredible time. I never knew being in a relationship could be so intense with feelings.

Yesterday was fucking torture, keeping my hands to myself for the whole day. Especially when I was in the pool and she strutted out wearing the sexiest thing I've ever seen. I wanted to empty the pool and take her there and then. In the end, I had to swim away from her for a few minutes until I managed to talk my erection back down. I'm sure she knew.

During dinner, the chemistry was smoking hot between us, and when we got back to the room, I thought I had died and gone to heaven as I unwrapped the best present anyone could ever give me. I slowly savoured undressing her. Just when I thought things couldn't get any better, her dress dropped to the floor and my eyes fell upon the underwear I'd picked out.

Jess Taylor is the sexiest and most natural woman I've ever known.

I hate the thought of leaving her for ten days.

We're in my car on our way to Glasgow. I turn my head and allow my eyes to linger on her for just a moment before turning back to the road ahead. She's totally relaxed, her hair looks amazing, yet she claimed this morning it was a mess, that's why she piled it up and pinned it in place. She has very little make-up on. Her face is fresh and beautiful. Picture perfect.

How the hell did I get so fucking lucky, having someone like Jess in my life?

Yes, she has issues that she's dealing with head on. But don't we all? Logan has said on more than one occasion that she comes with too much baggage, but I don't see it.

"Why are we here?" she asks, taking in our surroundings.

"I need to get my case from mine and we can stop off and see your parents."

"Are you sure that's a good idea?" she asks, frowning.

"Yes." I park the car in my drive and we get out. "Go in and see your parents. I won't be long."

"No. We can go in together."

"Okay."

It only takes a few minutes to grab my case, make sure everything is turned off, and lock up. I put the case in the back of my car, take her hand, and walk towards her parents' house. She tenses with each step closer we take.

"Jess, everything is fine, and we can't stay long. You need to drop me at the club."

She turns. Her mouth drops open and she stares directly into my eyes. "What do you mean I need to drop you?"

I hand her my car keys. "What I mean is you are dropping me off and you can look after my baby for me."

"There's no way I'm driving your car. Shit. I don't trust myself with it."

"I trust you." I lean in and kiss her, but our kiss is interrupted as her mum opens the front door.

"Elaine," I say, stepping back from Jess but still keeping her hand.

"Fletcher." Her eyes dart between me and Jess, and I see a

slight smile playing on her lips. "Jim is in the kitchen. Go on through."

I kiss Jess on the cheek and walk away. I'm not out of ear shot when I hear Elaine say, "You look radiant, sweetheart." I walk to the kitchen, grinning, because that *is* how she looks.

"Elaine said you were back," Jim says as I enter.

"Yes, but I've just picked up my case to leave."

"Ah, yes, football. I can drop you if you want, and I can take Jess to the apartment because I know it was your car you were away in."

"No, it's fine. I've given Jess my car key." He smiles and Elaine and Jess enter the kitchen.

"Do you have time for a cup of tea?" Elaine asks.

"Yeah, a quick cup," I reply, looking at Jess, who seems taken aback by her mum's attitude toward me. What Jess doesn't know and I won't be telling her is that the lovely Elaine and I have had words. Or rather, she told me in no uncertain terms what would happen to me if I messed with her daughter's fragile heart. I made it clear to Jim and Elaine I have no intention of hurting Jess. Elaine seems to be slowly coming around to that fact.

We spend the next thirty minutes with them. Jess tells Elaine about our time at the spa. Jim asks me some questions about our training and the games we'll be playing.

"Jess, we need to go. I don't want to be late and start off being in the boss's bad books."

"Yeah, I know, but I'm still unsure about driving your car."

I'm not listening to her. She's driving it. End of. And even if she doesn't use it when I'm away, at least it will be safer at hers in the secured parking.

Jim wishes me well with a pat on the back, but it's Elaine who surprises not only me but Jess too. "Have a safe journey, and good luck with the football," she says.

"Thank you."

I make my way to my passenger seat, leaving Jess saying goodbye to her parents. She tells Elaine they can go shopping one night after work to make up for not going yesterday. I watch as she kisses her parents and I feel a slight twang of jealousy. She is close to both of her parents; something I never had. I shake those thoughts to the back of my head where they belong. I only have a short time left with her and I don't want my low mood to ruin that.

"Right, are you really going to make me drive?"

"Yes," I say, sliding into the passenger's seat. She huffs before getting in the car and starting the engine.

For the first few minutes of our journey, her body is so tense, I almost tell her to stop so I can drive. But now she seems much happier. I might need to let her drive more often when we go out because I love watching her.

We pull up at the stadium and she parks the car. The bus taking us to the airport is already here. I can see the boss talking to Jackson, and Fran is standing to the side with their boys. I know how I feel at the thought of leaving Jess, but I have no idea how he must feel leaving Fran and the boys.

"I'm going to miss you," Jess says, turning to face me. My heart fucking aches right now. I reach out, take her hand, and pull her closer to me. She strokes her fingers gently across the palm of my hand.

"I'm going to miss you just as much." I press a soft, lingering kiss to her lips. "Do you want to come out and see Fran?"

She nods.

We exit the car and I take my case from the back. She waits, holding my car keys in her hand, staring at them. She's thinking; I can see the cogs turning. I hope she's not going to hand them back to me. I take her hand and we walk toward everyone. Most of the players are here, but there's still a few missing. Glancing around, I shake my head when I realise Logan isn't here.

"Jess, honey," Fran calls out. "How are you?"

I let go of her hand and Fran gives her a warm hug. "I'm good," Jess says.

"Just good?"

"I'm *very* good."

"Fletcher." Fran greets me with a smile.

"Well, Mr Adams, you are on time. I can only presume I have your lovely lady to thank for that? Jessica." Peter gives her a kiss on her cheek, and she blushes.

"Fletcher," Peter and Fran's boys call out.

"Hi, boys. Hope you're going to behave," I say. "And will you be watching the game?"

"We will only if you promise to score."

"Boys, you can't ask Fletcher to promise that," Fran says.

"Why not?" I ask, shrugging my shoulders. "Boys, I promise I will score at least one."

"In that case, make it count," Peter says, laughing. "Make it our European game."

Jess talks to Fran, and I notice some of the other wives and partners who are dropping off players look at Fran and Jess with displeasure. Yeah, I forgot how bad some of them could be. But what I also notice is neither Fran nor Jess let it bother them.

Logan finally arrives in a flashy Audi that doesn't belong to him. He gets out of the car and the driver swings her long bare legs out of the driver's side. The tall brunette from a few weeks ago. Jess is as surprised as I am, although I hope for different reasons. He grabs his case, gives her a quick peck on the cheek and says, "See you." His date looks stunned. She gets back in her car and speeds away without looking back.

I leave Jess with Fran as I go and put my case in the luggage area of the bus. "Didn't think you would have Jess here to see you off," Logan says.

"Well, she did drop me off."

He looks at Jess and then to my car. "Seriously? You're letting some chick drive your car?"

"Logan . . ."

"Yeah, yeah."

"Right, boys. We need to leave!" Peter shouts out.

Most of the players start getting on the bus, but I don't. I need to say goodbye to my girl.

I walk back toward Jess and she turns to face me, a hint of sadness in her eyes before she smiles. I reach out and pull her into my arms as soon as I'm close enough, and seal my mouth over hers. It takes her a moment before she responds. The feel of her tongue stroking sweetly against mine turns me on and I have to remember where I am.

Slowly, I pull back from her, and we're met with a chorus of cheering. But it's Fran and Peter's boys that make us laugh as they both shout, "Yuk."

"Now, don't take offense, but you two need to stop kissing like that in public," Peter says, smirking. "Now, come on. Get on that bus."

I watch as Fran wraps her arm around Jess's shoulder.

"Bye," I say softly, turning away from her. I don't look back, because if I do, I might not get on the bus at all.

Chapter FORTY-FOUR

Jessica

I NEVER IMAGINED OUR TIME apart would affect me the way it does. For someone who's only been in my life a short period of time, he consumes my thoughts. I've not been able to contact him for the last two days. Before that we spoke every night before I went to bed. Hearing his voice helped settle me. For some reason, I've been anxious this week alone in the apartment at night.

I think Scott has been playing heavily on my mind. There was no more contact from him until last Sunday night when Fletcher left. Purely coincidence, I hope. On Sunday night, I received another email asking to meet up. I didn't reply, but I did let the police officers dealing with the case know he'd been in touch. I then got in touch with my solicitor, Mr Jones, to see what could be done, and also let him know I wanted all loose ends with regards outstanding bills in joint names sorted.

Last Monday, I went to the bank during my lunch break to remove him from one of my accounts only to find out it was empty. I should've dealt with it before now. There wasn't much money in that account in the first place, so I ended up closing it.

I called my solicitor back to let him know about the bank, only for him to give me more bad news. It turns out there have been various credit cards taken out in the last few weeks in both my name and Scott's.

Mr Jones came out to the office to see me on Tuesday morning at the same time as the police officers. Lee stayed with me because I was feeling a bit low about Scott deciding to pop back into my life. As we were all sitting and talking, there was a flower delivery for me. My heart sank when I saw the same arrangement Scott sent me before, when I thought Fletcher had sent them.

Now, every day since, the same flowers have been delivered, and it's making me a little uneasy. I haven't mentioned anything about Scott in my conversations with Fletcher. I don't want him upset or to put him off his game, especially when there's nothing he can do.

So, here I am in work before seven a.m. to try and keep my mind occupied, sitting at my desk and drinking a cup of tea. My thoughts keep going to Fletcher. I know he travelled to Italy yesterday ahead of his game tomorrow night. But I wish I could talk to him. It might help.

On Sunday, I went shopping and out for lunch with Lee and my mum. Lee wanted me to tell my parents about Scott, but I didn't want to worry them. Mum and Dad went away yesterday for a wee two-night break and won't be home until tomorrow. I will tell them about Scott when they come home; no use ruining their time away.

I open my emails and I'm shocked to see there are loads from Scott. This is getting beyond a fucking joke. I open one, read it, and decide not to open the others.

You belong with me. Not him. That's all it says. I pick up my cup and throw it across the room. It smashes into a hundred pieces. Tears roll down my face.

I sit for a few minutes feeling sorry for myself before giving myself a kick up the arse. I go into the bathroom to clean myself up and make myself presentable before Lee gets here.

"What the fuck happened? Jess! Where are you?"

It's too late.

With a final glance in the mirror, I leave the bathroom. "I'm here and fine."

"Care to explain why there is a cup smashed all over the floor?"

"I'm just going to clean it up," I tell her.

"Jess, what's wrong?"

"Look at my computer." That's all I say, and set about cleaning up the mess I've made.

"Have you called the police?" Lee asks quietly.

"Not yet." She comes over to where I am and helps me up, and takes the dustpan and brush from my hands.

"Do you want to go home?"

"No, there's too much to do here and you're out all afternoon."

"Oh, yes. I have viewers for Mr and Mrs Richardson's house. The couple are young and want a project. They're not afraid to get their hands dirty. I'm going to keep everything crossed that they like the house and put an offer in, just so I don't need to deal with them again." I know how she feels. They are the most frustrating couple I've come across. "Okay, let's first call the police and then I'll make you another cup of tea."

"Thank you."

The police officers pay us a visit and they seem to be getting as pissed off as I am about Scott. They have been unable to track him down. Just as they're leaving, there is another flower delivery for me. The poor driver looks on helplessly, handing the flowers to the officers. I don't even look at the flowers; I just want all traces of Scott out of my life.

Lee and I work hard the rest of the morning. I was right; we're too busy to be dealing with anything else.

"Right, it's time for me to be heading out," she says, grabbing my attention.

"Okay, will you be back in the office?"

"Yeah, I should be back about four. Do you want to go out for a drink and some dinner when we finish?"

"Yeah, why not?"

"Okay, then I will see you later. Try and have some lunch."

"Yes, Mum. I'm actually just going to make myself some tea and toast," I tell her, standing up. We have a small kitchen in the back of the office, which is handy. We usually only make tea and coffee when we have clients in.

She leaves, and I go and put the kettle on and pop some bread in the toaster. This will do for now; hopefully I'll be hungry when we go out after work for dinner. My thoughts switch to Lee. She had a date on Saturday night and she seems really keen on him. She spoke about Josh all day Sunday when we were out. I did try to ask her about Logan, but her reply was that he's only interested in someone to fuck. There was nothing I could say to that given the fact it was a brunette with legs that went on for miles who dropped him off at the stadium.

I hear the front door open. "I'll just be a minute," I call out.

"Oh, take as long as you like. I'm not going anywhere." My legs tremble on hearing his voice, and my breathing quickens. I don't think I can face him. I look about for my phone to call someone but I've left it on my desk.

Taking a deep breath, because I know I have no option but to face him, I leave the kitchen and walk back into the front office with a fake smile on my face. "What can I do for you, Scott?" I take in his appearance. He looks as though he's been sleeping rough. His clothes are dirty and it looks like he's not shaved in weeks.

He shifts from one foot to the other. "How about you start by telling me why you haven't replied to any of my messages?"

"I have nothing to say to you, so why reply?" My eyes dart

behind him to my desk, where I can see my phone.

"Well, I have plenty to say to you." He moves a little closer. Then it hits me, the stench of stale alcohol. Oh, fuck. He's drinking again. But why I'm surprised by this, I don't know. "Why are you with him, Jess? Someone like Fletcher Adams is only going to use you for one thing."

"As opposed to you using me as a punch bag and sex when it suited you." The words leave me in a rush, and I should know better. His expression darkens, and all I see is hatred and rage.

"I came here today to apologise. I love you, Jess, and I can't stand the thought of you and him together. What is it? Is it the money you're after? Or maybe it's the fame, although I didn't really see you as one of those girls. The ones that hang around someone, trying to make some sort of name for themselves. Will we see you sell your story in the paper? Is that what this relationship with Fletcher fucking Adams is all about? You seeking your fifteen minutes of fame?"

"How fucking dare you? Get out of here, Scott. Anything we have to say to each other will be done through solicitors. I want nothing more to do with you." I try to stay calm but he's making me mad, standing there, mouthing off. If I could just get to my phone.

"Oh, we have plenty to say to each other." He takes another step closer to me. This whole fucked up situation takes me back to all those weeks ago.

I'm not the same person I was. I repeat this over and over in my head.

"We don't. I want you to leave. Just go."

I try to make my way around him to my desk, but he stops me, grabbing my arm and twisting it around and up my back. "Fucking hell. Let go of me!" I scream and lash out with my free hand.

He only laughs at me. "Was that meant to hurt me? You are

so fucking stupid," he snarls through gritted teeth.

"What the fuck do you want from me? I have nothing left to give you."

"I want you. I want our family."

"Our family. You took my son away from me!"

His grip loosens and my arm falls to the side. His posture stiffens. "A son? It was my son you were carrying?" He turns away at my words, but this is new information for him. We've not really had time for a discussion about it.

"Yes. His name is James."

"My son wouldn't have been called James. Why would you name my son without consulting me first?" he asks quietly, with tear-filled eyes. "Why would you keep all this from me? Why?"

"Why? You really have to ask that question? Because you took him from me! You killed my son. You murdered him." I lift my hand and slap him as hard as I can over and over. He stands still in front of me. I finally stop hitting him and he laughs. His face is red and already swollen, and my hand stings.

"Is that all you have, you stupid, stupid fucking girl. I fucking love you, and what do you do? Disrespect me. You don't deserve my love. You are nothing more than a cheap whore, running after some equally daft footballer who has more money than sense."

He reaches out, grabbing my hair so tightly my neck tilts back and I'm looking into his eyes. Eyes that are dark, and that I no longer recognise. I continue to lash out against him because there is nothing else he can take from me.

I kick out at him.

"You bitch!" He punches me in the stomach, knocking the wind out of me, all the time still pulling at my hair. It feels as though my neck might snap at any moment. Tears roll slowly down my face.

He's a fucking mad man.

He drags me into the middle of the floor. Where is someone when you need them? I draw in a deep breath and scream as loud as I can, hoping and praying that someone, somewhere will hear my cries for help.

He repeatedly punches me in the face. My eyes start to close and I'm fighting a battle to keep them open.

"I hate you!" I scream. "I wish you were dead because I'll never love you. I'll never want your hands on me."

"Oh, Jess. Here's the thing. If I can't have you, no one else is going to have you or want you."

He swipes my feet from under me and my weak body falls to the floor. He continues kicking my head, my body, then my legs. I don't even have the energy to try and protect myself from his vicious beating.

I can hear his voice but it's floating in the distance. But I know he's still close because he's still beating me. Everything goes dark and calm. The darkness takes me away from all the pain.

Chapter FORTY-FIVE

Fletcher

RIGHT NOW, I'M SURE ALL the players are feeling the same way as I do, and want to kill Jackson. He is the reason we've had our phones taken from us. The boss saw our phones as a privilege and used it as a punishment for Jackson's drunken behaviour while we were training.

"Okay, lads. Gather around," the boss calls across the football pitch. We make our way to the sidelines where he's standing. The heat is almost unbearable. I'm glad the game is tomorrow night; hopefully it should be a bit cooler because I don't relish the thought of playing football in this heat for ninety minutes.

"That's us for today. We'll go back to the hotel. There's nothing more that can be done . . ." I let his voice trail off, already knowing the drill. We have the day to relax and stay away from the bar. I wonder how many of the lads will stick to that rule. Then we all meet back up for dinner tonight. That's Peter's way of making sure we stick to his rules.

At least we only have two more days until we're home and I get to see Jess. I'm sure Peter will give us back our phones tomorrow after the game, because I need to call her. Peter had also asked hotel management to remove all phones from our bedrooms. I thought that was a bit extreme, but he's the boss, after all. And all this because Jackson didn't stick to the rules laid out to him. I've missed hearing her voice the last few nights and I need to let her know what time to pick me up from the club on Thursday.

"Fletcher," Logan says, nudging me. "Come on. Time to travel to the hotel. What is wrong with you? You thinking about Jess?"

"Of course."

"Fuck, you have got it bad."

He really has no idea.

Chapter FORTY-SIX

Jessica

BEEP. BEEP. BEEP. THAT BLOODY noise is making my head hurt. I want to open my eyes, but I'm scared. From the noise, I already know I'm in hospital, *again*, which means someone came to help me. Someone managed to get Scott away from me.

Someone is holding my hand. I hear a door opening and footsteps crossing the floor. I try to open my eyes but it's taking too much energy.

"Can I get you anything, sweetie?" a soft, kind voice asks.

"No, I'm okay." It's Lee who answers the question. Lee. She's here with me. God, my best friend is by my side, as always.

"You've not moved all night. I'm going to get you some sweet tea. Although, you should also try and eat something to keep your strength up. Your friend is going to need you when she wakes up."

"When do you think she will?" Her voice sounds so pained. I attempt to squeeze her hand and I try harder to open my eyes. She has to know I'm awake. "Jess? Nurse, please tell me I'm not imagining it?"

"No, sweetie. You're not."

Finally, I manage to open my eyes. They're sore and heavy. Lee moves from the chair she's been sitting on and stands closer to me. Tears roll down her face. "Oh, Jess." I can hear the sorrow and relief in her voice. She moves closer and hugs me, and I wince from the pain. "Sorry."

"Don't be."

"Jessica, I'm going to get the doctor, let him know you are awake. Then I can start to check you over," the softly spoken nurse tells me.

"Can I please have a drink?" I croak.

"Of course you can. Just let me adjust the bed and help you." The nurse helps me into a sitting position before leaving the room. Lee holds the water while I take small drinks through a straw.

"Jess, I thought I had lost you yesterday," she cries, pulling the seat closer, sitting down, and taking my hand.

"No. Looks like you're stuck with me. What time is it?"

"Nine a.m. Who did this to you?"

"Scott. He arrived shortly after you left."

"Thought so. That bastard. The police are here. They will want to talk to you."

"What time did you come back to the office?" I ask.

"About four, and I found you there . . . just . . ."

"Lee, it's okay."

The door opens and the nurse and doctor come in. The doctor explains my injuries, mostly cuts and bruising, two cracked ribs, but tells me I'm a very lucky young lady. He should try telling that to my body, because it doesn't feel like it. He continues to give me a thorough examination. His hands are cold against my almost fevered skin.

"Can I get up?" I ask when he finishes, because I don't want to stay here. I want to go home, and the sooner the better.

"Yes, but the first time will be hard because of your injuries. If you want, we can try just now."

I nod at the doctor.

Lee moves the chair out of the way and the nurse comes to

my side, and the doctor is beside her. The nurse pulls the covers down and I gasp, seeing my legs. There's no clear skin to be seen, it's all black and blue bruising.

Shit!

"Jessica." The nurse says my name softly. "I should warn you, this is going to be uncomfortable."

She holds one arm and the doctor holds the other, and I pull myself up. Lee is standing in the corner of the room, watching me through tear-filled eyes. I take a step, and boy does it fucking hurt, but I carry on taking another and another. Lee smiles but it doesn't reach her sad eyes.

"How does that feel?" the doctor asks.

"I won't lie, it's bloody sore. Can I ask, is the rest of my body as bad as my legs?"

"Now it's my turn not to lie," he says. "Jessica, yes. I've never seen bruising on a patient as widespread as yours."

"Can I see?"

"Jess . . ." It's Lee's voice. I turn and she shakes her head from side to side.

"Lee, I have to see. I have to know what he's done."

The nurse leaves the room and I use the time to sit back down on the edge of the bed. The doctor asks a few more questions. After several long minutes have passed, the nurse enters the room with a large mirror. She gives Lee the mirror to hold and comes back to help me.

"Are you sure about this?" she asks as I stand. I nod. "Okay, underneath this gown you are naked. We had to remove everything when you were admitted yesterday. We won't be able to remove the gown because of the IV line, and I'll hold all your bits and pieces."

It's only now I realise she means the catheter. Under other circumstances I would probably be embarrassed with this, but I'm not. I'm sure the nurse and doctor have had to deal with a lot worse than me.

I walk the short distance to Lee with the support of the nurse and doctor. I gasp when I see my face. My eyes are swollen so badly, it's no wonder it hurt trying to open them, and the bruising has covered my entire face. It's a bloody mess. God, I'm surprised Lee even recognised me.

The stranger staring back at me is lost. Looking at myself in the mirror, I could be anyone.

The nurse loosens the gown at the back and slides one arm out. She holds the gown so I can see my body. What the fuck did he do? Again, there's not a part of my body I can see clear skin.

"I'm sorry, Jessica, but the back is the same," the nurse says, putting the gown back on me.

"I need to go to the toilet."

The doctor looks at me and back to the nurse. "Okay. I don't see the problem because you're on your feet, although I would prefer someone with you."

"I'll be here," the nurse says. "We just need to sort you first." The doctor leaves the room and takes the mirror with him. I lie back down for the nurse to do what she needs to do before I can go to the bathroom. She helps me in, and stands by the opened door with her back to me. Even trying to sit down hurts.

I finish up, wash my hands, and go back into the room. Lee is sitting back in the chair and looks a bit better than she did moments ago. The nurse helps me back into the bed. "Now, we know you were attacked yesterday afternoon, so when did you last eat?" the nurse asks.

"Monday night. I was in the middle of making something when he came in."

"Okay, in that case, I'm going to arrange some breakfast for you both, because . . ." She turns to Lee. "You need to eat." Lee smiles and agrees with her. "Jessica, are you up to answering some questions? If not, I can ask the officers to come back later."

"No. I may as well get this over with."

"Okay," she says with a smile, and leaves the room.

The officers come in and both look visibly shocked by my appearance. We go over everything that happened yesterday. Lee holds my hand as I go over the events. She cries along with me, and I have to stop talking a few times. The officers ask if I need a break, but I tell them no, I need to get this over with. By the time I finish reliving what Scott did to me, I'm sobbing uncontrollably. Lee holds me. I learn that Scott isn't in custody because they can't track him down.

Which means he is still out there. Fear soars through me at that thought. I don't want to be that woman who lives in fear.

The officers apologise but say they also have to take some photographic evidence before leaving me to rest. It's harder getting the photographs taken than I thought it would be. Maybe that's because when Lee helped lower the hospital gown, one of the officers couldn't hide his shock when he said, "Fuckin' hell."

When they finish with me, they apologise before leaving. My body sags against the bed, and the nurse comes back in with a tray of food.

"Breakfast for two." Her smile is full of warmth. "If you manage to eat, Jessica, we might be able to remove the IV line."

"Thank you," I say, and she turns and leaves us to eat. Neither of us says a word, but we do manage to eat, even if we play with some of it.

"Jess, I've not been able to let your parents know," Lee says as I push my plate away.

"They'll be home tonight. I can call them later when I get home."

"What do you mean *get home*?"

"I'm not staying here. I don't feel safe. You heard the officers. He's still out there somewhere. The apartment has security. It's the safest place for me until he's caught. Please. My mind is made up. As soon as I have this out, I'm going home."

"What if the doctor says you need to stay?"

"Lee, I'm not staying. I will sign myself out if I have to. So maybe you should go and get the nurse for me."

She walks away from me, shaking her head in frustration.

Chapter FORTY-SEVEN

Fletcher

MATCH DAY. IT'S ONLY SEVEN a.m. here, and I'm already fucking nervous. I can't put my finger on it, but I get the feeling something is wrong. I wish I could talk to Jess; she might help calm my nerves.

This is such a huge match for us, but for once, there are no expectations. The Italian team is great, and even the media back home have already written us off in this game.

"What the fuck are you doing?" Logan asks as he wakens in his bed.

"I'm going to go for a run to clear my head. Do you fancy joining me?"

"I'll crack the fucking jokes." I should've expected his answer. "No, you go. I'm going to try and get back to sleep. Wake me when you get back for breakfast. I need to start the day off the right way."

I shake my head and leave our hotel room.

I'm glad he said no because I fancy some time alone. Some time to think about my feelings for Jess. Think of the meaning behind my feelings and what it means for us. Then I can focus on tonight's game, and after tonight, I can focus on seeing my girl tomorrow when we get back home to Glasgow.

Focus!

Chapter FORTY-EIGHT

Jess

"SO MUCH FOR FUCKING FLETCHER when I've needed to talk to him these last few days. Where is he?" I cry at Lee as I pace the floor of the apartment. I've walked from the living room to the kitchen over and over again. My body aches with every single step I take. Lee has warned me about wearing a hole in the floor, but I don't care. I don't care about anything again. I feel like I'm slipping down an endless black hole and there is nothing I can do to pull myself back out.

This last week has been crap, even by my standards. I don't know how much more I can take. My life is being ripped away from me by the one person I thought couldn't take anything else from me. God, how wrong was I? I thought he had done all the damage he could.

Why can't they find Scott? After everything that has happened this week, you would think the police would be closer to finding that worthless piece of shit. But no, all they can tell me is that they have every available officer looking for him.

Surely he just can't disappear into thin air?

Where would he go?

"Jess, that's unfair. He's in another country. Don't you think he would be here as soon as he could if he knew what had happened to you? Because I know he would be on the first flight home to be with you. To support you and care for you."

"Why the fuck is there no signal? Surely he must be able to call me?" As I pace the floor, I ask myself why I'm so upset. Why am I so desperate to call Fletch and hear his voice?

The answer is clear. I've fallen for Fletch.

"Jess, you have Fran's number. Call her." I wanted to call her this week when Scott's emails and flowers continued to haunt me, to see if she could get a message to Fletcher for me, but each time I picked up the phone, I decided against it.

"I can't. That would mean having to tell her everything."

"Jess, she is the only way you're going to get a message to him. I'm sure what you tell her won't go any further. She's a friend to you, and right now, you need your friends."

She's right. I know I should've done this at the start of the week, but I thought I could handle this on my own. I grab my phone and scroll until I reach Fran's number. Taking a deep breath, I press call.

"Jess, I was just thinking about you. I was going to call and arrange lunch or dinner. The boys have just had so much on since the team left."

"That would beee . . . nice." I take several deep quick breaths. I can't do this.

"Jess, honey. What's wrong?" I can hear the panic in her voice and I'm certain it echoes mine.

"I . . . I need you to get in touch . . . I need . . ." I drop the phone and Lee runs to me. "Please. You tell her. I can't."

"Fran, it's Lee . . . No, she's not good . . . I'll give you the short version . . . Her ex is a nasty piece of work who has decided, with Fletch being out the country, to up his harassment campaign against her. It's been really bad, and yesterday she was attacked . . . Of course you can come over . . . But she really needs to speak to Fletcher . . . Thank you, Fran. We will see you soon."

I sink to the floor, unable to stand any longer. Lee joins me and I hear her muffled sobs. She wraps her arms around me and I'm not sure how long we sit here before she speaks. "Fran is coming over and will call Peter. Peter took all the players' phones off them and locked them in a safe so they could concentrate on training and the game. She says their game should've kicked off. Do you want me to put it on?"

I nod. At least I know he's not purposely ignoring my calls now.

She turns the TV on, and yes, the game has started. My phone ringing startles me. I grab it, hoping it's Fletch, but I know it's not. He's on the screen in front of me. I look at the caller ID. My parents.

"Can you?" I ask, handing Lee my phone. Lee had called them earlier, but I knew they were out all day. She wanted to let them know about last night.

"Elaine . . . I think both of you should come over to the apartment . . . I tried calling but I forgot you were out of town yesterday . . . No, there was an incident last night. Scott . . . Elaine, I can tell you everything when you get here . . . Bye."

"I'm sorry," I say. "I don't know what to do."

"Jess, don't be sorry. I'm here to help you. Everything will be okay."

I turn my attention back to the TV. It will provide me with a much needed distraction. My parents are going to be so disappointed that I've kept this to myself this week. But I truly thought I could handle it on my own. I thought I was strong enough to deal with Scott.

Our tears stop falling and we sit on the floor watching the game. I can't take my eyes away from the screen in front of me. I've not seen Fletch in what feels like forever, and the last time we spoke was a few days ago. God, I miss him. I need to hear his soothing voice and feel his warm arms around me.

I try to concentrate on the game, and although it's nil-nil, we look the better team. Fletcher has come close to scoring twice now, and I'm sure it's only a matter of time. The intercom buzzes at the same time as the ref blows the whistle for half time, and Lee answers it.

"That was security. Fran is on her way up."

"Okay."

"Will I open a bottle of wine?" she asks.

"Why not? It might help ease my pain."

"Jess, the doctor gave you painkillers. If it's that bad, take them." Lee walks into the hallway and waits for Fran. After a few minutes, I can hear their whispered voices. I wonder what Lee is telling her.

"Jess, sweetheart." I turn my head on hearing Fran's voice. "Bloody hell," she screeches. She rushes toward me, pulling me to my feet, and wraps her arms around me. "Oh dear God. What has he done to our beautiful girl?" I pull out of her hold, feeling overwhelmed, and look at her. She's dressed in leggings and a T-shirt, no make-up on, and hair piled loosely back. She still looks beautiful.

I must look a state in comparison.

"Jess, you're my friend. I want to help. And why in God's name are you here at home and not in hospital?"

"I signed myself out. I didn't feel safe."

"Go on." Fran guides me to the couch, and we sit down. Lee comes through with three glasses and a bottle of wine. "I hope there's more of that."

"There is plenty where that came from," Lee says.

"What about your boys?" I ask Fran.

"I dropped them off for the night with my parents. Told them there was an emergency. So you're stuck with me until the morning." Her voice is sincere as she speaks.

I start at the beginning and tell her all about Scott and my baby, and everything that has happened since Fletcher has been out the country. She sits quietly, listening to every word I say, gasping at various parts of my story. When I stop talking, my eyes fall on the TV screen, and just at the right time.

Fletcher has the ball, takes a shot, and scores the first goal of the game. If I had the energy, I would leap up and cheer, but like everyone in the room, my mood is too subdued.

"Well, your man has got his goal," Lee states, trying to diffuse the heavy air that lingers around us. "And there's still time to get another." I watch him as he runs to the camera and blows a kiss before celebrating with his teammates. "See, he's still thinking about you."

"He's going to be pissed off when he sees me," I say with a tear rolling down my face.

"Don't be silly. How can he possibly be pissed off with you? That man loves you," Fran says, and Lee and I look at her. "What? It's true. You'd have to be a fool not to see it. Jess, he loves you. He might not have told you. Christ, he might not even realise it, but he does."

I try not to think about her words, even though I want to believe they're true. Because deep down within my heart, I know I've fallen in love with him.

The intercom buzzes. "That will be your parents," Lee says, going to answer it. I watch as confusion crosses her face as she hangs up. "It's the police. They're on their way up. It all sounds very official."

"Hopefully they've caught up with Scott and I can start to put this nightmare behind me."

Fran tops up the glasses whilst Lee goes to wait in the hallway. I sit, eyes glued to the TV screen, hoping for another goal for the team. There are only a few minutes left to play. I watch with interest as Jackson links up with Fletcher and he scores again. My eyes fill with tears as he does the same as last time, and blows me a kiss. The final whistle blows; our team is through to the next stages of this competition. Fran hugs me and cries.

Lee joins us with two different police officers from the ones that took my statement in the hospital. They both remove their hats. My body starts to shake uncontrollably.

"Sorry to disturb your evening, ladies," one says, looking at us then the wine, and finally, the TV.

"It's okay. Take a seat," I tell them, but they refuse. "I presume this is to do with my attack?"

"In a way, Miss Taylor." Lee joins Fran and me on the couch. My friends take a hand each, offering me their support.

"Tell us you have Scott in custody and he can't hurt Jess again?" Lee asks with her voice raised.

"Miss Taylor. We're sorry to be here under these circumstances, but I have to inform you that Mr Stevens was found dead earlier today, and as you are still down as his next of kin . . ." His voice trails off and I feel myself sink into the couch, only I'm not. Lee has moved closer and has pulled me into her arms. Fran is still holding my hand but also rubbing my back. I can't believe what I'm hearing.

"How did he die?" Lee asks the question that is on the tip of my lips, but I can't seem to find my voice to ask.

"He took his own life. We should have more details shortly. We found him after doing a search of your house."

"Why my house?"

"Because a neighbour reported seeing him hanging around and checking the windows and doors. The neighbour later saw a broken window at the house and called it in. As you know, we had a warrant out for his arrest."

"Why am I his next of kin? I shouldn't be, especially after everything he's done to me."

"We would have come to see you because of the delicate nature of the circumstances, but on checking his records, he has no immediate family and he still has you listed as next of kin."

I'm not sure my head can process the information I've just been given. I stand up, slightly dizzy, and walk to the window and look out across the Clyde. Tears fill my eyes. I'm not destined to be happy. Even in death, he's still going to continue to hurt me. Am I really that bad a person? Surely I've done something to deserve all this pain? But I can't work it out.

This must be Scott's idea of a sick joke. It can't be true. I turn back to look at the police officers and see sadness in their eyes as they look at me. After everything Scott has done to me, I can't believe he gets to have the final say. Tears blind me.

"This can't be happening!" I cry out.

"Jess, come and sit down," Lee says, taking hold of my arm. I try to walk with her but everything turns hazy. My focus is strained. The room starts spinning and all I see is darkness; it's calling for me. My legs crumble and I fall to the ground.

So many voices all talking at once; I don't hear the words. But I do hear my mother's scream. She's here.

I'm floating and I know the darkness has decided to keep me this time, and I don't have the energy to fight it.

"Get Peter on the phone now . . . I don't give a fuck who he's speaking to, and make sure Fletcher is with him . . . Do you think I would be screaming down the phone if it wasn't important . . . ?" I know that's Fran's voice; I hear it above the others. She's crying too, I can hear her sobs.

"Someone call an ambulance . . . Jessica, please. I need you to stay with me."

Just when I finally thought I was re-building my life, he comes along and takes it from me. I hate Scott with every breath I have left in my tired, weak body.

The voices stop.

To be continued

Books by KAREN FRANCES

The Captured Series

Family Ties a Captured Series Novella

He's Captured my Heart Book 1

He's Captured my Trust Book 2

He's Captured my Soul Book 3

She's Captured my Love Book 4

Captured by Our Addiction Book 5

A Beautiful Game Series

Playing the Game Book 1

Playing to Win Book 2 Coming Soon

About the Author

SHE CURRENTLY LIVES JUST OUTSIDE Glasgow, Scotland, with her husband, five children and two dogs, although she does dream of living somewhere warm and sunny. Her days are spent helping her husband run their busy family business. She spends some of her free time trying to keep fit and prepare healthy meals for her family, when their busy schedules allow them to sit down at meal times together. The rest of her free time she uses to plot and write and occasionally read.

17656371R00187

Printed in Great Britain
by Amazon